Sharon Milburn was born in Northumberland and after an eclectic mixture of occupations including teacher, census collector and gas board clerk, she now writes full time. *Lord Whitley's Bride* is her first novel. She lives in Australia.

LORD WHITLEY'S BRIDE

Edith Backworth, daughter of the local parson, leads a tranquil life in rural Northumberland until the tragedy of Waterloo propels her into London society. Charles, Lord Whitley, is still mourning the loss of his fiancée and friends when he is thrust into the unwelcome role of executor. His life is totally disrupted by the new Lady Edith's outspoken behaviour. He would like nothing better than to throttle her! But when Edith's murderous cousin, Bertram, covets her father's new title and kidnaps her, only Charles can come to the rescue . . .

SHARON MILBURN

LORD WHITLEY'S BRIDE

Complete and Unabridged

ULVERSCROFT
Leicester

First published in Great Britain in 2003 by
Robert Hale Limited
London

First Large Print Edition
published 2004
by arrangement with
Robert Hale Limited
London

British Library CIP Data

Milburn, Sharon, *1955 –*
   Lord Whitley's bride.—Large print ed.—
   Ulverscroft large print series: historical romance
   1. Aristocracy (Social class)—England—History—
   19th century—Fiction
   2. Love stories 3. Large type books
   I. Title
   823.9'2 [F]

   ISBN 1–84395–510–5

Published by
F. A. Thorpe (Publishing)
Anstey, Leicestershire

Set by Words & Graphics Ltd.
Anstey, Leicestershire
Printed and bound in Great Britain by
T. J. International Ltd., Padstow, Cornwall

This book is printed on acid-free paper

1

'I don't know how I am going to bear it!' Lady Louisa declared, throwing down her spoon. 'It is beyond anything! A mere nobody. A country parson, for heaven's sake, to usurp my brother's position. And isn't it just *like* my cousin Anthony to get himself killed as well? Before our engagement could be announced, too. Why could he not have been more careful?'

Lady Louisa's outburst shattered the gloomy silence pervading the dining-room of Lord Cramlington's town house. All over London women were dressed as Louisa and her companion were now, in unrelieved black, a colour that did nothing for the younger woman's sallow complexion. In the aftermath of the gallant but terrible victory at Waterloo the losses were keenly felt.

Charles Ashington, Viscount Whitley, struggled to keep his temper in check. 'I'm sure Anthony would have done everything in his power to postpone his death, Louisa, had he known how distraught you would become. You speak of it as if it were a personal affront!'

Lady Louisa had the grace to blush. 'After all it's not as if Anthony and I were so very well acquainted, my lord! But we were cousins and Mama arranged our marriage when I was in my cradle.'

Lord Whitley conjured up a mental image of the late Anthony. Marriage was surely the last thought to worm its way into a mind stuffed with fox-hunting, gambling and the cut of his uniform.

'Was *he* aware of that?'

Louisa's gaze dropped uncertainly. Seconds later she rallied. 'Of course he was! But it is all for nothing, after all. I shall be cast out into the street and *another* set in my place!' She lay back in her chair, one arm artistically shading her features from view.

'Oh, please do not distress yourself!' Louisa's female companion flew to her side, handkerchief and salts at the ready. 'Indeed it is a dreadfully lowering prospect, but you must do your best to bear up. After all, the heir has not, as yet, arrived! Who knows what may befall him upon the journey.'

'Thank you, Miss Berwick, for the happy thought.' Lord Whitley threw down his napkin, too sickened to remain at the table for another moment. 'Sharples and I will withdraw to the book-room and leave you to compose yourself, Louisa.'

The late Lord Cramlington's man of business was hard put to keep up with the long, limping stride of Lord Whitley as he left the room, calling loudly for the butler.

'Mr Sharples and I will finish dining in the book-room, Hartley. Please send Lady Louisa's maid to her at once. She is overcome with her grief . . . *again*.'

Once the butler was out of earshot his temper finally exploded. 'My God, Sharples, if I am forced to endure any more affecting attitudes and crocodile tears I shall go mad! Not a word of concern about her brother, or her father even, in all this time! And what about her poor cousin George, to die like that? An amputation and then mortification of the wound. How he must have suffered! But does she even mention him? Have you detected *any* trace of sorrow not motivated by self-interest? She is totally devoid of finer feelings.'

He paced up and down the room, for the thousandth time cursing the wound in his thigh as sharp pain clutched at him. Oh, God, what if he was to end up like George? The prospect could not be borne. He would shoot himself first.

'Anthony never once considered marrying Louisa and who can blame him? The poor devil is well out of it, if you ask me.'

Sharples cleared his throat. 'I realize you are under considerable stress, my lord. Indeed the whole business must be most repugnant to you. I find it very strange that Lord Cramlington should have requested *you* to carry out his wishes. I would have thought someone closer to his own age; a friend, one of the family, perhaps. Even entering this house each day must bring back so many memories of happier times. You should not have to bear the responsibility, and so I told his lordship. You have your own wound to consider.'

Lord Whitley felt a shiver of fear. The last thing he wanted to think about was his wound. 'Forget it, Sharples, it's nothing. A mere nuisance.'

'A ball lodged too deep to be removed can hardly be termed a mere nuisance,' Sharples demurred.

'Anyway,' his lordship continued, determined to turn the conversation, 'Lord Cramlington regarded me as one of the family, even though Chloe died more than three years ago. I still cannot believe she and Louisa were sisters. She was so good, and so beautiful, yet Louisa . . . '

He pulled himself up. 'If Chloe had lived . . . ' The loss tore at him again. Three years meant nothing. Thirty years would never erase her memory. 'If she had lived we would be husband and wife and Louisa would now be my responsibility anyway. As it is I shall never marry. No one could compare with my darling. Apart from all that Richard was my closest friend. Most certainly I will take care of his sister. There is no one else she can turn to now save her Aunt Seaton. But Louisa doesn't make my task any easier, does she?'

Sharples smiled sympathetically. 'No, indeed. Perhaps we may instead discuss the Reverend Backworth. The letter regarding the succession should have reached him by now, but he won't know of his lordship's death. It will be quite a surprise when he discovers he's the fifth Lord Cramlington. Will he be residing here?'

'Of course!' Lord Whitley's black eyebrows shot up. 'It's *his* house now, after all! It's not his fault he's the heir. He'll no doubt be bringing his family with him, too. I hope the housekeeper will be able to cope. Mrs Anstey doesn't seem to appreciate disruption to her routines.'

'I should imagine there'd be few problems. There's only the one daughter, a Miss Edith Backworth. Mrs Backworth died back in the year one, or so I believe.'

Lord Whitley smiled unpleasantly. 'Well, I

hope *Lady* Edith is up to snuff. We'll have every damned fortune-hunter in London nosing round in no time.'

'Not to mention the match-making mamas,' Sharples added wryly. 'The reverend will no doubt be in need of a countess, too.'

'Oh, my God,' Lord Whitley groaned. 'That's all I need.'

★ ★ ★

'Miss Edith! Miss Edith! . . . Oh, where *is* the girl? Edith, you come out at once!'

Edith Backworth looked down from her perch in the limb of her favourite apple tree. Well screened from the vulgar gaze of passers-by on the road, she was equally well hidden from the searching scrutiny of her one-time nurse, now standing arms akimbo in the kitchen garden.

For a moment longer Edith tried to ignore the summons. The August sun streaming through the leaves dappled her body with warmth, whilst the gnarled trunk at her back gave her a feeling of solid dependability. She had first climbed this tree as a broken-hearted five year old, and its comfort had never failed her in the fourteen years since.

The copy of the *Gazette* she had been avidly consuming was less than half-finished.

Lord Wellington was such a hero she wanted to read every word of his dispatches. The temptation to close her ears was great, but Edith knew what the outcome would be. Suppressing a sigh, she swung down from the branch before Agnes could catch sight of the swirl of petticoats, or, even worse, a pair of shapely ankles.

'There you are at last! Where have you been? No, never mind. Your father is looking for you, and mighty put-about he is, too. You're to go directly to the study. The mail came in, and there's a letter from London.'

'London? Who could be writing from London?' Edith enquired, her interest caught.

'I'm sure it's not my place to question the reverend, any more than it is yours to go scrambling about in nasty trees. At your age, too! Many a girl younger than you is a mother already. Yes, it's all very well to smile, but I've been telling you times out of mind it isn't fitting for the parson's daughter to go acting like a hoyden. It isn't fitting for any genteel young lady, especially one as is related to earls and viscounts, if you ask my opinion, as I'm sure I don't offer until I'm asked.'

Edith straightened her face as best she could, conjuring up a demure expression that didn't fool either of them. Agnes sighed as she shooed her charge towards the house.

'This is what comes from having no mother, and a father too bent on 'educating' his only child to teach you anything useful, like how to catch a husband!'

Edith paused for a moment to survey herself in the hall mirror. There were no dried leaves or bits of twig in her abundant dark curls, but the back of her gown was marked with moss stains from the tree. Papa never said a word, but for a man so scrupulously neat in his own appearance anything less than perfect grooming would cause an expression almost of pain to cross his features.

From the front the pale sprigged muslin looked deliciously fresh. A less modest girl would have admired her own appearance. Dark, lively eyes lit an animated face graced by a clear complexion only lightly touched by the summer sun. Edith never gave her looks a thought as she snatched up a shawl to hide the evidence of her climb before tapping on the study door.

The Reverend Richard Backworth sat behind his oak desk, clutching the mysterious letter from London. A slim, elegant man just entered on his forty-third year, his distinguished features held no trace of their habitual good-humour. Whatever the news had been, it wasn't good.

Edith hurried to his side, exclaiming in

astonishment. 'Papa, whatever can be the matter? You are distressed!'

Her father swallowed once, then again. Indicating the letter, he finally found the words. 'I have had the most unhappy news, Edith. Please sit down.'

Thoroughly mystified, Edith did as she was bid. It was only then she noticed that the paper he held in his hand bore a wide black border. Someone had died.

Her father appeared to search for the right approach. 'I am very sorry to inform you of the deaths of three of our cousins: Richard, Anthony and George. The facts were not at first clear, and the letter was misdirected. It has taken some time to reach us. Edith, it is so tragic: Richard and Anthony fell at Waterloo, whilst George succumbed to the wound he sustained at Quatre Bras. He died of a fever three weeks ago.'

The desperate battles had been fought over two months previously, but, as her father said, news took time to travel, especially to the wilds of Northumberland.

Edith gasped. 'How dreadful!' She tried to think, but her relations were so confusing. 'I'm sorry, Papa, but I don't exactly recall which cousins you mean. There are so many Richards and Anthonys, not to mention Georges. Are they from Mama's family, or yours?'

He sighed again. 'I'm referring to Richard Backworth, Viscount Holywell, and his first cousins. Young Anthony and George were the same age as yourself, give or take a year or so, and Richard himself only two and thirty.'

'Oh, Papa, it is a terrible thing. Lord Cramlington must be distraught.'

Edith had never paid much attention to the family history, but she did know something of the house of Cramlington. The first earl had been her great-great-grandfather. The deceased hero of Waterloo would have become, if he had been spared, the fifth earl.

'Edith, you don't understand, do you?' Her father's voice sounded strained. 'It is all very complicated, but I will try to explain it to you. The first Lord Cramlington had three sons, namely the second earl, then Anthony and then Edward, who was my grandfather. My great Uncle Anthony had only daughters. Richard, the second earl, had only one surviving son, another Richard, who became the third earl. His sons were the present Lord Cramlington and the late George, who was the father of the Anthony and George who have just now died.'

He paused for a moment.

Edith puzzled the relationships in her head, not quite sure what Papa was trying to tell her. Suddenly, a shiver touched her spine.

She felt the blood drain from her face as the enormity of what he was saying set in.

'Your father was an only son and *my* Uncle George died of the inflammation of the lungs in January.'

'Exactly. He was my elder brother. He has no sons still living. Now I am informed that the fourth earl, my second cousin, was so greatly afflicted by all this sad news that he suffered a palsy-stroke. He is gravely ill. We have been summoned to his bedside.'

He glanced at the letter, and then turned stricken eyes on his daughter.

'Edith, I am now the heir to the earldom.'

Edith slumped back. Too shocked to feel anything for a few moments, sadness for the lives cut so short started to overwhelm her, mingled with other, more personal emotions. Her gaze wandered randomly around the shabby, comfortable study. Rays of sunlight slanted through the windows, illuminating the gold blocking and the rich reds and browns of the well-used volumes in the bookcase. Dust motes wafted in the still air. Only the ticking of her mother's carriage clock on the mantelshelf broke the silence. For the past fourteen years, ever since Mama's death, she had loved this room, often reading quietly in the corner whilst her father wrote his sermon.

One letter and it was all lost to her. No! It could not be.

'But Papa, surely there is some mistake. We are the merest connections to the Earls of Cramlington, after all. Cannot we give it up?'

He sighed. 'There is no mistake. I am the most senior descendant in the male line from the first earl. There *is* no one else.' He sounded lost. 'No one.'

'But what of my cousin Bertram?' Edith felt no affection for her cousin, who had married an iron-master's daughter for her money and now resided on a country estate in Norfolk, aping the gentleman. He could be married to a cottager's daughter if only he could be the heir!

'Bertram is my younger brother's son. He is *my* heir. No, it is my duty, Edith, to the family name. I shall write to this attorney at once.' He looked around at his beloved books, his expression wistful. 'No matter what that duty will cost us.'

★   ★   ★

Later, when the golden afternoon had faded to lingering twilight, Edith plucked some blooms from the flower garden and walked the few steps to the churchyard. In the shadows of an ancient yew she knelt by her

12

mother's grave and ran her fingers over the headstone in the way she had done so many times before.

'Oh, Mama, can you believe what has happened?' She placed the roses on the grave, tidying up the odd weed that the sexton had missed. 'We are to go to London. Who knows when next I will talk to you like this? I will try to look out for Papa, but indeed, how shall I know how to go on?'

She sat back on her heels, gazing round at the square Norman tower of the church and the familiar monuments that surrounded it. 'If only you could be with us, all would be well. I must do my best for Papa, though. He cannot look after himself: he is too good, and too unworldly.'

She mused for a while, pondering on the opportunities that might present themselves to the daughter of the heir to the Earldom of Cramlington.

'I wish I might find a man I can love, and be married, to be as happy as you and Papa. I could be presented, and take to the floor at Almack's with a dashing hero in a red coat. He would have dark hair, and laughing eyes, and love no one but me.'

She sighed as the air began to cool around her. 'I am being fanciful, I know, but to meet someone other than the curate, or Squire

Jesmond's son, who thinks of nothing more than hunting . . . '

She scrambled to her feet, briskly brushing the dirt and withered grass off her dress. 'Papa will want his supper. I must see to him.'

★　★　★

Edith peered out from her corner seat as the coach swayed and lurched out of Newcastle and over the Tyne before picking up speed as they reached open country. Amazed, she turned to her father. 'Is not the pace incredible? I've never known anything like it!'

Reverend Backworth smiled. 'Indeed, yes. I believe twelve miles per hour is common. I only hope I shall not become carriage-sick.'

Hastily Edith looked back out of the window. What an unpleasant thought! She should think about something else. Would anyone be there to greet them? Would they be invited to stay at Lord Cramlington's town house in Grosvenor Square, or would they perhaps stay at a hotel? The thought sent a shiver of excitement down her spine. Edith Backworth putting up at a hotel, for all the world like a great lady. No one would ever dream she had been plucking chickens for Papa's dinner the day before!

A long and tiresome ride soon dulled her

first enthusiasm. Her dismal black garments, so recently worn for her Uncle George, were hot and uncomfortable in the stuffy interior of the coach. The August sun beat down mercilessly, while the wind of their passage was sufficient only to circulate the dust thrown up by the horses' feet. Her first experience of an inn, when they stayed the night in Grantham, did little to enthuse her. Clean and reasonably comfortable as it was, there was not a book to be seen, and loud, raucous noises sounded from the tap room until well into the night.

A pall of brownish haze in the sky ahead finally alerted Edith to the fact that the end of their journey was at hand. Half dead from exhaustion, she summoned up the interest to look out of the window. For the past few hours the traffic had become more frequent, with the guard constantly blowing blast after blast on his horn to command right of way for the mail. All the passengers had sat up nervously as they crossed the infamous Finchley Common, but to Edith its only significance was its proximity to the metropolis.

Now and then a clarion call sounded behind them and a team of fine blood horses would swing out to pass, but slap-up-to-the-echo conveyances with the speed and nerve to

15

overtake the mail were rare.

Edith watched for a glimpse of one of the spires of London. Her immediate impression as they entered the first streets was not favourable: the people, so many of them it seemed as if a giant ant's nest had been stirred by a stick; the noise, compounded of a thousand shod hooves clattering over the roadways and the cries of the street vendors. Worst of all, the stench. Edith was used to the country smell of horses and cattle but here in the confined spaces the stable stink was multiplied a thousand times. Also there was the foulness of countless cesspits and privies, together with filth streaming down makeshift channels in the meaner streets. Added to the odour of the untold thousands of unwashed bodies, the result was overpowering. Edith held a vinaigrette to her nose as the coach finally swung into the yard of a prosperous inn. The din diminished, but only marginally. The smell remained as bad as ever.

Stunned and bewildered by the assault upon her senses, Edith descended stiffly from the coach. Utterly bemused by the hustle and bustle she took a few steps, trying to sort out the various scents and sounds. She stood in the middle of the yard easing her cramped limbs whilst her father and Agnes went to attend to the luggage. Waves of sound crashed over her. Would the tumult never cease? A post horn blared loudly, whist the guard gesticulated and screamed like a madman. Suddenly, she flew backwards through the air as an iron hand clamped around her waist.

Lord Whitley was not in a good mood. His leg pained him, a constant, ominous reminder of what might be to come. For the second time in as many days he was forced to hang around this devilishly noisy inn, dancing attendance upon a miserable preacher from some outlandish backwater. Northumberland, for heaven's sake! It may as well have been the moon. The distance involved meant no one could give him any precise information as to when the man would have received Sharples' letter or indeed whether he would leave everything and come at once.

Lord Whitley's lip curled. Who wouldn't drop everything when summoned to such a position? Twenty thousand a year, at the very least, going on Sharples' figures. From country parson to one of the richest men in England! The mail yesterday had carried no passengers from the far north, though. Surely he would arrive today. Lord Whitley very much doubted he could endure another day of his self-imposed task. What could he do if the man failed to arrive? Someone other than a lawyer should inform Reverend Backworth that he was now the fifth earl.

Taking a vantage point as far away from the rush as he could manage, he watched as the weary passengers descended, each in their turn straightening stiffened limbs. There was no one who resembled the person he was looking for, or a daughter, until at last he caught sight of a young woman, simply dressed but obviously not of the labouring class. She wore black, too, which further confirmed his suspicions. So this was the new Lady Edith, was it? Lord Whitley made a thorough appraisal as she moved away from the coach. He'd seen greater beauties before, but there was something about her carriage and her dark eyes which drew a flicker of interest. Her complexion was surprisingly good, but those clothes! Something would have to be done.

As he moved forward to find the girl's father a horn sounded. Both the guard and the ostler shouted a warning, but the girl made no attempt to remove herself from what was obviously a very dangerous place to contemplate the glories of the metropolis. Without thinking he lunged forwards just as a chaise swept in under the arch. He reached her a bare second before the team crashed over the spot, drawing to a halt in a plunging, flourishing style that would have led him to dismiss *his* postilions instantly if they had treated any of his cattle that way.

All this registered dimly on his subconscious as he fought the pain that shot through his thigh. Gritting his teeth, he forced himself to master the grinding agony until it subsided into a dull ache once again. As his perception returned he became aware of a smell of violet-scented soap and a very shapely body clasped in his arms. Dusky curls peeped out from under a round bonnet, but he was unable to see the woman's features. It took a few seconds longer to realize that she lay limp in his arms. He swept her up and carried her to a nearby bench, clenching his jaw at the effort required.

'Madam, are you hurt? Come now; answer me if you please! Did the horse strike you?'

Dazed, Edith stared down. There was a long smear of slime extending over her glove that had not been there seconds earlier. Her knees trembled with sudden fright as she at last recognized it for what it was; lather from the chest of the offside leader. She had been that close! Suddenly, the sounds and smells disappeared as a wave of red heat threatened to overwhelm her. She would have buckled again had it not been for the arms around her, which held her up with an iron force. The pressure released at last as she was picked up like a feather, allowing her to suck in a lungful of air. Dimly, Edith realized that a man was talking to her. Fighting for control, she tried to concentrate on the face shifting in and out of focus. Intense dark eyes, just now frowning, stared down at her. With a rush of confusion she also became aware of an arm supporting her back and a hand extended round her ribs to the point where it brushed the underside of her breast. Even through the thick cloth of the travelling pelisse she wore she could feel the heat of his embrace seeping in. With a gasp of horror she struggled to thrust away his support and sit up.

'Easy does it!' The hand slipped downwards, much to her relief. 'Don't try to stand, yet.'

The voice was soothing and calm, the cultured tones of a gentleman. She breathed deeply, recovering her equanimity before daring to look him in the face. Edith's rescuer smiled slightly, although no warmth reached his eyes.

'I wonder if you could be Miss Edith Backworth? My name is Whitley.' When she made no response he tried again. 'Lord Whitley. I have come to meet Reverend Backworth and his daughter.'

'Sir!' Her father had finally managed to reach them from across the other side of the yard. His face was drawn with horror. 'I saw what you did, sir! My precious Edith, are you hurt? I did not think he could possibly reach you in time.'

She straightened her bonnet, desperately wishing that the heat would leave her cheeks. She had never felt so embarrassed in her whole life!

'I am quite well, Papa, only shocked. The noise is so bewildering I did not realize the chaise was coming.'

'Surely you heard the post-horn? It was loud enough to waken the dead.'

Lord Whitley had finally removed his hand altogether. Edith suppressed a sigh of thanks. If he continued to act as if nothing out of the common place had happened, then she must force herself to do likewise. She took refuge in what was left of her dignity.

'Yes, my lord, I did hear the post-horn. I simply didn't realize that it meant the chaise was coming into this yard.'

'I see. Pray tell me what you thought it meant.'

'I . . . I . . . ' Edith felt another wave of colour flood her face. How dare he be so contemptuous? Deliberately she turned her back. 'If you will excuse me, I'll wait inside the inn, Papa, whilst you arrange the baggage.'

Reverend Backworth frowned at her lack of manners. 'My dear, surely you are going to thank his lordship? If it hadn't been for his quick thinking you might have been seriously hurt.'

Edith sketched a curtsy. 'Thank you, my lord, for your service.'

He raised his glossy beaver a few inches to reveal equally glossy black hair. His gaze trailed languidly from her countenance down over her figure.

'My pleasure, Miss Backworth. Definitely my pleasure.'

Edith felt her face glow with a new heat. Anger boiled up in her again, mixed with embarrassment. She pulled herself together. Wretched, odious man! With an exclamation of rage she whirled on her heel and hurried away, taking care this time to see that the yard was clear.

Her father did not join her for some time. When he did finally appear, that insufferable man was still with him. As gently as he could, Reverend Backworth informed his daughter of the situation.

'Edith, my dear. My cousin Lord Cramlington did not recover from his ailment. I regret to tell you he has died.'

No! It could not be! Edith felt stunned by the news. Somehow, all along the tedious journey she had imagined that the fourth earl would be miraculously restored to health by the time they arrived. She didn't want papa to be an earl. It wasn't until the landlord himself had brought a tray of refreshments, his nose nearly touching his knees, that she realized all the bowing and scraping and 'my lord' this and 'my lord' that were addressed to her father, and not, as she had first supposed, to Lord Whitley.

Lord Whitley took pity on her. 'You look bewildered, Lady Edith. Perhaps you would care for some refreshments; maybe a glass of ratafia?'

Lady Edith? Was he talking to her? Edith Backworth a *ladyship*? It was too absurd a notion to be considered for an instant! What was the man still doing here, anyway? He wasn't family.

'His lordship has brought his carriage to collect us, my dear,' the reverend explained. 'Would you care to eat a luncheon here, or press on?'

'Press on? Are we going to a hotel?'

'No, to Lord Cramlington's . . . I mean to our new house. Apparently the entire estate has passed to me. Lord Whitley is the executor.'

It was all too much. Edith allowed herself to be handed into a luxurious barouche. Her father placed a travelling rug across her knees before he settled himself beside her, whilst Lord Whitley took a place opposite. She smiled a little, wondering when Lord Whitley was last obliged to sit forwards, but there was too much to think about to allow herself to worry overmuch about him.

A footman must have been on watch; before the coach even drew to a stop the doors of the imposing mansion were flung open. A phalanx of lackeys surrounded the butler, with the housekeeper and housemaids lined up further inside the hall. As Edith was ceremoniously passed along the line in the wake of her father she realized that even the scullery-maids had been fetched up to greet the new lord and his daughter. She smiled at the knife-boy, an urchin of no more than ten or eleven, who turned bright red as her gaze fell on him. They all looked so wary!

The housekeeper, Mrs Anstey, conducted her up two flights of stairs to a set of apartments consisting of bedroom, dressing-room and boudoir, all overlooking the square. Within seconds, a maid arrived with a can of hot water. Agnes unpacked a morning gown, which was whisked off to be pressed, while Edith washed away the stains of the journey. What luxury! Abundant hot water, her favourite violet soap and towels of the finest linen. Edith admired the exquisite band of lace along the hem of the towel. She wouldn't have been ashamed of wearing such workmanship, yet here she was drying her face with it.

As soon as her hair was reduced to something like order and the gown was returned, she scrambled into it and made her way down. Uncertain which direction to go she hesitated for a few moments in the hall, debating which of the doors in front of her would lead to the drawing-room. She heard voices to her left and went to investigate.

'Really, Louisa, you could have shown your cousins the courtesy of receiving them. I was astounded that you left Mrs Anstey to conduct Lady Edith to her room.'

There was a loud, ungenteel snort. 'You expected *me* to stand in a draughty hallway for a country nobody and his dowdy daughter? You must be mad, Charles! They deserve no mark of respect from me, I can assure you!'

Edith froze. Is that what they thought of her father? Of her?

'Tell me, what is she like, this Edith?'

Edith was about to storm into the room, then changed her mind. Eavesdroppers rarely hear good of themselves, she knew, but it would be interesting to find out what Lord

25

Whitley had made of her.

'I wasn't overly-impressed. Dowdy, as you said, but that can be set to rights. She has a neat figure and passable good looks. Fine eyes. Obviously she needs a good deal of town bronze. Being nearly run down by a post-chaise taught her not to stand and stare like a yokel, I should imagine. And then that father of hers didn't have the sense to know she was in danger, either. I feel he would be more at home with his flock than with the society we keep.'

Lady Louisa's reply was never uttered as Edith sailed into the room, her head held high. Dowdy, was she? A provincial nobody to be set to rights by the likes of Lord Whitley? How dare he!

Lord Whitley looked slightly taken aback, but only for a second or two. He very swiftly recovered his poise, moving across the space separating them to offer his hand.

'Lady Edith! We had thought you resting. May I present you to your cousin? Louisa, this is Edith Backworth.'

'From Northumberland,' Edith interposed. 'The country yokel. How do you do, Lady Louisa? I do trust that I have no straws sticking to my clothing, or anything else equally objectionable!'

2

A dull flush rose into Lord Whitley's face. Whether it was caused by anger or embarrassment Edith had no idea, but she wasn't going to wait to find out. She pressed home her attack before her courage failed.

'And as for you, my lord, my father may well be a country nobody, but he is most certainly the gentleman! You could do a great deal worse than study not just his manner of address but also the true dignity of spirit that goes with it. You might be a nobleman, but that is a mere accident of birth: gentlemen are distinguished by their breeding, or so I do believe.'

'What *outrageous* impertinence! Who are you to criticize your betters?'

The furious comment came not from Lord Whitley, but from Lady Louisa. She sprang to her feet, her face pale with rage. Edith, her temper well up, surprised even herself.

'I am now the daughter of an earl, madam, just as you are. Before today, I thought of myself as a parson's daughter. If yours is an example of how I must behave in my new position, I would that I had remained in my former state!'

'Perhaps we should all remember our positions,' Lord Whitley interrupted. 'Brawling in the drawing-room with your father hardly cold in the ground is not seemly, Louisa.'

Lady Louisa swelled with rage. 'Brawling? You accuse me of brawling? I would never dream of such vulgarity! I do not consider a well-deserved reprimand to a common upstart *brawling*. You forget yourself, sir. I will leave you to enjoy your low company as best you may!'

She swept out of the room without so much as another glance at Edith.

Lord Whitley glowered as the door closed with a decided bang. His lips thinned to a narrow line and his eyes spoke volumes. After a moment, he turned to Edith. 'Do you not consider, ma'am, that your remarks were most ill-judged? Louisa has been deprived of her brother, her father and the man she planned to marry. What is more, her position of safety and comfort in this house now resides on your father's whim. Surely she is entitled to feel upset?'

Edith had had sufficient time to regret her outburst. It was not so much the criticism of herself that had upset her, after all, but the slight to her father. She was forced to acknowledge the truth behind Lord Whitley's words, much as it galled her. Lady Louisa had excuse for her behaviour, but not this man!

'Perhaps, my lord, Lady Louisa might not have become so upset if *your* choice of language had not offended me so.'

'Then I must apologize. I should not have voiced my opinion.'

Edith seethed. He didn't apologize for his opinion, merely for having voiced it! The man was insufferable! She strode over to the window and stood looking down at the street. Her breath surged in and out of her lungs as she fought with herself. Had none of these people any consideration for her feelings? For her poor papa? He had done nothing to deserve their insults and their scorn! Angry fingers wiped away a tear of rage that was threatening to spill.

'I am sorry that you are so overset.' The voice came from close behind. Edith whirled around to find Lord Whitley looking down at her. His features were schooled into a semblance of politeness. The hard look in his eyes had faded, to be replaced by an expression close to sympathy. For the first time she noticed the marks of suffering around his eyes and mouth. She recalled his limp, and the slight stumble he had made when he descended from his carriage. Conceivably he, too, had reasons for his temper.

'Perhaps we are all overset today,' she admitted, grudgingly. 'We must all learn to make the best of things.'

'Indeed.' Lord Whitley nodded. 'I will take my leave of you. I shall be calling on Lord Cramlington in the morning to discuss legal matters. I trust I shall see you in better spirits then.'

Edith curtsied slightly. 'Good day, my lord.'

The new earl and his daughter sat in splendour at the dinner table that evening. The covers had been laid fully twenty feet away from each other, but Edith very swiftly moved to her father's right hand side, ignoring the disapproval of Hartley. The two of them regarded each other rather forlornly as the soup was served.

'Well, my dear, and what do you think of your new home?' her father enquired.

Edith didn't know what to say. 'I suppose I shall grow accustomed,' she replied, 'but it is all so very strange. I do not think Louisa and I shall rub along very comfortably.'

Lord Cramlington sighed. He too had suffered the sharp edge of Louisa's tongue when she had been persuaded to join them earlier for a dish of tea. His fond belief that she would take Edith under her wing had vanished in a very few seconds.

'It leaves us uncomfortably situated, for you must have a chaperon who can tell you how to go on. Someone who knows the latest modistes and all that sort of thing. Someone who can take you into society, and escort you to all the parties. I am not acquainted with anyone that I can ask to perform such duties.'

'I am in mourning, Papa. I have no wish to go into society at present. Agnes can look after me.'

Her father would have none of that. 'For the degree of your relationship I think that three or four months' mourning will be quite sufficient. You must certainly make your debut at the start of the season, even if you are still in black gloves. There are more things to do than dancing, my dear. There will be concerts, assemblies, lectures, museums and libraries to visit and my time will be wholly taken up with business for a considerable period. As good a creature as she is, Agnes would be completely unsuitable for such a position. No, I must seek advice. Lord Whitley will know what to do, I am sure.'

'Pray, Papa, do not think of asking Lord Whitley to advise you!' The very thought of his condescending patronage appalled Edith.

'I cannot wish to be beholden to him.'

'But we *are* beholden to him, my dear, and very much so. I noticed today that you have taken him in dislike, although I cannot think why. I must ask you to treat him with civility. He has been most kind.'

Uncomfortably aware of what her father's reaction to her outburst that afternoon would have been, Edith felt the tips of her ears grow warm. She had not been civil to Lord Whitley, and well she knew it. She swallowed hard. 'Of course, Papa, if that is your wish. I am sure I have enough breeding to be able to cope with Lord Whitley.'

Her father smiled. 'Thank you, my dear. And I am sure we can put our heads together and come up with something to suit.'

The next morning as Edith descended to the breakfast-room, she stopped short at the sight of the hall piled with trunks and boxes. Before she could summon Hartley to discover what was happening, Louisa swept out of the book-room. She stopped when she saw Edith on the staircase.

'I have just informed your father that I refuse to remain under the same roof as you for another instant. Now that I have been driven out of my own home, I shall have to cast myself on the bosom of my mother's family in the hope that they will take me in. I shall reside with my aunt Seaton. I do not bid you farewell. I have nothing more to say to you!'

Edith waited until Louisa was out of earshot, together with the fawning Miss Berwick. 'And good riddance too!'

Her father sat behind his desk, a pained expression on his face. Edith hurried to his side. 'I am sorry, Papa.'

'Is it true, Edith, what Lady Louisa has told me? That you have driven her away?'

'I don't know what she told you, Papa, but I will not permit anyone to insult you in my hearing.'

He sighed. 'What are we going to do with you, Edith? First Lord Whitley and now Lady Louisa. We must pray that she will come around.'

'We are much better off without her, Papa. Now at least we may be comfortable.'

'But you have no other female living here, Edith. It is very irregular.'

Edith racked her brains to think of something to take the look off his face. She hated to see her father upset. 'Lord Whitley will be here this morning. I have no idea why he was made executor, but since he is, he might as well make himself useful. Remember your plan to ask him to recommend a suitable lady?'

Her father's brow cleared marginally. 'Ah, yes. He will know how to go on. And Edith, I have remembered why Lord Whitley has such close associations with the family. He was engaged to be married to Louisa's sister. Lady Chloe died of fever nearly three years ago, whilst his lordship was serving in the Peninsula. You were most likely too young to take much notice at the time.'

Edith vaguely remembered the death of her cousin, but not the fact that she had been engaged. 'Oh, I am sorry for him, then. There appears to be a great deal of bad luck associated with this family, does there not? Only Louisa, ourselves and Bertram remain.'

Her father sighed. 'No more so than many another in England at the moment, my dear. The casualty lists from Waterloo were enormous.'

Lord Whitley, it appeared, had the perfect solution to Edith's problem. Within a very few days he arrived at the house with Mrs Augusta Venables in tow. It was difficult to assess her age, but Edith gauged it to be around four or five and thirty. With clear, milky skin, huge pansy eyes and fine blonde hair hidden almost completely by her cap, she had obviously been a great beauty. In her widow's blacks she looked as fragile as a porcelain doll. Lord Whitley was obviously fond of her.

How fond exactly? Edith's suspicions as to the precise nature of the relationship existing between these two simmered as she watched them.

Her qualms, however, were very soon laid to rest.

Over a dish of tea, Augusta revealed some of her history as she smiled fondly at Lord Whitley across the room.

'Charles and my late husband were the greatest of friends. I think of him almost as a brother-in-law, they were so close. Colonel Venables was his superior officer in the Peninsula campaigns, until he fell at Salamanca. I owe Charles a debt I can never repay. Despite his own wound he searched for hours until he found my Henry.' She broke off, sipping at her tea until she blinked away a tear that had crept into her eye. 'Henry died in his arms, comforted by his friend. Charles was able to bring me a final message. I shall never forget his kindness.'

Kindness wasn't a trait that Edith had associated with his lordship, but she was quite prepared to admit that Augusta must be a better judge of his character than she. Perhaps he wasn't all bad.

'So, Lord Whitley received his injury at

Salamanca.' She watched his limping progress across the room with a new interest. Edith had read every word of the dispatches from Spain. 'It must have been most severe.'

'Oh, no, my dear Lady Edith. Charles was wounded in the shoulder at Salamanca. This present affliction dates from Quatre Bras. Charles concealed it as a mere scratch until he was carried from the field at Waterloo. His bravery is astounding!'

There was little Edith could do but agree. Any wounded hero of the Waterloo campaign was allowed his share of testiness. As the gentlemen joined them she smiled up at him. Lord Whitley's expression changed to one of astonishment.

'Augusta has been with us for less than half an hour and already you are looking at me more kindly! She is a magician. Your father and I have agreed that if anyone can bring you into society she is the one to do it.'

It was Edith's turn to be astonished. Her charitable feelings disappeared in an instant. 'Is it such an onerous task, my lord?'

Lord Whitley coloured slightly. 'I beg your pardon. If ever there is a person who could take one up the wrong way it must be you. I simply meant that Augusta is related to or well acquainted with every hostess of note in town. Moreover she has the time to devote to the task. And,' he added, smiling down at his friend's wife, 'she has promised me to obey Henry's wish and cast off her mourning. He never wanted you to pine, my dear madam, you know that.'

Mrs Venables tried to smile. 'I always obeyed my husband. After three years I still miss him dearly, but life must go on.' She reached out to take Edith's hand. 'It will *not* be so very onerous a task, my dear. You are one of the most beautiful girls I have seen in a long while, and definitely not in the common style. Do you not agree, Charles?'

Edith nearly giggled at the expression on Lord Whitley's face. It was patently obvious that he did *not* agree!

'Of course, you must be a better judge than I, ma'am,' he managed. 'I have not been in town for several seasons now.'

'I can assure you that the beauties lately have been no less than insipid. Lady Edith will take the shine out of all of them.'

'She will?' He did not appear to be convinced. Before he could say anything more however, Lord Cramlington intervened.

'It's agreed then, is it?' he enquired. 'Will you help us out, ma'am?'

Augusta looked at Edith, then back at the earl. 'If you would like to have me, it would be a pleasure.'

Anything was better than Louisa. Edith smiled. 'We would be honoured, Mrs Venables.'

As it turned out, Mrs Venables fitted into the household much more easily than Edith had anticipated. They very soon discovered a mutual love of literature, especially the works of Herrick. Being obliged to wait one morning to be attended at the silk warehouse, the conversation naturally turned to his lines on the topic.

'So truly *melodic*, do you not think, my dear Lady Edith? There is such magic in his style.'

'Indeed, ma'am. *Whenas in silks my Julia goes*,'

'Oh, yes! *Then, then, methinks, how sweetly flows . . .* '

They finished in unison, ' *. . . that liquefaction of her clothes.*'

Augusta sighed. 'My dear Henry was used to read to me from the *Hesperides*, although there were some parts he judged unsuitable for a lady's ears. He would call me his Julia, even when I was dressed in sensible broadcloth and half-boots! Of course, that was when we were much younger, newly married, in fact!'

'And you could still be taken for Julia, ma'am! I can quite imagine you in silks upon a dance floor.'

'There was little call for that in Spain, although we did have our moments in the winter quarters. Still, we must not linger over the past. Tell me what you prefer, my dear. With your colouring you can quite easily wear some of the bolder colours. What of this blue velvet for a riding habit?'

'Wait? Do you not know who I am? I am not accustomed to waiting!'

Both Edith and Augusta started at the sound of the loud, angry voice. Before they could do more than exchange speaking glances, Lady Louisa swept into view, the ubiquitous Miss Berwick not far behind. Louisa pulled up short at the sight of Edith and her companion. Her eyes narrowed to venomous slits.

'You!' she exclaimed, in accents of utmost loathing. She turned on the unfortunate proprietor in a fury. 'Obviously the tone of this establishment is sadly lacking. You might be prepared to attend to the wants of a parson's daughter before those of a Lady of Quality, but I shall not so demean myself. I shall transfer my considerable patronage to another emporium, one where the clientele is more to my taste. You had best attend this . . . female.' Louisa's gaze swept insolently over Edith. 'Obviously, she is sadly in need of whatever assistance you are able to afford her.

Come, Miss Berwick. I have no wish to breathe this contaminated air for another second!'

'I always knew that Louisa was vulgar, and now I have ample proof of it.' Edith had not before heard her companion speak so coldly. Augusta's eyes flashed. 'You are well rid of her, my dear.'

Edith stared at her cousin's departing figure. What gave anyone the right to behave in such an outrageous manner? Suddenly, she recalled the look on Louisa's face when she had first caught sight of her. Her anger evaporated in a flash. Hastily, she tried to suppress a giggle.

Augusta looked at her in surprise. 'Are you not angry?'

'Not nearly as angry as Lady Louisa is going to be when she sees me in my finery!'

By the time they left the warehouse, their footman was loaded down with packages. Edith felt torn between delight at the purchases they had made and guilt at the wicked extravagance. Her companion must have suffered a twinge of conscience also. Once they were settled in the carriage Augusta mentioned it.

'It is so good of your father to provide me with a dress allowance! It was not a thing I had looked for, I assure you, but he insisted.

His generosity is beyond belief.'

'Yes, Papa is generous, and he likes nothing better than to be able to exercise his generosity. Don't think anything of it, ma'am. We both need to present a modish front, and you would not have incurred such expenses if it was not for my benefit.'

'I am grateful, nonetheless. And I do think it sensible of him to permit you to go into black gloves at the end of the month. Full mourning for a distant cousin you have never met does seem a trifle unnecessary.'

'Papa will observe the entire six months, however. He thought it only proper.'

'Well, the case is not quite the same, of course. He will not be wishful to go to as many balls and assemblies, and even if he does go, no one would expect him to dance. But you, my dear Edith, are a different proposition. It is my opinion you will become all the rage when the season opens.'

Edith laughed. 'I have no desire to become 'all the rage', ma'am. I'll enjoy myself for the season, which is what Papa wishes, and then we can be comfortable back in Northumberland.'

'Ah, yes! At Cramlington Priory, of course. But not, my dear, in the winter! I am persuaded it can be sadly uncomfortable so far north.'

'At least we won't have to go far for our coals! Papa tells me he is the owner of at least five prosperous collieries.'

'He is to be congratulated! I am sure the whole of London depends on coals from Newcastle in the winter. Ah. Here we are! Let's see what Mrs Bell can suggest for all these riches.'

Edith was as keen as Augusta to enter the modish salon. 'As long as the first garment is my new riding habit, I'm happy to go along with whatever she suggests, as I must and I will have my rides. It is impossible to walk in town as I was used to do, but my rides I will not give up.'

Edith might have thought that she didn't care overly for clothes, but when the boxes started to arrive in Grosvenor Square she was as anxious as any young girl to have them carried to her room immediately. With her hair dressed in one of the becoming new styles she was astonished at the transformation in her appearance. What with the hats, the shawls, gloves, boots, fans, slippers, reticules and all the hundred and one other necessities, the place soon looked like Aladdin's cave. Her conscience smote her from time to time, but Augusta only laughed.

'I can assure you that by some standards you have been fairly modest in your purchases, Edith. Gloves and slippers will only last for a single evening, unless you are amazingly fortunate and they do not become soiled. You cannot appear at a ball in the same dress on more than two occasions without being considered a dowd, either.'

Edith flushed at 'dowd'. Lord Whitley's words still rankled, even though she knew that he would be very hard put to use the description now. In her trim-fitting riding habit with its audacious feathered hat and fall of lace at her throat she thought she looked the picture of fashion. Not the blue velvet, however, but a much more practical grey broadcloth.

Her companion sighed as she looked in the mirror. 'I still think the velvet would have looked dashing. That dark grey is so sombre. I do believe it works, though. The white of the ostrich-plume and lace highlights the perfection of your complexion.'

'Oh, ma'am, pray do not!' Edith wasn't used to being praised.

'No, no, I assure you!' Augusta insisted. 'The elegance of your carriage is shown off admirably, too.'

Edith had to laugh. 'Indeed! All I need now is for Papa to engage a groom for me and provide a hack. I can take all the exercise I require, then.'

On a mild morning early in November, Edith finally descended the shallow flight of steps at the front door to her waiting horse. Dawn triumphed with its battle over night as Rogers, her new groom, hurried to throw her up. Newly promoted from stable-boy by Lord Cramlington, he was very conscious of his duty. He kept a wary eye open until he could judge her ability. Her father had taught her well, however, and Rogers soon relaxed.

Her new mount was a beautiful bay mare, with intelligent eyes and a soft mouth. A powerful hunter, not a town hack, she looked to have the staying power and intelligence Edith loved in her horses.

She laid a hand on the shining neck in front of her. 'I shall call you Glory.'

Fretting to be away, they walked sedately through the streets until they reached Hyde Park, Glory ignoring such distractions as mongrel curs and pieces of paper blown across her path with a well-bred disdain.

Once through the gates, Edith urged her horse forward. The mare responded with alacrity, breaking smoothly into a fast canter, which very soon stretched into a gallop. At this early hour of the morning there were very few other riders in the park and the sense of freedom made Edith laugh with the sheer joy of living. The last of the autumn leaves scattered in a bronze shower as they raced along in their mad dash, the only sound that of the thundering hooves. Too soon she dropped back to a more sedate canter, not wishing Glory to be overworked on her first outing.

Rogers caught up to her. 'My lady!'

Edith laughed. 'I know, I know, Rogers, but I couldn't help it! Isn't she beautiful?'

'That she is, my lady. Lord Cramlington is a good judge of horseflesh, from what I've seen. He spent nearly two hours going over the late earl's stable. Lady Louisa's nags weren't good enough for you, not by a long shot! Downright slugs, I call them! He did too, but then Lady Louisa couldn't hold a candle to yourself, beggin' your pardon, ma'am.'

'Oh, yes. My father loves his hunting. Squire Jesmond always supplied mounts for him during the season, and often consulted Papa about his purchases. He said he had an eye.' Edith suddenly recalled that she could well be accused of gossiping with the servants, but his words still left a warm glow inside her. So Lady Louisa wasn't much of a horse-woman, was she?

Walking sedately towards the main gates, Edith noticed an exquisite black trotting towards her. Lost in admiration of the animal's magnificent conformation, she failed to notice the rider until he was almost up to them. Lord Whitley was certainly a judge of horseflesh if he had had anything to do with the purchase of the black.

His lordship touched his crop to the rim of his hat as he pulled up beside her.

'Good morning, Lady Edith. I'm surprised to see you out at such an hour. I thought young ladies enjoyed their beauty sleep.'

'Good morning, my lord. I was of the impression that gentlemen rarely keep such early hours either.'

He looked around at the nearly empty park. 'I fear you may be right, ma'am. That's a neatish-looking mare you are riding. Surely she's a trifle high spirited for a lady?'

'What, my Glory? She's perfect. Not one to take the shine out of your own mount, however. I've never seen such a magnificent animal.'

Lord Whitley laid a hand on the sleek black neck. 'Ah, yes. Satan is a prize indeed.'

The stallion flicked back an ear as if to hear more clearly. Lord Whitley smiled and murmured to the animal, allowing Edith to see a softer side of him she had not previously witnessed as he spoke to his mount. In a moment or two, however, he looked back at her.

'I beg your pardon, my lady. Were you on

your way home already, or would you care to take a turn with me?'

Glory was still fresh, so Edith obligingly turned back along the row. Lord Whitley set Satan to an easy canter, a pace that soon had the black fretting at the bit. It was obvious to Edith that the stallion longed to stretch out, just as she had herself a little while previously. In a spirit of mischief she set her heel into her horse's flank and gave Glory her head. The bay bounded away, gaining a good start while Lord Whitley collected his startled wits. In seconds, however, he was after her, urging his mount to a gallop. The stallion caught up to the smaller bay with apparent ease. Thundering along neck and neck, Glory vainly tried to match her companion, but he very soon pulled away. As the mare began to labour Edith reined back and was again sedate as Lord Whitley returned to her.

They walked along back to the gate over a carpet of fallen leaves. Vapour rose in lazy drifts from the hides of the heated animals to add to that produced from their nostrils. A squirrel, not yet fully prepared for the winter, scurried out of their way with a frightened chirp.

'Well, whatever other talents you might have, ma'am, I take leave to tell you that you have an uncommonly good seat on a horse.'

Lord Whitley smiled as he indicated their surroundings. 'Although this is not, perhaps, a good place to choose for a gallop. Allow me to take you to Richmond Park one morning.'

'I doubt if my companion would approve. It was only with the strictest of instructions to Rogers that she permitted me to ride today. Mrs Venables is not a horsewoman, or so she informs me.'

Lord Whitley bowed. 'I spoke without thinking, ma'am. Of course it would be most improper of me to be alone in your company. We could, of course, make up a party.'

'But then we should not be able to have our gallop, would we, my lord? You would be mindful of your guests and keeping pace with the slowest of the riders.'

She had annoyed him again. Perhaps he didn't care to be countered like that. Well, that was just too bad.

They had reached the park gates again by this time, where Rogers was awaiting them. Edith held out her hand. 'Thank you, sir, for your company.'

'No, indeed. It was my pleasure. In your presence I can be nothing less than entranced. I shall see you home.'

Edith bit down on her lower lip. If only she could be sure that he was referring to her conversation, but she'd seen the almost blatant sweep of his gaze across her figure. Was this his way of punishing her? Or did he imagine that she liked to be ogled? That perhaps females would welcome such attentions? In London society who knew what standards of conduct prevailed, but Edith had been more modestly raised. Feeling the colour mount in her cheeks she turned for home without reply.

3

Perhaps she had dropped her guard, thinking her mare had perfect manners, but when it happened Edith received such a surprise that for a second she was slow to react. Rogers and Lord Whitley had dismounted and the groom was just reaching for Glory's bridle when a wretched donkey pulling a trades-man's cart brayed loudly. The mare shot up on her hind legs, squealing with terror.

For an instant Edith thought she would fall and with frantic fingers grabbed for the mane to steady herself. Lord Whitley leapt for the mare's head, as did the groom. It was only when his leg collapsed under him that anyone remembered his wound. The sight of the sprawled body and flashing hooves filled Edith with terror. Rogers hurled himself between the horse and Lord Whitley, but not before Edith felt a solid thud as one of Glory's hooves landed on flesh. The sickening jolt caused her to cry out with fear, not for herself but for the man now lying on the road in a crumpled heap. As if held in the grip of a nightmare, her body would not obey her wishes. Why was everything taking so long?

She must go to his aid. He was hurt. Perhaps . . . perhaps he was dead.

The hideous idea acted like a goad to jar her out of her stupid shock. She scrambled out of the saddle, fumbling to free her foot from the stirrup. She had to get to him.

At last she could throw herself beside him, uncaring of the danger from her mare's wild plunges. An ominous red stain darkened his breeches.

The screams and commotion had swiftly drawn a crowd. Hartley and two of the footmen hastened to help Edith, whilst the driver of the donkey cart ran to the assistance of the harassed Rogers, who had three horses to deal with.

Edith thrust her handkerchief over the injury in Lord Whitley's thigh. It was obvious that the blow from Glory's hoof had split open his half-healed wound.

'Hartley, find Mrs Anstey immediately. Send the knife boy for the nearest surgeon. Tell him to run all the way.'

The flow of vivid scarlet showed no sign of diminishing. There must be *something* she could do!

'You two, help me to take his lordship inside.'

The two footmen gathered up the semi-conscious viscount. Edith kept up a determined pressure on the blood welling past her fingers, but she was doing very little good. The fine leather of his riding breeches would have to be cut away immediately if she was to prevent him bleeding to death.

Abandoning her plan to have him carried to a bedchamber Edith directed the footmen to the book-room, where Lord Whitley was laid on a sofa. The housekeeper came running with a razor and some linen and between them they managed to slit his boot and breeches to reveal the ugly gash. Edith winced, but her resolve held firm. One of the footmen turned green and vanished, but the other helped her to wrap several hastily torn bandages around the leg. Mrs Anstey fluttered around, making exclamations of horror as she summoned burnt feathers and hartshorn. When they arrived she supported Lord Whitley's shoulders and attempted to revive him.

'No, don't do that!' Edith looked up from her work. 'Lay him flat. The leg should be raised, not his head. We've done all we can to prevent the bleeding until the surgeon arrives. Let's get him up to the bedchamber.'

The crowd around the door to the book-room was sent about its business with a few well-chosen words, apart from the four stout men Edith commanded to carry his

52

lordship. With the greatest of care they eased him off the sofa and away up the stairs, where Mrs Venables and Edith's father had just emerged from their rooms to find out what had caused the commotion in the house. Augusta turned so faint at the sight of the blood-soaked pair that Edith had to send the housekeeper to her aid. Her father, however, was made of sterner stuff and rushed to assist, not wasting time by asking questions.

When Lord Whitley was laid on the bed Edith left him for a few moments with her father and the footman. While they stripped off the rest of his clothes and eased him into a night-shirt, Edith took the opportunity to shed her own soiled habit and wash the blood from her hands, all the time shaking her head at the uproar around her. The chambermaids ran about in hysterics, carrying cans of hot water and linen this way and that, not knowing what they were to be doing or where they were going without the housekeeper to direct them.

The boy sent to fetch the surgeon had been extremely fortunate to find Sir James Walgrove still at his breakfast table in his residence two streets away. By the time Edith had calmed the chaos, Sir James was at the door. Not for the first time she wished for the presence of Agnes, who would have taken charge of the situation with her customary northern sense. However Agnes had gone back to Northumberland, to see to the packing at the vicarage. If anything was to be done, Edith was the one who was going to have to do it.

Her father accompanied Sir James to the patient, whilst Edith waited anxiously by the door. Her father came out to her quite soon after.

'Sir James informs me that he must probe the wound again. He has a very poor opinion of the job done by the army surgeons. We must be quick if we are to save Lord Whitley. Can you find someone to assist him?'

Edith mentally passed the chambermaids under review, dismissing them all instantly. Between the lot of them they had no more sense than a wet hen. The housekeeper was no better, exclaiming in repugnant denial when Edith came to find her in Augusta's room.

'I wouldn't know what to do, my lady!'

'Very well.' Edith looked at the woman scornfully. 'You remain with Mrs Venables. I will assist the surgeon.'

Mrs Anstey gasped with horror. 'Your ladyship! It isn't fitting! A young girl like you can't go into a sick-room! A nurse will have to be sent for.'

'And in the meantime his lordship will have bled to death.'

Mrs Venables struggled to rise. 'It is my place to assist the surgeon. It was only the shock of seeing the blood which turned me so faint.'

'Madam, pray sit down again.' Augusta was no more able to assist Sir James than she was to fly. 'It would be far too distressing for you. I am quite capable of helping. Don't torment yourself. I'll go and prepare.'

It was one thing to appear calm and collected in front of Augusta, but Edith felt a qualm of apprehension when she entered the sick-room. She had never even seen her father in his nightshirt, let alone a comparative stranger like Lord Whitley. Swallowing hard, she tried her best to appear brisk and business-like, smoothing the clean apron she had donned to conceal the tremble in her hands.

Sir James straightened from taking a pulse. His eyebrows shot up as he looked at her, but he made no comment. Instead he issued a rapid stream of commands, which had Edith scurrying to obey. It wasn't until she was actually standing beside the doctor, holding a bowl for him whilst he probed for the ball that she had time to take another look at Lord Whitley.

Oh, the poor man! Her heart contracted with instant sympathy as she took in his appearance. Mercifully unconscious, his skin had assumed an unhealthy, grey tinge, with dark shadows under his eyes. There was a sheen of cold sweat across his brow and his breathing was laboured. He looked so young and so helpless she found it hard to believe that she was looking at the same person who had been so urbane and self-assured barely an hour before.

'Demme, what a mess! Oh, I beg your pardon, your ladyship. I can't believe the condition of this wound.' The surgeon muttered and exclaimed as he worked. At last he grunted with satisfaction, holding up a bloodied pair of forceps. Something rattled into her dish. Edith made out a flattened lead ball, together with what appeared to be a tiny scrap of material. It must have been driven from his clothing into his flesh when the ball first struck. Edith shivered. Her head pounded as the bile rose up in her throat. How had he ever managed to conceal this appalling wound?

Sir James examined the dish and its contents. 'I believe that the ball deflected off something solid before striking the thigh muscle. See this misshapen area? If that had happened in the leg the bone would have been shattered at the very least. How anyone could have missed it is beyond me. The Duke must have little better than butchers working for him. It's a scandal. Lord Whitley is an exceedingly fortunate young man that this accident happened when it did. There is infection here that could still kill him.'

Edith tried to make an intelligent comment, but all she could do was desperately strive to swallow the nausea threatening to overtake her as the room swayed before her eyes. Sir James must have realized her predicament for he threw a cloth over the dish and sent her dashing for fresh water and linen as he began to clean and tend the wound. By the time she returned, Edith had conquered her nausea, if not her fear. At last he was finished.

The doctor shook his head. 'I am still not completely hopeful of saving the limb, or even his lordship's life, but with careful nursing he might pull through. If the infection spreads, however . . . the next few days will be critical.'

He gave Edith a detailed list of instructions regarding hot fomentations, laudanum and other medications. Finally, he prepared to leave. 'You will have to expect a deal of fever and delirium, my lady, but I shall send an attendant to instruct his lordship's valet. They should be able to deal with him. I'll call again this evening to see how he is progressing. I see no need to bleed him at present. In the meanwhile, I suggest . . . ' he paused for a moment, regarding the inert form, ' . . . is his lordship married?'

Edith shook her head.

'Very well. I suggest his parents be sent for.'

At the door he paused. 'You did well, my dear, very well. I'll inform the earl of that.' With a nod of his shaggy head he departed.

She felt the blood drain from her face as the import of the doctor's words struck home. Edith fell into the chair set close to the bed and raised trembling hands to her face. Hot and cold shivers racked her body as reaction set in. What had she been thinking? If only Agnes had been here, or . . . or anybody!

A low groan sent her bolt upright. How could she be wallowing in self-pity when here was Lord Whitley so desperately ill! Reaching for the bowl of lavender-water she had set close by, she dipped a cloth and gingerly dabbed it across his face. His eyelids flickered, but didn't open. Feeling bolder, she smoothed the pillow under his head then raised a single finger to the lock of hair that had spilled across his brow. Gently, she eased it back, sliding her palm across his sweat-soaked hair as a wave of fierce compassion filled her. If Lord Whitley was to die . . . Well, he wouldn't die, not if Edith Backworth could prevent it! Filled with a stubborn determination, she set to work.

Hartley leapt to his feet in consternation as a miniature whirlwind swept into the servants' quarters. His first thought was to scan the board to see which of the bells had been overlooked.

'No, no, Hartley, I didn't ring the bell. I don't have time to bother with that nonsense.'

She scanned the assembly, looking for the cook. In seconds he was dispatched to prepare the most nourishing broth he could muster. The chambermaids were told in no uncertain terms how they were to behave in and around the sick-room and a footman was delegated to assist until Lord Whitley's valet could be fetched. Finally she turned to the butler.

'Hartley, I fear Mrs Anstey is still recovering from the shock of this morning's events, but I am sure I will be able to count on you.'

Dazzled by Edith's smile, which for a second or two replaced the determined frown on her face, Hartley could only nod.

'Excellent. Please send round to the stables

to have the boys spread a thick layer of straw in front of the house. The racket those carriages and carts make is enough to make anyone ill. The noise must be reduced. We shall make every effort to keep Lord Whitley as comfortable as possible.'

By the time he had thought of a suitable reply, she had gone.

'Well, I don't know, I'm sure,' one of the chambermaids began, but Hartley turned on her.

'And that's the way it should be, Sarah. I believe you heard my lady's instructions?' His gaze swept the room. 'All of you?'

He returned to the silver he had been polishing, a half-smile on his lips. Compared to Lady Louisa, Lady Edith was like a breath of fresh air!

Edith's short-lived bravado faded as soon as she returned to the bedchamber. Lord Whitley moaned softly, his head turning from side to side in a feeble effort to find release from the pain that caused the sweat to bead on his brow. She felt so helpless. Surely there was something more the doctor could do?

By five o'clock, Edith was ready to tear her hair out. Apparently Lord Whitley's valet had been given leave and was nowhere to be found. The attendant Sir James had promised to send was watching by the bedside of a dying patient and could not be with them until the morning at the earliest and Augusta still succumbed to swoons every time she attempted to rise. Edith had left her father alone with the invalid for no more than a few minutes and found him attempting to give Lord Whitley a glass of claret when she returned. He had shrugged his shoulders apologetically when the danger of his actions was pointed out.

'I'm sorry, my dear, but I have not the faintest notion of how to care for a sick person.'

Edith dispatched her father to the book-room to pray for Lord Whitley, which was a skill he had in abundance. It would also keep him out of the way.

After watching the clumsy efforts of the footmen to change a nightshirt she knew that delegating his care to them would be disastrous. Perfectly willing to follow instruc-tions as they were, they too had no skill when it came to nursing. Once they had finished their task she dismissed them.

'Fetch some clean linen and fresh lavender-water, then find out if Mrs Anstey has been able to procure those items I need for the fomentations. I shall have to apply them myself.' She stopped as a low growl issued from her stomach. The light had faded, and she had left the house for her ride before breakfast. With a weary hand she pushed a straggling lock of hair from her forehead. 'Oh, and be so good as to have a tray of dinner sent up for me. I cannot leave his lordship.'

The doctor arrived just as she finished her meal. He hummed and tutted so much that Edith began to fear the worst, but at last he straightened.

'There's no sign of the infection spreading. Tonight will be the test, I believe. If his lordship has the strength to conquer the fever his excellent constitution should pull him through. He must be watched closely.'

Edith nodded. 'My father and I plan to take turns to sit with him. Papa will fetch me instantly if he shows any signs of rousing.'

'Excellent, my dear, excellent. Just remember to be prepared for some delirium. His fever will undoubtedly rise.'

When the laudanum administered by the doctor took its effect Edith left Lord Whitley with her father whilst she retired to her own chamber to snatch a brief rest. Midnight brought her back to the sick-room, after almost two hours of sleep. On her return she found her father leaning back in the big chair, his eyes closed.

He jerked upright. 'My dear, you startled me.'

'Go and rest, Papa. I'll watch his lordship. Have the fomentations been applied?'

A guilty flush gave her the answer she didn't want to hear. Swiftly she crossed to the little table near the window and prepared fresh cloths. Her father ran to assist her, eager to atone for his neglect. The wound looked harsh and ugly by the light of the working candles her father held for her as she replaced the dressings. The skin around the purpling gash had a red, angry appearance and even to Edith's inexperienced touch felt unnaturally warm. She uttered a prayer of desperation. Not an infection! Surely Lord Whitley didn't deserve to lose his leg. There was no way she would allow it to happen.

By two o'clock he had started to toss and turn on the pillows. His face was flushed and his unseeing eyes glowed bright with delirium. She found it extremely difficult to change his dressings and keep them in place without him tearing at them. Where earlier he had sweated, now he felt hot and dry with the mounting fever. Edith attempted to lift him off the bed as she held a glass of water to his lips, but both glass and contents were sent flying as he grabbed at her wrist.

'More powder! We must have more powder. Have it brought forward at once.'

For a second, she felt at a loss, but when he

repeated his command more urgently, realization set in. He thought he was on the field at Waterloo. Before she could reply he began again.

'No! Do not take me away. I must stay with my men. I forbid it, do you hear? I forbid it. I will not go.'

'Shhh. All is well. Lie still. Please lie still.'

His eyes flew open once again. 'Chloe? Is that you?' A frantic hand reached out to grasp the fabric of Edith's sleeve. 'My darling, where have you been?' The hand slid further up her arm to clutch at her shoulder. His voice broke into a half sob. 'Please help me, Chloe.'

Edith swallowed hard. She wasn't Chloe. There was no possibility of her being found. Lady Chloe had been dead for years. What was she to do?

'Try to rest, Charles. We'll talk in the morning. Let me smooth your pillow.'

'No! Don't go. Don't leave me again.' Just as Edith leaned forward to turn the pillow he made a sudden grab for her and pulled her down on to the bed beside him. Edith was so startled she could do no more than gasp as he buried his head into her shoulder and enclosed her in an incredibly powerful embrace. His parched lips began to move over her neck, murmuring with a frantic desperation. The rough growth on his chin scraped over her flesh as she tried to pull away. He was going to kiss her!

The sensations that flooded through Edith were incredible. Shock, panic, worry that he would hurt both himself and her were all displaced in an instant by the overwhelming flood of compassion as his lips touched hers. Even in his delirium the longing and tenderness were manifest. How he had loved his Chloe!

When she could, she eased back gently. 'Charles, can you hear me?'

His hold relaxed slightly, although his eyes remained glazed and unseeing. Growing bolder, she freed a hand to stroke at his hair.

'Charles, my darling, you're ill. You've been injured and need to rest.'

The gentle whisper in his ear seemed to soothe him. Edith continued to talk. She told him about her home in Northumberland, about visiting her mother at the churchyard and her favourite apple tree in the orchard. Slowly he relaxed. When at last he fell back into an uneasy sleep Edith held her breath and began to inch her way off the bed. Finally she could roll free. With hasty motions she smoothed her hair and clothing and tucked the sheets more securely round his long form. At the window, she laid her burning forehead against the cool of the glass and pressed her fingers to her cheeks. Her knees trembled. Her throat felt dry and she found it difficult to swallow. What a thing to happen!

Embarrassment flooded through her until she had to sit down. Try as she might, she couldn't compose herself. He was ill, desperately ill. He didn't know what he was doing. His actions were not meant for her, but a long-cherished love who existed only in his memory. His embrace didn't shame her. It was her own response that filled her with mortification. For an instant, until sense reasserted itself, she had longed to return his caresses. If only that love *had* been meant for her!

On two other occasions during that endless night Lord Whitley called for his Chloe. The second episode occurred just as her father slipped into the room. Edith held a finger to her lips in warning, and then bathed Lord Whitley's face with a cool cloth.

'I'm here, my darling. I shan't leave you. Try to rest, please.'

Once he was calm, she beckoned her father out of the room and then almost threw herself into his arms.

'Oh, Papa, I feel so distressed! The heartbreak that poor man has suffered. He believes me to be Lady Chloe. He will be so

66

angry when he finds out I have deceived him. I didn't know what else to do.'

Tears of exhaustion and strain rolled across her cheeks as she gave way to sobs. 'I feel as if I have been eavesdropping on an intimate conversation.'

'Shush, Edith. I am sure his lordship will have no recollection of any of the events of this night. You have been a brave, good girl, but you must go and rest now. Try to sleep — '

A loud crash from the chamber startled them both. Edith flew past her father into the room. Lord Whitley had flung out an arm and swept the bowl of lavender-water to the floor. He lay slumped to one side and very still. Filled with dread she rushed over to take his hand. To her surprise, it felt cool and damp. She felt for the pulse, then laid a hand on his forehead. It came away covered with his sweat.

She fell to her knees, clutching his hand to her bosom. 'Oh, thank God, the fever has broken.' Closing her eyes, she muttered a heartfelt prayer. Seconds later she began to bustle about.

'Papa, you must help me change his nightshirt. If he should take a chill after all this . . .'

Somewhat bemused, her father followed

her instructions, holding up the patient as Edith eased the damp garment away. Quickly she washed his chest, back and arms with some water that had been warming over a spirit stove on the hearth, then dried him with a soft towel. Her fingers lingered for just a moment on a line of raised and puckered flesh. The ugly scar on his left shoulder must be the legacy of Salamanca. Augusta had told her about a shoulder wound.

Taking extra care, she eased a clean nightshirt over his head, then turned away as her father finished the change. Her spirits were so light she felt like singing. He would recover! He wasn't going to lose the leg. She felt sure of that now.

Waves of weariness rolled over her. Vaguely she recognized the fact that her father had taken her arm. Somehow, she reached her room and sprawled across the bed. She knew nothing more.

Edith awoke to the sound of a street vendor outside her window. Warm and content, she snuggled under the covers for a moment. Before she could drift back to sleep however, memory flooded in. With a startled cry she leapt out of the bed. Someone had removed her shoes and tucked her under the blankets but she remained fully dressed, her hair a bedraggled mess half pinned up and half tumbling round her shoulders. She almost pulled the bell cord out of the wall in her haste. By the time the housemaid arrived with a can of hot water, she had shed her dress and petticoat and reduced her hair to something approaching order.

'How is Lord Whitley this morning?' she demanded. 'Has the doctor called?'

'Yes, my lady. He's in with him now. The attendant arrived, and also his lordship's valet. Very put about *he* is, I can assure you. There's been a bustle in the servant's hall today.'

She relaxed slightly. 'Oh, *is* he now? Find me the blue cambric, then you can see to my hair, and *I* shall see to this valet.'

Ten minutes later, Edith greeted the doctor as he left the sick-room. The smile on his face told her all she wanted to know.

'Well, my dear. A very neat piece of work, if I do say so myself. I won't say that all danger is passed, but my man is quite capable. What his lordship needs now is rest and nourishing food. He seems to be sleeping peacefully. Did you have a quiet night?'

A quiet night? Edith thought for a moment about her fears. She smiled. 'Not exactly, Sir James. As you predicted, there was some fever and delirium, but Lord Whitley has an excellent constitution.'

'Fine, fine. I shall call this evening. You needn't worry your pretty head any longer.' He pressed her arm briefly, and then departed for the book-room to impart the good news.

She tapped softly at the bedchamber door. A stranger, impeccably turned out as a gentleman's gentleman, opened it immediately. Obviously this was the missing valet.

'Good morning. I am Lady Edith.'

He bowed slightly. 'Tate, my lady. His lordship's valet.'

'I'm glad to find you here, Tate. We could have done with you yesterday. May I come in?'

Tate looked startled for a moment before assuming a very correct expression. 'My lady, his lordship is indisposed.'

There was nothing to do but sweep past him with an air of authority. 'I'm very well aware of that fact, Tate.'

The capable-looking attendant rose from the big chair next to the bed. She acknowledged him briefly, then took a swift appraisal of the sleeping viscount. His face had recovered much of his colour, his breathing looked even and relaxed and his pulse felt steady.

'Good. All is well.' Next she inspected Tate's arrangements, checking that he had sufficient quantities of medicaments and lotions. Everything appeared under control. Obviously there was no further need for her services. Edith felt both relieved and disappointed.

'Ahem.' Tate stood politely by the door, but his posture was so rigidly eloquent that she wasn't fooled.

'That's quite all right, Tate. I'm going now. Obviously Lord Whitley is in very capable hands. Let me know immediately if there is any change, or if there is anything you require.'

He bowed, opening the door for her. 'Certainly, my lady.'

Why did she have the distinct feeling she'd been firmly dismissed? He'd rather walk over hot coals than ask her for help, Edith felt sure. No matter. Lord Whitley would get well. With a little grin, she ran to find Augusta.

For a moment she felt a flick of surprise to see her father engrossed in conversation with a strange lady. Who would be calling at a time like this? *Oh, goodness, it was Augusta!* She had dressed in a new gown of lavender silk, made up high to the throat with a little ruff of lace. The cap on her golden hair, made of finest lawn edged with thread-lace, was white, not her customary black. The effect was both startling and extremely becoming.

'Why, Augusta, how beautiful you look this morning!'

Mrs Venables coloured. 'Thank you, my dear. I am so very sorry to have been of such little help to you yesterday. What news is there of his lordship?'

'He appears to be resting more peacefully, but I am banished from his chamber. His valet has no opinion of females, I fear.'

'Good. I'm so glad that dear Charles is . . . is . . . ' She paused, then made a gallant recovery. 'I am utterly determined to undertake my duties more seriously from now on. You must leave Lord Whitley to the experts, and *I* must consider you. Would you like to take a drive in the park? The weather is very mild today.'

Inspiration flashed into Edith's brain. 'Oh, I have a great deal to see to this morning, but perhaps Papa would like to take you out. After the shock you received yesterday you need to recover your spirits. Don't you agree, Papa?'

Lord Cramlington smiled down at Mrs Venables. 'I should be extremely happy to escort you, ma'am. If you will permit me, you do indeed look a trifle pale. Allow me to order the horses brought round.'

Augusta objected, but she was no match for Edith and her father combined. Less than thirty minutes later, well tucked up against the cool breeze, the two drove off toward the park. Edith watched them go with a half smile on her face. She couldn't remember her father being so taken with anyone. He had never so much as uttered a syllable to her, but she was well aware of how lonely he must be. Perhaps he would find her chaperon a congenial companion.

'My lady, may I have a word?'

Edith turned to find a grim-faced house-keeper looking at her. The smile vanished from her face. 'What is it, Mrs Anstey? Is there a message from the sick-room? His lordship? Is he — ?'

'No, my lady. I have no knowledge of sick-rooms, nor do I wish to. I will not have anything to do with the goings-on in this house.'

4

'The scandal is sure to get out, and I am not prepared to be associated with such immorality. I have my reputation to consider. I have always kept a respectable house.'

Edith groaned silently. Now she was in a fix. Why did the stupid woman have to cause a fuss now, of all times? If Mrs Anstey had been so worried surely *she* could have sat with Lord Whitley last night?

She smoothed her forehead, trying to push away the headache that threatened to blossom at any moment. 'Mrs Anstey, there was no impropriety. My father assisted me, after all.'

'I have no intention of remaining another instant in an establishment where the mistress is so lost to decency and good manners as to sit half the night with a gentleman, in his *bedchamber*, no less, and on her own! There were never such goings-on in poor dear Lady Louisa's time, nor did she ever think it necessary to circumvent my authority and enter the servant's hall. I will be a laughing stock among my acquaintance!'

So that was the real problem. Edith lost her

temper. 'Thank you, Mrs Anstey, for your observations. Where, pray tell me, should I have nursed his lordship? In the front hall? Of course, I shall not detain you. You may go.'

'There is the matter of my wages. I have given long and faithful service to this family. I should be paid to the quarter day.'

Now she was going too far! 'Do not take me for a fool, Mrs Anstey. You were well provided for in his late lordship's bequest. Out of good will I shall pay you for October and November, but do not press my generosity. I shall instruct Mr Sharples accordingly.'

'I am being robbed! The world will hear of my treatment at your hands!'

Swelling so much that Edith had a ludicrous mental picture of her stiff black bombazine splitting down the bodice, the housekeeper swept out of the room. Edith's sense of the ridiculous got the better of her. Poking her head around the door she called after the departing woman, 'Do give my regards to poor dear Lady Louisa, won't you?'

When Augusta and her father came back from the park, Edith found it hard to give them the news of yet another upset.

Her father sighed deeply. 'My dear, what have you done?'

75

Mrs Venables flew to her aid. 'Nothing at all, my dear sir! There can be no question of impropriety. Your daughter acted with more courage and ability than I possessed yesterday, and so I shall tell Lord Corbridge when next I see him. It is through Edith's efforts that his son's life has been spared. Might I also say that I have considered this house to be very ill run? A new housekeeper will not go amiss.'

In the face of her father's open-mouthed astonishment, Edith smiled her gratitude. 'We don't need a new housekeeper. I'll send for Agnes immediately. I miss her so, more than I imagined. What do you say, Papa?'

Lord Backworth hadn't quite recovered from Augusta's spirited defence of his daughter. He regarded her with undisguised amazement, mixed with admiration. Obviously he found it difficult to concentrate on Edith's suggestion.

'Papa, what do you think? Shall I send for Agnes?'

'Er . . . whatever you consider necessary, my dear. You are the mistress here.'

'Good, it's settled then. I shall inform Hartley immediately.'

Edith waited for him to reply, but no answer was forthcoming. All he could do was stand there. Augusta began to realize that something was wrong and blushed under Lord Cramlington's continued scrutiny. Edith glanced from one to the other, opened her mouth to say something, but thought better of it. Feeling distinctly *de trop*, she left.

The butler stood very correctly at attention in the book-room when he responded to her summons. Her heart plummeted as she looked at his impassive countenance. Would he leave, too? Had she sunk herself beyond redemption in the eyes of all the servants? She should have left Lord Whitley to bleed to death and then they all would have approved of her.

As Edith informed him of the change in arrangements his expression remained fixed, but was that just a twinkle of approval in his eye?

'So, until Agnes, er . . . Mrs Fenwick, can return to us, we shall have to manage as best we may.'

'If I may be so bold, my lady, I believe we shall manage very well. Mrs Anstey will not be missed, by me at least.'

Edith blinked hard. Goodness! What had she stumbled into here? 'Have there been problems, Hartley?'

He sighed, just enough to convey his sentiments, and nodded in a most dignified manner. 'Yes, my lady. I do not believe Mrs Anstey recovered from the death of her mistress, the late countess. We shall go on much better, now.'

Somehow she felt immeasurably relieved to have won his good favour. 'Indeed, I hope so, too. Will you advise me, Hartley? Can you think of any pressing obligations?'

Hartley pondered for a moment. 'We could well expect a visit from Lord and Lady Corbridge. Lord Whitley is their only son and I believe the family is very close.'

'They don't own a town house?'

The butler shook his head. 'No, your ladyship. Lady Corbridge dislikes the town racket intensely. I believe the earl puts up at Reddish's Hotel whenever he comes to town.'

'Well, naturally, they will have to stay here. Send Sarah to me immediately, please. Inform cook that we may have visitors and warn the stables also. We must make sure that they will be comfortable.'

Hartley bowed. 'As you wish, my lady.' He started to turn away, then paused. 'If I may be so bold, when the late countess was alive this house was noted for its hospitality. It is a tradition I would be happy to see revived.'

The old fox! Beneath his crusty exterior Hartley was a gem. Edith smiled at him. 'Thank you. I am delighted to hear that.

Once his lordship has recovered his strength we should see about some entertainment for him. I'm sure his close acquaintance will want to visit.'

'I'll make sure his lordship's man spreads the word. If that will be all, my lady?'

Edith nodded. 'Yes, thank you, Hartley, for now.' She maintained her posture until the door closed behind the butler. As soon as he was gone she danced a little jig and laughed with relief. Her heart lighter than it had been for some time, she sped off up the stairs to supervise the preparation of the rooms for Lord Whitley's parents.

There was still no sign of Lord and Lady Corbridge by the time the doctor called that evening, so Edith conducted him to the bedchamber herself. Tate managed to convey his outrage at her invasion of his master's room without any incivility, but a faint movement from the bed diverted her attention from him immediately. Lord Whitley had regained his senses. Still extremely weak he submitted to the doctor's ministrations, even managing to answer him with a degree of civility. The crease between his eyes told its own story, as did the lines on his face and the sudden tightening of his mouth as the doctor examined his dressings. All the same Edith could discern a vast improvement.

It wasn't until the doctor addressed a remark to her that Lord Whitley realized she was present. Astonishment and chagrin flashed across his features.

'My lady!' He was too weak to bellow, but Edith had no doubt about his feelings. She crossed the room to stand close to the head of the bed. For a moment, she felt the upwelling of emotion that had bound her to him the night before. What would he do if she reached out to smooth his hair?

'How do you do, my dear sir? You gave us such a fright. I am so very glad to find you better at last. The doctor has given us a good account of your progress. Are you aware the ball has been removed from . . . your . . . limb?'

She faltered to a halt. Lord Whitley lay looking up at her as if he couldn't believe his eyes. Was something amiss with her attire? One thing was certain, he wasn't happy to see her. She turned away to rearrange the lotions on his night stand, aware of a flush of embarrassment creeping into her cheeks.

His voice soon had her turning back to the bedside. 'Thank you, ma'am, for your kind attention. I shall go on well now, so please do not discommode yourself further on my account. Indeed, I beg your forgiveness for the disruption caused. I must return to my own lodging in the morning. Tate will answer to my needs from now on.'

Leave? He couldn't leave! He'd kill himself. 'Oh, you mustn't think of moving until you are well, my lord. I quite forbid it. I . . . that is we would not want you to risk any infection. You must build up your strength.'

'You are too kind, ma'am. I must insist — ' He broke off.

Edith watched as exhaustion claimed him once again. Compassion swelled inside her and forgetting all her reservations she laid a hand on his brow. Her breathing constricted without warning as she touched his skin. If her presence was going to upset him, then she'd stay away. Already he had become important to her, although she couldn't think why. To be the cause of a setback would be unthinkable. She fought off a sudden desire to kiss his cheek.

'Shh. Don't try to talk. Truly, it is no trouble at all to have you in the house. Don't worry. I'm well aware that some gentlemen can't abide a female fussing round them when they don't feel quite the thing. I won't disturb you any further, I promise. You have Tate to see to your needs now.'

He wanted her out of his room. Edith bit down on her lip. She should have known that he would resent her seeing him like this. Did he have any recollection of the previous night, though? By the look on his face he knew nothing of it. He would no sooner willingly embrace her than he would shoot himself.

'Goodnight, my lord. I hope you sleep well.' Gathering up the remains of her dignity she ushered the doctor out. 'I'll see you to the door, Sir James.'

Lord Whitley waited until the door closed, then turned a wrathful eye on his valet. Weak though he was, Tate was subjected to the full force of his displeasure. 'What were you thinking of, Tate, to allow Lady Edith into this room?'

The valet fidgeted around, smoothing linen and straightening the bottles arranged by Edith not five minutes previously. 'I am exceedingly sorry, my lord, but I am informed that her ladyship has supervised your care personally. Sir James mentioned to me this morning that you owe your life to her.'

'I'll be damned if — ' A sudden thought struck Lord Whitley. 'Is it true what she said, that the doctor has removed the ball?'

'Apparently so, my lord. Her ladyship assisted him.'

'Good God.' Lord Whitley stared up at the ceiling. Emotion made him dizzy for a moment until he forced his tired brain to concentrate. That damned ball had gone!

Gingerly he tried to wriggle his toes and was rewarded with a stab of pain. Truly, his leg was still there. It had been saved. He wouldn't shuffle out his days as a helpless cripple! Weak tears threatened to spill, but he blinked them away. Only foolish females cried. Still, the relief almost overwhelmed him.

But Lady Edith had assisted the surgeon? How could any gently born girl do such a thing? Surely all her sensibilities should have been outraged. It was all too much to comprehend. As his eyelids pressed down and he drifted off to sleep, his thoughts started to wander. His precious Chloe would never have done anything so . . . so ungenteel. He thought of his dream, where she had soothed his brow with lavender-water. He could even smell the fragrance of lavenders blended with violets. Had Chloe worn violet scent? He was too tired to remember. The cloth had been so cool and refreshing as she had comforted him. Those dark eyes had smiled down on him, filled with compassion and love.

. . . Yes, that's what a real lady would have done. Why did she have to die?

His last thoughts before sleep claimed him returned as always to his lost darling.

'Chloe, my dearest. I love you.'

Tate looked up from his work. 'I beg your pardon, my lord?'

But Lord Whitley lay fast asleep.

★ ★ ★

After breakfast, Augusta and Edith made a quick foray to purchase some trifles for the sick-room and to add a few welcoming touches to the visitor's chambers. They hurried home as soon as they could, in case Lord and Lady Corbridge had lodged for the night close to London. Not really expecting anyone before noon at the earliest, Edith felt dismay when the butler admitted them to a front hall stacked with boxes and portmanteaux.

'Oh, Hartley! Lord Corbridge has arrived already? He must think us most inhospitable not to have been here to welcome him. Is my father with him? What have you done with her ladyship? I must go to her immediately.'

The butler helped her with her braided pelisse before replying. His attitude appeared very constrained. Edith frowned.

'What is it? Is something wrong?'

'I have shown the visitor into the morning-room, my lady. It is a Mr Back-worth. I believe he is wishing to reside here for some time. As you have not left any instructions about the matter I have not as yet had his boxes sent up.'

'I should think not! My cousin Bertram? When we are expecting other guests?'

The mansion in Grosvenor Square was one of the most imposing in London, but even so it only possessed six bedchambers large enough for family and guests. Augusta, Edith and her father took up half the available space, whilst Lord Whitley occupied the fourth chamber, with the dressing-room used by his attendant and valet. There was simply nowhere for Bertram to go.

Exasperated, Edith turned to her companion. 'That is just like my cousin, to expect to be waited on hand and foot. He has ample means to put up at the best hotel in town, but he is so tight-fisted he would foist himself off on to anyone in the slightest degree related to him. He is sadly out of luck this time, however!'

As she finished speaking a footman ran to the door to admit her father, who carried a book under one arm. She hurriedly informed him of the circumstances. Lord Cramlington sighed at the sound of his nephew's name. A pained look crossed his face.

Edith hugged him. 'Don't you worry, Papa. You are far too gentle to deal with the likes of

Bertram. I shall speak to him!'

Hartley led them to the morning-room. Edith stifled an exclamation of annoyance at the sight of her cousin, dressed from head to toe in deepest mourning. His gaze was just then fixed on an ornament from the mantel, which he held in his hand. Her antipathy hardened into something far stronger. What was he doing? Evaluating the furnishings, perhaps working out what might come to him in the course of time?

Bertram caught sight of them. Showing no signs of embarrassment he welcomed them into the room.

Exactly as if he owned it already! Edith fumed.

'My lord! Uncle! We live in unhappy times, do we not? Indeed, I was excessively shocked when I heard the lamentable tidings. Pray, sit down. Allow me to felicitate you on your good fortune.'

Bertram was an upright young man, very close in age to Edith, but already his flesh had started to thicken round his waist. His dark hair bore evidence of his valet's laboured attention in the modish, but highly unflattering, style he had assumed. Lines of discontent pulled down the corners of his narrow lips. As ever his eyes were set too close together for Edith's liking.

Almost eighteen months previously, Bertram had married at a scandalously young age. His wife, Catherine, was not one of the gentry. In fact, Edith had even heard her father refer to Catherine's papa as 'that vulgar mushroom', which for him was strong language indeed. Something dreadful had happened, but Edith had been carefully shielded from the worst of the gossip. It had been rumoured that her late uncle had threatened his only son with a horsewhip if he should disgrace the family with such a low connection, but the match had been made anyway. Uncle Frederick had died falling from his horse the day after Bertram and his new bride returned from their honeymoon.

After introductions had been made, Augusta rang for refreshments. Edith cast around in her mind for something to say.

'Have you just come down from Norfolk, Bertram? We thought you quite settled in Norwich.'

To her astonishment, Bertram produced an elegant handkerchief and dabbed at his eyes. 'The doctors advised me that a change of scene would be beneficial to my health. My distress over certain events proved too much for my constitution.'

'But surely you didn't even know the late

earl? I had scarcely heard of my cousins, either.'

Bertram's expression turned from melancholy to pained surprise. 'Lady Edith? Is it possible you have not heard? Has my letter been delayed?' He reverted to his former despondency, looking from Edith to her father and back again. 'Indeed, I can see you do not know. My beloved wife, my Catherine, has left us.'

'Left us? You mean she has died?'

He nodded solemnly. 'Last Thursday sennight. I departed for town immediately following the funeral. My heart is broken.'

Poor Catherine! Edith had never liked her cousin's wife over much. She had been a miserable, sickly creature, and vulgar, too. She had, however, possessed a fortune of ten thousand pounds, which had attracted Bertram from the outset, despite his father's outraged opposition.

'I . . . I collect she had a sudden illness?'

He sighed again. 'Alas, no. My darling fell down the stairs. An apothecary was fetched immediately, but there was nothing to be done. Her neck was broken.'

Augusta gasped with horror. Edith and her father exchanged startled glances. She could think of nothing to say. A broken neck! His father had met with exactly the same fate.

Lord Cramlington stepped into the breach. 'Her family must be distraught. She was their only daughter, was she not?'

Bertram nodded his head. 'Alas, yes. Their only child! I fear the shock almost deranged my poor dear father-in-law. His lamentations and accusations were wild to the point of madness.'

'Accusations? What can you mean?' Something was wrong here; Edith could sense it. By the look on his face her father must have had the same thought.

Her cousin flicked his handkerchief. 'Please do not concern yourself. As if I did not take the greatest care of my sainted Catherine. A mere misunderstanding, that is all. But tell me about yourself. I can see you have already acquired a modish wardrobe, Cousin. Are you to be presented?'

Edith followed his lead and allowed the conversation to be diverted. Bertram, however, had not quite done.

'Of course, in my position as heir I too will have to attend one of the Regent's soirées. I will assume a modish face for the *ton*, much as I would prefer to live retired with my misery. My darling Catherine insisted that I did not mourn her. As much as I desire to wear the willow, her wishes must of course be sacrosanct. You, sir, will naturally decide to make me an allowance out of the estate. I thought I might impose on your hospitality whilst we come to the arrangements and I look around me for some suitable accommodation.'

Edith sucked in a deep breath. Her fingernails nearly pierced the palms of her hands. What impudence! Why did he need an allowance? To walk in here, brazenly demanding money *and* free accommodation to boot. She'd soon put a stop to that!

'I am sorry, but that is impossible.' Edith tried her best to smile. 'We are all in an uproar here. You cannot know, of course, that Lord Whitley has suffered a serious accident. He is at present lying upstairs in the best spare bedchamber, and we are in hourly expectation of his parents, Lord and Lady Corbridge.'

Bertram gasped. 'How unfortunate. It is exceedingly inconsiderate of Whitley to impose himself upon you in this manner. I am seriously put out to hear of it. What shall I do now?'

Calm, Edith, she told herself. *You must be calm.* Don't embarrass Papa. 'I suggest you repair to a hotel. There are several passable ones to be had, you know.'

'But the expense! They will all be quite ruinous, I am sure. I have already brought my boxes here.'

'It will only be until you establish yourself in lodgings. I believe there are genteel establishments in Half Moon Street. A man of your experience will no doubt very soon make himself acquainted. Unless you decide to retire to Norfolk, after all.'

'No, no. I shall not do that. My Catherine did not wish it.'

Edith couldn't wait to get the creature out of her sight. She rose to pull the bell. 'Hartley will know what to recommend. I'll have him send word to the stables for the carriage. It's the least we can do.'

'I cannot like it. There must be somewhere you can put me. I am family, after all. Mrs Venables could move to one of the servant's rooms.'

What, have Augusta move to one of those horrid, poky rooms? And how dare he talk like that when her friend sat in the same room as him, too!

'Mrs Venables can do no such thing! She is by no means regarded as a servant. I am sorry Bertram, but the facts are plain. You have not been invited to stay and there is no room for you.'

Forty minutes later, protesting and complaining, Bertram was finally driven away from the door, his boxes piled in beside him. Edith shuddered as he cast her a final, malevolent look.

She returned to the drawing-room. 'At last! I thought he would never take himself away. The man is an underbred oaf.'

'Edith, my dear!'

'I'm sorry. Papa, but I cannot like him. The manner in which he treated Augusta was quite shocking!'

'Indeed!' Lord Cramlington leapt to his feet and took Augusta's hand. 'That is quite true. I cannot forgive him for it. I am so sorry, my dear, that my nephew was so abominably rude.' He gazed into her eyes for a few seconds. 'Pray, do not hold it against us.'

Augusta looked embarrassed. Looking back at Lord Cramlington, she tried to speak, but no words came out of her mouth. Edith coughed, bringing her father back to his surroundings. With a start, he dropped Augusta's hand and blushed.

Edith hadn't quite finished with Bertram. 'Do you not think it strange? As soon as he hears of your elevation to the peerage his poor wife suffers such a tragic accident! A broken neck, no less, just as happened to my uncle Frederick, although the circumstances were different. And when, pray tell, was Catherine able to instruct him not to mourn if her neck was broken? I have a right to my suspicions.'

Her father tried his best to pooh-pooh such flights of fancy, but it was obvious to Edith that he was more than half-convinced himself of Bertram's guilt.

Just as Augusta and Edith were on the point of retiring to change for dinner, a commotion in the hallway betokened a new arrival. Accompanied by a tall officer in a scarlet uniform, Lady Corbridge was announced. A plump, motherly sort of woman, she looked dreadfully anxious. In two strides, Edith crossed to her to take her hand.

'Good news, my lady! Lord Whitley is recovering. Indeed, Sir James was even able to remove the ball from his wound.'

As soon as the words left her mouth, Edith felt a flush of mortification rise to her cheeks. What was she thinking of? This wasn't some anxious mother, but a peeress of the realm. 'Oh! I am sorry.' Hurriedly she sank into a curtsy. 'I beg your pardon, ma'am. You must think me horridly forward!'

'Of course not! What glad tidings! I have been so worried.' The countess tried to smile but her eyes filled with tears. Hastily, she searched in her reticule for her handkerchief.

Thank goodness she hadn't been offended. To give her a moment of privacy, Edith addressed the officer who had entered. 'Sir, you must forgive me. I didn't quite hear what

Hartley said when you came in.'

'No need to apologize, ma'am. I only stopped to learn the news of Charles. I'm his cousin, you know, Giles Ashington. I happened to be visiting my aunt when the word came. As my uncle is severely indisposed, I offered to escort her ladyship. Now that I know Charles is to recover I'll take myself off at once. You must be wishing me to the devil.'

There was a family resemblance, although Edith privately thought Lord Whitley had finer features. Captain Ashington possessed a much more friendly, open countenance, however, and right now he positively beamed with delight. A certain gleam of appreciation entered his expression as he gazed at her.

'Top fellow, Charles, and a dashed good officer. You have my heartfelt thanks, ma'am, for all you've done, as you'll have the thanks of all his friends. I'll spread the word.' Instead of shaking her proffered hand, Captain Ashington raised it to his lips and kissed it.

'Oh!' Edith didn't quite know what to do about the frank admiration, or the kiss, which caused a shiver to run up her arm. No one had ever kissed her hand before. Perhaps she should just ignore them both.

'Please do, and I expect Lord Whitley will be well enough to receive visitors by the day after tomorrow. We shall be delighted if any of his friends should wish to call.'

'That's devilish good of you, ma'am. He can be sure of seeing me. Pray tell him I haven't forgotten about the monkey I lent him at Brussels! I hope I shall also find you at home when next I call?'

He looked so anxious Edith smiled. 'I should be most happy, Captain.'

Refusing an invitation to stay for dinner, Captain Ashington lingered only to exchange compliments with Lord Cramlington and Mrs Venables, whom he knew well from the Peninsula, before taking his leave. Edith turned back to the countess.

'Let me take you up, ma'am. I'm sure you're very eager to see for yourself how your son is faring. Indeed, I haven't been permitted to see him myself today. Not even Tate could refuse *you* admittance, though!'

Although the valet looked anything but pleased, Edith was right. At the sight of the countess he bowed low and held the door for the ladies to enter. Lord Whitley lay propped by several pillows. Freshly shaved and with his hair neatly combed, he looked to be much improved in health. Now that the colour had returned to his face, Edith lost the lingering worry that had been nagging her.

'Charles, my dear boy! What a fright you

have given me.' Lady Corbridge gathered him up into her arms and pressed him to her bosom. After bestowing a kiss upon his forehead, which Lord Whitley took in good part, she stepped back from the bed.

'There. I am done with my fussing. And you are to be better than ever, or so I hear.'

'Certainly, Mama. Did you doubt me?'

He looked so handsome smiling up at his mother with a fond humour lightening his countenance, Edith felt a pull of strong emotion. Such a little time ago he had lain weak and helpless in her arms. A wave of heat swept over her at the thought and she pressed her hands to her cheeks to hide the blush. She could not betray herself now. Fortunately, they did not notice.

'I suppose you'll be waltzing with your latest flirt before a sennight is out,' Lady Corbridge exclaimed. 'And after alarming us so, too. You were not yourself when last I saw you, even though you insisted that you were well.'

A shadow covered Lord Whitley's expression for a moment. 'I'm sorry to have been the cause of anxiety to you, Mama. There was some infection already present which had been affecting my constitution. Indeed, for a while I, too, thought . . . ' He did not finish his sentence, but rallied in a very few seconds. 'Enough of that. I am mending very well now. Sir James assures me that all I required was his expert attention to make a full recovery. He doubts if I will even limp too badly. Though I do not expect to be dancing next week, I'll take my chance to engage Lady Edith here for the first waltz at Lady Sefton's ball when the season opens.'

So he had noticed her, hanging back behind the ample figure of his Mama. What else had he noticed? Oh, dear! Edith mustered up her best smile and sketched a curtsy.

'My lord is too kind. I will, however, hold you to that promise. It will give you something to look forward to. Also, Captain Ashington sends you his greetings and will be waiting on you shortly. I believe there is a question of some money owing?'

'What, is that reprobate Giles returned to our midst? There's not a female in fifty miles will be safe. I must get well, if only to keep that young devil in check.'

What a thing to say! After the captain had so obviously been concerned about him, too. 'Your cousin appeared to be a most gentlemanly officer. So friendly and open a disposition must only suggest a good character.' She paused to give him the full benefit of her stare. '*Others* would do well to emulate him. Now I must leave you and her ladyship to talk. I only wished to ascertain for myself that your health is improving.'

Despite the circumstances, Lord Whitley managed an exquisitely graceful nod of the head.

'I beg your pardon, madam. I stand, or should I say, lie corrected. My cousin Giles is all you say and more. Indeed, he is a paragon of all the virtues. You obviously have a much better understanding of his character than I do. I have only known him since he was born. I bid you good evening.'

He'd done it again! Edith fumed as she waited outside the bedchamber. Why was it she couldn't open her mouth in Lord Whitley's presence without making a fool of herself? He brought out everything that her father so abhorred in her character. Muttering to herself, she marched up and down the upper hallway, waiting to conduct the countess to her bedchamber. It was a good job that Bertram hadn't found out Lord Corbridge's room would be vacant now. She couldn't have stood to have him in the house as well! One odious, overbearing guest was quite enough, thank you!

Suddenly, she grinned. What a relief to be fighting with Lord Whitley again! She must speak to Augusta immediately about engaging a dancing master. The waltz, indeed. The thought of whirling round a ballroom in his lordship's arms filled her with an unexpected throbbing warmth. She looked at her reflection in a mirror.

'I must have some lessons. Augusta will know the best masters. I wonder what Papa will have to say about the waltz?'

5

'I . . . beg your pardon, Papa. *What* did you say?'

Edith had to sit down. No, she had to stand up again and pace over to the window. She couldn't remember when she had last felt so astonished. She mustn't have heard him correctly. It couldn't be true!

Only yesterday Agnes had returned from the North and Lord Whitley had made his careful departure, his mother and his valet almost elbowing each other aside in their anxiety. Lord Whitley had refused all offers of help, even managing a small bow as he bade her goodbye. Edith had felt desolated to see him go. Now this!

'And I thought it would be devilish flat around here!'

Her father didn't hear her unladylike language, which was just as well. Instead, he tugged at his neckcloth. His face had acquired a scarlet hue and he appeared to have trouble breathing. 'I said, I want to marry Augusta. If you do not mind *too* much? Of course, if you are set against it I quite — '

What Lord Cramlington was about to say was smothered as she cast herself into his arms and hugged him tightly. 'Oh, Papa! How wonderful! I thought from the first that you could be good friends, but I never for a moment suspected . . . What did she say when you asked her?'

'You don't object, then? You don't think I'm dishonouring your mother's memory?'

Edith sighed, then blinked furiously to chase away the tears. Dear Papa. How she loved him. He looked like a little boy caught in mischief. He had mourned her mother for nearly fifteen years and yet here he was, worried that he might be thought disrespectful to her memory.

'Mother would be so happy for you, Papa. We both know it. You have been lonely for far too long.'

'You think Augusta would entertain my proposal, then? A lady so charming and beautiful could have her pick of suitors.'

'You haven't asked her yet?' Edith managed a watery chuckle. 'Oh, Papa, you are too absurd! Don't you know what a fine catch you are? Half the females in London will swoon with envy at Augusta's good fortune. Once the banns are read there will still be time for a Christmas wedding, then my new mama can present me when the season opens. I suggest you go and find her right now, before your courage fails.'

'Yes, you are right. Of course you are right.' Lord Cramlington paced around for a moment or two. With the air of one about to have a tooth drawn he pulled himself erect. 'I will go and find her at once.'

'And I will tell Agnes the news, and have Hartley fig out the best champagne from the wine cellar.'

The brilliant smile she bestowed upon him lasted until he hurried from the book-room, leaving the door ajar in his agitation. Edith leaned against it until it shut with a soft snick. Instead of pulling the bell-cord for the butler she let her thoughts drift back to the faint memory of her mother. Silly, inconsequential things blotted out more important considerations. Mama had been so fond of snowdrops. It wouldn't be long now before they bloomed once again in the parsonage garden. Edith had always gathered the first handful to place on her grave. Who would do it this year?

Enough! Briskly she walked over to the bell and tugged. At the approach of footsteps she pinned a smile to her face. Just as the door handle turned, she murmured under her breath, 'I love you, Mama.'

By the time the butler entered she had

pulled herself together.

'Hartley, we have work to do. My father has gone to pay his addresses to Mrs Venables! I have no doubt that very soon we shall have a new countess to be mistress here. Please send Mrs Fenwick to me in the book-room and then find a bottle of the best champagne.'

Agnes so far forgot herself as to sit down in one of the studded leather chairs as she grappled with the news.

'Married? Oh dear Oh Lor! Whatever shall we do with him? Married?' Eyes wide with shock, she stared at Edith in amazement. 'I never ever thought of such a thing.'

'I am very happy for him, Agnes, as you must be, too. Augusta is exactly the wife he needs right now.'

Agnes's handkerchief hid her face for a moment or two, then her common sense reasserted itself. 'Well, it's busy we're going to be, my lady, and that's no error!'

By the time Edith sought out her father they already had a lengthy list of tasks prepared.

Augusta looked radiantly happy. Any lingering doubt vanished as Edith clasped her in an embrace. Papa deserved this, as did Augusta. They were two of the gentlest, kindest people she had ever known. Anyone but a fool could see that they would deal extremely well together.

Edith beamed at them. 'A Christmas wedding, then. No sense in waiting, is there? It will be very private, but it would have to be so in any case, as you are still in mourning, Papa.'

Augusta nodded. 'I agree. I thought I might ask Charles to lend me his support. He is closer to me than any brother.'

'Lord Whitley to lead you to the altar?' Edith hadn't thought of that. So she would see him again, and soon. A small glow ignited under her ribs. 'That would be ideal. He is sure to approve.'

She couldn't resist just a *little* teasing. 'And you, Papa? Will you invite my cousin to be your groomsman?'

Her father actually shuddered. 'I think not. We only require two witnesses. We might even dispense with the banns, irregular as that is. A special licence can well be granted in such a case.'

Edith kissed his cheek.

'Very wise, Papa. With luck, Bertram will not get to hear of it until after the knot is tied.'

Lord Cramlington gathered his dignity. 'I am not afraid of Bertram's opinion, Edith.'

Discreet as they were, rumours of the impending marriage flew around the clubs and drawing-rooms as if on wings. No doubt some footman or parlour maid chatted to a friend and, say what they would, most employers were not above listening to servants' gossip.

On a visit to Hookham's lending library Edith and Augusta were the recipients of all sorts of vulgar stares and probing comments, although no one was quite brass-faced enough to ask the question directly. Edith felt a mounting anger as she perceived Augusta's embarrassment.

'I think we should leave. You are being made very uncomfortable, ma'am.'

Augusta sighed. 'I shall have to grow accustomed, I suppose. The biggest drawback to marrying your dear father is that I shall have to be a countess. I am used to being an unimportant widow.'

'Never unimportant to your friends, and they, after all, are the only people who count.' Edith cast a scornful look at a badly dressed woman who was regarding them like something in a milliner's window.

They were almost to the street door before disaster struck.

'Well, Mrs Venables! I collect you are to be offered congratulations.'

Augusta quailed under the malicious glare. Edith watched her try to act normally. 'Good morning, Lady Louisa. I hope you are well?'

'Not as well as you, madam. You have stolen a march on the rest of society, have you not? The parson caught in his own mousetrap, no less! Was Lord Whitley also one of your dupes, or did you scheme this up between yourselves?'

What a low, underhand accusation! Edith stepped slightly in front of her friend. 'You are insulting, Lady Louisa. If you do not wish to be civil, I can see no reason at all to speak to you. Come, Augusta. We have much to do.'

Edith started to brush past Lady Louisa, but the infuriated woman reached out and grasped her arm. Almost hissing with spite, she thrust her face close.

'Not so fast! I will not be treated in such a manner by a country nobody. Stop and consider for a moment. When you are presented with a brother twenty years your junior you will have plenty of time to decide whom he most resembles, your sanctimonious parson father or the man who has had this woman any time he liked for the past three years! You are a fool.'

That she had once thought the exact same thing herself only added to Edith's rage. Even a passing acquaintance with Augusta, or with Lord Whitley for that matter, would be enough to establish the honourable nature of their characters. Louisa was prepared to defile them both for no reason whatsoever, except spite and jealousy.

'And you are a foul-mouthed liar. If I were a man I would call you out. Keep your wicked slander to yourself! Take your hand off my arm this instant and *never* presume to address me again.'

Feeling sicker than she would have believed, Edith linked her arm with Augusta. 'We need some fresh air, ma'am. Sometimes the close proximity of the vulgar becomes too much to bear.'

Refusing to so much as glance back, Edith thrust her chin into the air and marched towards the door.

Lady Louisa's voice carried across the room. 'Charles never did have any taste or discretion. He should have chosen me, not wishy-washy Chloe, but they were much alike, my sister and this . . . trollop. You will regret to the day you die saying such things to me, parson's brat!'

Once in the carriage Edith had to thrust her own feelings aside as Augusta dissolved into helpless tears. She hugged her close and exclaimed fiercely, 'I don't believe a word of it, do you hear? She's a spiteful, vicious cat.'

'To say *such* a thing, and of Charles, too, who has been so much the gentleman, and all that is kindness . . . ' The sobs came again, more fiercely than before.

'Remember her remark about his having no discretion? It's my belief she's hated him ever since he chose her sister to marry instead of her. You've presented her with the ideal way to strike at him as well as me, and she doesn't care if she destroys your reputation in the process! I will speak to Lord Whitley.'

Augusta flew up at that. 'Oh, no! You must not! Promise me that you will never breathe a word of this to a living soul.'

'But — '

'No! Promise me. I cannot bear to have such accusations repeated. I cannot marry your father if they become known.'

Edith subsided. 'Very well. I promise not to speak about it, but only so long as that *harpy* does not repeat her remarks. It is to be hoped she has thought better of them!'

Her hopes were in vain. At an unheard of hour the next day, Lord Whitley arrived at the house. Her heart pounded with an unexpected thrill of excitement when his name was announced, but one look at his face told her he had not come to pay a social call. Her heart sank as she curtsied in answer to his abrupt bow.

'My lord! I am so pleased to see you so much improved. You are hardly limping at all.' She felt proud of her composure. Her voice sounded quite normal, even if her pulse still beat uncomfortably fast.

'I haven't come here to chat; I want to know what the devil is going on.'

Without waiting for leave he sat in a chair near the fire, glowering at her as he eased his leg into a more comfortable position.

Well! What rag-bag manners! She wasn't going to sink to his level. Instead, she smiled sweetly. 'It is a pity, is it not, that your disposition has not improved along with your recovery in health.'

'Cut line!' Obviously, Lord Whitley was not about to avail himself of social niceties. 'If Augusta is hurt by the petty wranglings of your damned family I shall know who to blame.'

What? How dare he speak to me like that! Whatever had she ever done, apart from being born, of course? It was Louisa who had caused the trouble, from start to finish. Edith kept her voice as calm as she could.

'Meaning me, I suppose?'

His scorn should have withered her on the spot. 'You suppose correctly. I should never have introduced her to you. Once you had so thoroughly antagonized Louisa her nasty tongue was bound to cause harm, but that it should reflect on Augusta is the outside of enough.'

That he should think so badly of her hurt deeply, more deeply than she would have thought possible. Her hands clenched together in her lap as she fought for control. She lashed out at him. 'And on you also, if what you have heard is the same vile slander that she hurled at Augusta yesterday.'

He looked even angrier, if that was possible. A pulse started to beat at his temple as his hands clenched on the arms of his chair. 'You mean she has been here, venting her spite?'

'No. Hartley would no longer allow her to cross the threshold. We had the good fortune to meet my cousin in Hookham's. Half the world must have her tale by now.'

Lord Whitley actually swore. Before Edith could protest he hauled himself to his feet and stood towering over her. Her gaze travelled from the fob on his pristine waistcoat, past his intricately-tied neckcloth, to meet his eyes. Her heart skipped a little at his proximity. He was such a tall man and so . . . so masculine that her mouth dried up with sudden tension.

His fingers curled into ominous, powerful fists. 'Tate only informed me that he had heard gossip concerning Augusta in the tavern. I had no idea she had been subjected to harassment in public. Where is she now?'

'With my father.' There was the faintest tremor in her voice. She hoped that he had not heard it. She would not let him intimidate her like this. She sprang to her feet and faced him, proud that her legs did not buckle. 'And if you, sir, cannot moderate your behaviour and language you will find yourself out on the street. I am not one of your low friends.'

A look of menace crept into his expression. 'Try it.'

In shocked silence, she stared at him.

Almost immediately he shook his head. 'No, I beg your pardon. Of course you are quite right.' He sucked in a huge breath, then another one, fighting for control. 'We must work together to decide what is best to be done.'

Edith blinked hard as she, too, drew in a long breath. For a moment the ferocity in his voice had frightened her, and badly. Lord Whitley would make a fearsome enemy. She wouldn't let him see how badly he had shaken her, though. She couldn't. Sitting down as gracefully as she could to disguise the trembling in her knees, she tried to be brisk and business-like. 'They must be married immediately, of course. Augusta swore to me yesterday that she would not go through with the ceremony if you or my father were to become the object of scandal.'

111

His scornful expression returned in full measure. Obviously he was not yet in control of his temper. 'The wedding should go ahead? You don't believe Louisa, then? You don't think me an unprincipled blackguard attempting to foist off my mistress on to one of the richest men in the land?'

He should never have mentioned the gossip. That he would do so clearly indicated his contempt for her. Edith stood with great dignity. So close to Lord Whitley that she could clearly discern the tiny flecks of colour in his dark eyes, she subjected him to a hard stare. Cold rage filled her.

'You missed out the part about your bastard.'

Fire leapt from his eyes, but before he could speak she plunged on. 'Sir, your character is entirely unknown to me, but I have far too high a regard for Mrs Venables to think her capable of such behaviour. I would never doubt *her* for an instant.'

Lord Whitley looked as if he would like to throttle her. His breath rasped in and out, fast and furious. He actually raised a hand, but controlled himself, barely.

'Would to God I had never met you. No one has ever insulted me in such a fashion before without regretting it, but despite what you think of me, I am neither mean nor petty

112

enough to vent my anger on a mere female. We must work together to ensure Augusta's happiness, then you may go to hell for all I care.'

Almost pushing past her in his haste he hurried from the room, his limp much more pronounced this time. Edith bit her lip, torn between fury and a wish to call him back, to tell him that she had never doubted him for an instant. Her anger fled, leaving her deflated and sad, with tears pricking at her eyes and a lump of emotion in her throat. What had she said? Along with the anger, just for a second she had seen the hurt in his eyes. The gossip had wounded him, impugned his honour. *She* had wounded him. The thought gave her no pleasure. She wanted to run after him, to tell him that she knew him for an honourable, trustworthy gentleman.

Almost acting on her impulse, she stopped instead. What of him? He had wounded her just as badly, and with no cause. Anger was one thing, but what was it he had called her? A mere female? Contempt hurt more than anger ever could. My Lord Whitley would live to regret *that* statement, whatever else happened between them. She'd see *him* in hell first.

The wedding took place in St George's, Hanover Square, on a Thursday morning.

With but four days to Christmas it was barely light and the December chill kept all save the most hardy or unfortunate off the streets. Only a couple of busy brown sparrows stopped to watch as the modest chaise drew up at the front steps. No bystanders observed as Lord Whitley handed Edith down and, unsmiling and silent, marched behind the happy couple to where the clergyman waited at the altar. This was not the marriage they had first imagined, with Augusta led down the aisle by Lord Whitley, a few chosen friends looking on. No, today only the four of them walked through the echoing silence of the great building. Agnes and Hartley waited for them, the two of them the only others privileged to witness the wedding.

Edith's feelings fluctuated as she watched her former companion become her new mama. She choked back tears at the sight of her father, so proud and happy, untouched by any of the innuendo and slander that had passed him by unnoticed. She felt like cheering or clapping when he made his vows in a firm, confident voice. Augusta had looked strained and nervous before, but now she glowed with an inner happiness that no unkind words could mar. Wearing a sky-blue velvet walking dress with a matching ermine-trimmed pelisse and carrying an ermine muff, she looked extremely beautiful and absurdly young. Edith sighed with admiration mixed with a strange type of envy. Would anyone ever love *her* half as much?

Momentarily forgetting her antagonism, Edith laid her hand over Lord Whitley's as they followed the earl and countess out of the church. 'Isn't it wonderful?' she declared. 'The bells should be ringing and the crowds cheering. I am *so* happy for them!'

He looked down at her, a quizzical expression on his face. 'You really are pleased for them, aren't you? I wasn't sure quite how you would react, in the end.'

She paused to stare at him. 'What did you expect? Jealous tantrums because my nose has been put out of joint? You need another branch of the family for that, my lord.'

'I do, don't I?' He waited as she surged forwards to hug her new mama, then continued, 'No doubt you think you've put me in my place. Instead of arguing with you, my lady, I think I should get Lady Cramlington out of this wind. She is becoming chilled.' The smile he bestowed on the new countess was almost dazzling.

Edith shivered and pulled her ermine-edged pelisse more tightly around her. What about her? Would she be allowed to freeze to death here on the street? She knew she was the picture of fashion, but a heavy travelling cloak would have been much more sensible, together with a snug, round bonnet instead of her dashing cap with its plume of ostrich feathers. Only dowds dressed for convenience, however, and no way was his lordship going to have the chance to bestow *that* description on her again!

Perhaps he thought that his words would be sufficient to snub her in return. Ha! She'd show him! She adopted the gracious air of condescension that her cousin Louisa used to such extent. 'You will have me quite in charity with you, sir, and you will be the hero indeed if you can procure a hot brick for my mama at the same time!'

His eyes gleamed as his riposte cut back. 'You almost unman me, Lady Edith! That I should be pleasing to you is *always* the object of my *every* desire. Alas, a hot brick is beyond me, but a hot breakfast she shall have! Here is the carriage now.'

Edith fumed. Sarcastic devil! She desperately cast around in her mind for a suitably cutting reply as she allowed him to hand her into the conveyance. Augusta's puzzled gaze slid from one to the other as she settled herself beside her new husband.

The expression on Augusta's face gave Edith a check. What must she be thinking?

Instead of a withering remark, she tried to smile. He would suffer. One day, he would suffer. For now, however, she would have to bide her time. Despite thoughts of boiling certain persons in oil, or sticking a hatpin in a most uncomfortable place, she made a silent vow not to be the one to spoil Augusta's day.

On the short ride home she kept up a flow of light chatter, being very careful to not so much as glance at the infuriating man sitting beside her. No matter how hard she tried to ignore him, however, it was impossible not to be aware of his masculine presence. There was the faintest whiff of clean soap, that muscular thigh clad in elegant pantaloons intruding on her vision and the modulated tones of his speech as he addressed Lord Cramlington. From shoulder to hip she could feel the heat of his presence, no matter that the coach was chill. It was unnerving.

Over breakfast, the four of them composed a suitable notice to be sent to the newspapers. Edith still fumed over Lord Whitley's sarcasm. Horrible man! What had ever induced her to think that he was a gentleman? She vented her spleen by imagining Bertram's face when he read his *Morning Post* the next day. It would quite spoil his breakfast. One could only hope so, anyway.

She was startled out of her reverie by a question posed to her by her father.

'Oh, I beg your pardon, Papa. I was not attending.'

'I asked, my dear, what you thought of his lordship's scheme that we should form a party at Bedebury.'

He waited, then took pity on her obvious ignorance. 'You have most certainly not been attending. Would you like to go to Lord and Lady Corbridge's home and spend Christmas with them?'

With them, certainly, but with their odious son as well? Edith looked doubtfully at Augusta.

'What of you, ma'am? Should you like it?'

'Yes, indeed. Dear Lady Corbridge expressed the idea to me before she left. And her husband, the earl, is much recovered, but pining for company. I think he and Richard would deal admirably together.'

Richard? Oh, Papa! Edith felt quite foolish. Of course, Augusta could call him Richard now. But what of this visit? There was no hope for it, was there? She sighed and tried to smile.

'I shall be delighted to go to Bedebury.'

Suddenly, Edith caught sight of Lord Whitley in the looking-glass over the sideboard. Silently eating his breakfast, he nonetheless exhibited a smile of malicious satisfaction on his face. Her stomach filled all of a sudden with a hundred butterflies as he glanced up and caught the reflection of her scrutiny. His whole body stilled as he stared at her, his expression changing slowly.

Lord Whitley's voice sounded suspiciously soft as he broke off his gaze to address Lord Cramlington. 'Might I make a suggestion? It is always so disagreeable to be obliged to travel three in a carriage. I should be happy to escort Lady Edith to Bedebury in my chaise tomorrow morning. As I am not yet well enough to ride so far it would provide me with some company and you with some more space and privacy.'

Augusta beamed at him. 'That's an excellent idea, Charles. I'm sure there could be no objection. What do you say, Edith?'

What did she not have to say? She could think of nothing more improper. Dear, sweet Augusta would never think the man capable of any low behaviour, but she knew better. It would be impossible to appeal to Papa either. He would never think evil of anyone. She swallowed and nodded her head. Just let him try anything! She'd make sure she had *two* hatpins with her!

Lord Whitley positively smirked with triumph as he looked at her. What had she done now? At Bedebury she could well be in his power. Did he plan to take his revenge on her there? Or would he make use of the hours she would have to spend alone in his company along the road?

6

Cousin Bertram must have felt too ill to consume a proper breakfast. Well before ten o'clock the next morning he presented himself at the door, dressed all by guess. He held a copy of *The Morning Post* in one trembling hand.

Edith sat alone in the morning-room, busy at the escritoire by the window. Wearing a carriage-gown of heavy navy merino with a gold brooch at the throat, she was attempting to take her mind off her meeting with Lord Whitley that morning. He had arranged to call for her at ten, so that the journey to Bedebury could be undertaken during the short daylight hours. Augusta and her father had departed to Reddish's Hotel the evening before and she would not see them again until they met in Buckinghamshire.

She looked up from the letter she was writing and raised an eyebrow at the sight of her cousin. 'Good morning, Bertram. How good of you to call.'

'I demand to know the meaning of this . . . this . . . ' Words failed him as he thrust the offending notice under Edith's nose. 'Has

121

my uncle run mad?'

Before she could reply he whirled away and paced up and down, clearly displaying an intense agitation. Edith bit her lip to hide her glee.

'Why, Bertram, whatever do you mean? I think it very kind of you to present yourself at such an early hour to wish him well.'

Her cousin gasped. 'Wish him well? I wish him to blazes, and that bitch with him!'

Bitch? He dared to call Augusta a bitch? Something snapped. In less than a second, anger completely overwhelmed any previous feelings she had experienced.

'Be silent!' Edith stunned both herself and Bertram with her vehemence. 'Have you lost your senses? How dare you insult Lady Cramlington in such a manner? Look beyond your self-interest for once in your miserable life. I cannot think why you have put yourself in such a passion in the first place. It was only natural for my father to marry again, especially in his new position.'

'Natural? You call it natural for a man old enough to be a grandfather to be marrying again? It's disgraceful! I shall be a laughing stock!'

'If you are, it's because you have made yourself into one.'

Bertram seethed. A murderous expression

closed his narrow eyes to slits. 'You go too far, Cousin. When we are married I shall curb that tongue of yours, and take great pleasure in doing it.'

Astonishment robbed Edith of all power of speech. She gaped at him in open-mouthed stupefaction for several seconds until she collected her wits.

'Have you lost your mind? I should sooner marry the stable-boy!'

'Nonsense!' Bertram crossed the room to stand close, too close for Edith's peace of mind, but she wasn't about to let him know that. All the same, she felt a lurking taste of fear. He stared down at her. His nostrils looked pinched and white, a sure sign of his anger.

'Our marriage is the obvious solution. Once I become the earl I shall hold the purse strings and the title. You will have nothing, unless I choose to bestow it upon you.'

Once he became the earl? Over her dead body!

Or . . . Dear God! Suddenly the fear she felt blossomed into something much more sinister. Almost panic-stricken, she stared back at him. Perhaps not *her* dead body, but her father's? Twice now she had suspected Bertram of a dark deed. Would he be ruthless enough to go through with such a dreadful act? The suspicion hardened into certainty. The look on his face left no room for doubt. He would kill his own mother to gain an earldom.

Struggling to maintain her composure, Edith rose and thrust herself past him. Standing with her back to the window, she stabbed her chin forward. 'You have forgotten my eighty thousand pounds, my dear cousin. The first thing my father did was to arrange with Sharples to have that amount settled upon me. If you were to become earl tomorrow I feel you would discover the purse strings to be well and truly loosened!'

'Eighty thousand . . . ' He actually lost colour. He made a quick recovery, however. 'It is folly to split the inheritance in such a manner. Why, everything not entailed would be lost if you demanded such an amount! Only our marriage would bring the estates back to good order.'

He cared for nothing but the money, did he? Contempt struggled with her anger, but for now the anger won out.

'I suggest you depart, at once. Do not return without an invitation, which will be a long time coming. I shall leave instructions with Hartley that you are not to be admitted. *If* you should have the temerity to approach me again, I shall call the watch! I will never marry you, Bertram, and I sincerely hope that I shall have the pleasure of holding a new Viscount Holywell in my arms before the coming year is out.'

Bertram snatched a figurine off the mantelpiece and threw it into the hearth with almost explosive force. His face ugly, he turned towards Edith with his fists clenched.

In that moment, she feared for her life. Terror clawed at her throat at the insane look on his face. With hands stretched out behind her, not daring to take her attention from him for a second, she fumbled for something, anything, which might be used as a weapon.

He advanced, snarling. 'She may well present my uncle with a bastard brat, but don't count on him surviving his childhood. I *shall* inherit the title, just you wait — '

What Edith was to wait for was never uttered as a strong hand seized Bertram by the back of his collar. She almost screamed with the shock of seeing Lord Whitley pounce upon her cousin and shake him within an inch of his life. Neither of them had heard the door open, which made the vision of him descending like a vengeful angel all the more surprising and shocking.

She had never felt happier to see anyone in her life.

With a last oath his lordship threw a

gasping and retching Bertram on to the floor. He stood over him, looking down in a most menacing manner. Edith shivered.

'Stand up, you coward! Or crawl like the worm you are!'

Bertram looked up at Lord Whitley's expression and menacing stance. He swallowed, then attempted a smile, which instead turned his face into a ghastly mask. Struggling to his feet he backed away, hands outstretched to ward off his lordship. His retreat halted suddenly as he hit the doorframe. Bertram jumped with fright, then turned and fled.

Lord Whitley started to follow him but pulled up short and clutched his thigh. With an even more colourful oath than his first one he gave up the idea of pursuit.

'Don't stop until you reach Half Moon Street, and not even then if you know what's good for you!' he shouted. Turning his attention to the gaping butler, who had been standing transfixed all the while, he glowered.

'Lady Edith does not wish to inspect your teeth, man! Fetch her some refreshment to the book-room, and send a maid to clean up this mess.'

Hartley shook his head as if to clear it. 'At once, your lordship! Lady Edith's maid has already departed for the country. Shall I send

Mrs Fenwick to her?'

'I shall attend to her ladyship. Get about your business!'

Hartley vanished without another word as Lord Whitley took hold of Edith's unresisting arm and led her from the room. He pressed her into one of the leather chairs in the book-room and refused to allow her to speak until he poured her a glass of wine and insisted that she drink. Edith looked at him in bemused wonder.

'Well, my lord, I can see that you are a man of action.'

Lord Whitley extracted the heavy, bronze paperweight from Edith's left hand. She hadn't realized she was holding it.

'It would appear, milady, that you were contemplating some action of your own before I intervened.' Suddenly, he grinned, a look of pure boyish delight that almost made her heart stop. 'Good for you!'

Edith fought for control of her feelings. She must remain calm at all costs and not follow her desire, which was to cast herself into his lordship's arms and weep on his shoulder. 'You cannot imagine the number of times I have wished I was a man when I have had dealings with Bertram. Allow me to tell you, Lord Whitley, that I admire your conduct excessively!'

He sobered. 'Ah, if you were a man, none of this would be happening.'

'Or I might well have already found myself with a broken neck! My cousin is evil. Pure evil! I shall never allow him to come anywhere near Augusta, or my father.'

'Do not distress yourself. If Mr Backworth is stupid enough to make any further threats I shall deal with him. *Personally.*'

Lord Whitley paused. He drew in a deep breath. A ghost of a smile appeared on his features. There may even have been a glimmer of amusement in his eye. 'There is at least one neck I have been wishing to wring for quite some considerable time. Your cousin Bertram will make a suitable substitute, however.'

She felt herself blushing. There was no need to enquire which neck he meant! She really didn't feel like starting the old arguments again right now. She pushed herself to her feet, surprised at how unstable her knees felt.

'Perhaps we should be on our way,' she suggested. 'Otherwise darkness will have fallen before we reach our destination.'

'Indeed we should, but I am first charged with a message from your new mama. I have persuaded her not to start out today. She and Lord Cramlington will take a day to rest, then join us at Bedebury tomorrow. She bade me wish you a safe journey.'

'She . . . what?' Edith felt the floor kick up under her. Rather than fall, she sank back into her chair. 'I am to go to Bedebury on my own?'

Lord Whitley smiled. His words were soft when he replied.

'Oh, no, my lady; you are to go to Bedebury with me.'

★　★　★

Her maid and Rogers had left with Glory and the baggage at first light, so Edith had only a small portmanteau and her reticule with her as she entered his lordship's post chaise. She was determined not to let him upset her. She had had enough upsets already today. No, instead she thought of her journey from Newcastle. There could be no comparison! Edith sank back against luxurious, crimson velvet squabs and obligingly lifted her feet to allow Agnes to slide a hot brick under them. Hartley himself tucked a rug across her knees and lowered the window shade a fraction so that the weak sunlight did not irritate her eyes. Lord Whitley settled himself beside her in the opposite corner. The door closed. They were off.

She glanced dubiously at the few inches of space that separated them. How confined she felt. With only the post-boys to drive the team, there wasn't even a coachman on the roof to hear if she called for help.

Why had he separated her so neatly from Augusta's care? What did he have in mind? She spent the first twenty minutes of the journey wondering what Lord Whitley planned to do to her. Well, she wasn't going to behave like a ninny, whatever he did. She had her two hatpins, after all, and they were proceeding down the king's highway. She could always jump out and run. With his bad leg, he wouldn't be able to catch her! The thought cheered her up immensely.

Lord Whitley stared out of the window as the chaise rattled over the cobbles. His gaze took in nothing of the passing scene as his mind grappled with the events of the morning. The unexpected and lately unaccustomed physical activity thrust upon him at the sight of the enraged Bertram had drained him of his strength. That damnable wound in his thigh throbbed like the very devil, too. Anger surged anew as he thought of any man offering violence to a female, no matter if the particular female had more than once driven even him to consider battery at the best and murder at the worst. Gentlemen considered before acting upon their desires. At least, they should do so . . . *he* hadn't considered his wound or the company present when he had seized that miserable coward by the scruff of his neck, had he?

Lord Whitley pondered. Lady Edith had insinuated herself into his life. From their first meeting she had demonstrated time and again how unsuitable she was to be a lady of high degree. Her outspokenness and rash defence of her father no matter what would have been enough to condemn her to other more gently nurtured females, but was that the limit of her faults? By no means! Add to that a lack of respect due to his position, an amazing tendency to answer back at even the faintest excuse, and an unbecoming lack of delicacy. His stomach roiled at the thought of her tending him on his sickbed. It was impossible for her to have any sensibility!

A vision of her braining Bertram with the paperweight popped unwanted into his head. What other female he knew would have contemplated any such action? Not many. Not *any*, if the truth were known. What other female had ever driven him to behave so rudely, and yes, it had to be admitted, *not* in a gentlemanly fashion, at times?

And yet she had her qualities. He was a fair

man, able to judge in a calm and dispassionate manner. She was a loyal and loving daughter, good to the servants, never peevish or spiteful. No, there was not a devious bone in her body. She had been so good to his mama, too. Indeed, it was Mama's urging, as well as that ungentlemanly desire to get the better of her, which had prompted him to issue this invitation in the first place. Poor Mama! She had been making any number of attempts over the past two years to thrust eligible females in his way whenever he had chanced to be in England. Edith was the latest in a long line, and by far the most unsuitable.

He shook his head. 'You are out of luck this time, Mama!'

'I beg your pardon, sir?'

Lord Whitley was recalled to his surroundings. Lady Edith sat beside him, looking uncommonly handsome in her stylish bonnet and blue outfit. She had a quizzical expression on her face and a wicked twinkle lurking at the back of her eyes. The drab little dowd of his first meeting had long since vanished. Indeed, Augusta had been right when she had told him that Edith would be a beauty. He forced himself to be polite as he thought up an excuse for his comment.

'Mama hoped we'd arrive early at Bedebury.

By the looks of the weather, she'll be disappointed.'

'Oh! How long do you think the journey will take?'

'If these horses sprouted wings, it would still be too long for me,' he snapped.

'Oh!' Lady Edith raised a hand to her face and turned away, but not before he saw a flash of pain in her eyes.

Immediately he regretted his outburst. Now look what she'd done! Reduced him to incivility, like any lout in the street. Why did she always bring out the worst in him? Before she could reply further he held up his hand. 'No! That was very bad of me. I beg your pardon. I do not know why I spoke to you in such a manner. Forgive me, please.'

She looked doubtful for a moment, then ventured a tentative smile. 'Perhaps your wound is paining you?'

If only he could blame it on that! A craven person might do so, but not him. 'No, I have not that excuse. I . . . ' He couldn't think of anything as he looked into those trusting eyes. Given other circumstances, a flirtation would have passed the time very agreeably, but this lady had no idea how to be a flirt. She would take him seriously, and that would never do.

Edith broke the awkward silence, unknowingly coming to his rescue. 'My cousin

Bertram is enough to cast anyone into the dismals. I wish I *had* thrown that paperweight at his head. He frightens me.'

Lord Whitley impulsively reached for her hand. 'Don't be frightened. I shall never allow him to harm you, or your family. Please remember that all you have to do is send word.'

His reward was a beaming smile that brightened up the whole chaise.

'Why, thank you, my lord,' she told him. 'I'm sure I can deal with the likes of Bertram, but I appreciate your concern nonetheless, especially considering the circumstances.'

'Circumstances?' Lord Whitley frowned. 'What circumstances?'

'Why, only that you are desirous of wringing my neck yourself, of course!'

There was a moment's silence as he regarded her mischievous face. He flexed his fingers. 'Lady Edith, do not push your luck!'

★   ★   ★

Bertram Backworth adjusted his fresh neck-cloth. He inspected his reflection more closely. There was no sign of the bruising on his neck. Perhaps no one had noticed his abrupt departure from his uncle's house. Moyle, his useless Irish valet, would never breathe a word to a living soul, on pain of instant dismissal. It was just possible that gossip about this morning's events would not get out.

How dare the man treat him in that fashion? If he had not been taken by surprise from behind in that low and underhand manner he would have given the upstart viscount the thrashing he deserved!

Bertram whipped up a self-righteous anger as he thought of his misfortunes. All of his plans had gone awry.

Once he realized how close he stood to the earldom he had seen to it that Catherine had not hindered his progress. How he had grown sick of her snivelling and whining! All he'd had to do then was move in with Edith and his uncle, offer her marriage to give him some respectability, then ensure that his new father-in-law had an unfortunate accident. Within a suitable time, of course. Six months would have lulled any suspicions. But what had happened? He had been thrown out like some chimney sweep's urchin, that's what! Treated with no respect for his position or his dignity. Cousin Edith had a lot to answer for, even before this morning's events.

Yes, she would be sorry. He gave one last twitch to his neckcloth. Anger he could have dealt with, but her contempt was too much!

And now that other bitch would have to be got rid of, too. Oh, yes, they would be sorry, all of them, before Bertram Backworth was finished with them! Slowly, he began to smile. His fingers drummed a slow beat on the dressing table as he thought. He nodded to his reflection. Yes, he would do it!

'Call a hackney for me, Moyle! I am going to visit my cousin, Lady Louisa.'

★ ★ ★

Ominous clouds darkened the already miserable atmosphere as Lord Whitley's chaise made its slow way south and west. There had been delay after delay. First the late start, then just past Hounslow, a carter ahead of them had lost his load of coal, blocking the road for at least an hour. They had made the best of it and taken shelter at an inn, which would in other circumstances not have received Lord Whitley's patronage. One look at the coffee-room confirmed his suspicions, but it was quite out of the question to take Lady Edith to a private parlour. At least the coffee was hot and passable.

Freezing rain swept across the bleak landscape of sodden fields and leafless trees. Edith gazed out at the dismal view, thanking heaven that she had not been brought into the world destined to be a post-boy. Since she had made the remark about wringing necks Lord Whitley had chosen not to talk to her unless forced to do so by common civility. The incident with the carter had further darkened his disposition and so she had been left to entertain herself. As the rain continued to rattle against the windows even her own company began to pall.

Twenty minutes earlier, one of the leaders had picked up a stone and gone dead lame four miles from the nearest inn. After a hurried conversation, the front pair had been unhitched and left with their post-boy to make the best time they might to shelter. With only the tired wheelers instead of the full team, the chaise crept onwards. The minutes crept even more slowly.

At last Lord Whitley broke the silence. 'I am sorry for the delay, but we shall soon be at The Green Man Inn. After a hot drink and a chance to refresh yourself you will not find the rest of the journey quite so bad.'

'I am quite comfortable, thank you, my lord. I wish the same could be said for the post-boys, in this weather.'

Lord Whitley glanced out of the window and shrugged. 'They are well paid for their service. I've had them out in worse than this.'

His complacent attitude nettled her no

end. Even a fight would be better than the silent treatment. 'No doubt! I'm sure the welfare of your servants comes low on your list of priorities.'

Lord Whitley rose to the bait just as she had hoped. 'Then you are wrong! What would you have me do? Tuck them up beside a nice cosy fireside when we reach the inn? We would be obliged to spend the night, if not several nights, waiting for the weather to break. Or is that what you had in mind?'

Edith gaped at him. What was he suggesting? 'It cannot be far to Bedebury, surely? We have been an age upon the road. I could probably walk more quickly across country.'

'Could you indeed? For your information, no one under my protection goes traipsing off across the countryside! But you are right. The Green Man marks the start of the last stage. It is only another five miles or so to my parents' home. With a fresh team we should make it in thirty minutes.'

Three miles on from The Green Man, with the coach lamps gleaming strongly in the dusk and a new team of bays trotting along at a spanking pace, Edith began to think of supper and a warm bed. Fatigued by the events of the day, she searched for the first sign of the lights that would mark the gatehouse at Bedebury.

Suddenly the chaise gave a sickening lurch and skewed sideways. Edith tried to scream, but an enormous weight thrust all the air out of her lungs and left her gasping for breath. Her head thumped against the side of the chaise. Only the padded squabs and her bonnet prevented her head from hitting the window frame with considerable force. The worst of the impact was cushioned but she still felt dazed and bruised. Thank God the window had not shattered!

An elbow in the ribs identified the cause of the weight crushing the life out of her. Lord Whitley had been thrown from his seat.

All was chaos outside as the horses reared and plunged, neighing with terror as their riders tried to calm them. The carriage came to rest tilted at a drunken angle. The nearside lamp had gone out, so Edith could see nothing as she fought to escape from the corner where she had been thrown. Her back was wedged against the window, her bonnet rammed down over her eyes and her legs tangled up in her petticoats.

'Get off me, for goodness sake!'

'I'm trying! Keep still, woman. I have no wish to injure you further.'

Someone opened the door from the outside. In an instant the weight was gone as

Edith heard a slithering and a thumping splash, followed by a loud curse.

Lord Whitley had fallen into the ditch.

An anxious voice sounded from the darkness. 'My lord! Are you hurt? The axle has broken. We're in the ditch.'

Edith managed to push her bonnet up out of her eyes and drag herself to the doorway. She could see the black, oily gleam of ditchwater churned up into a million reflections as Lord Whitley struggled to his feet. He almost snarled as he pushed away the proffered help.

'You surprise me, Tom! I never would have guessed. Go to Lady Edith's aid, you snivelling fool!'

The unfortunate post-boy appeared in the doorway. Edith saw at a glance that she would have to jump, or be carried. She didn't like the thought of that. The lad didn't look strong enough to carry a fly.

'Stand aside. I can get myself out of this.' She gathered up her skirts, not caring about the amount of limb visible to anyone who might chance to look. With a nimble leap she cleared the ditch and landed on the bank at the far side. Keeping her balance with difficulty on the wet and muddy turf she then pondered her position. Immediately in front of her a stone wall blocked all access into the fields for as far as she could see. She could, perhaps, re-cross the expanse of ditch water a little further along, but that would take a leap of prodigious proportions. She was stuck!

'Obviously you are not badly hurt.'

She whirled round to find Lord Whitley staring at her. Up to his knees in water, he had lost his hat and his cane. The carriage lamps had been relit and the light silhouetted his form, making his expression almost impossible to read. His eyes were visible though as he stood with his fists on his hips glaring up at where she stood on the relative safety of the bank. It was all she could do not to laugh out loud. What a picture he presented!

'How do you plan to extricate yourself from *this* mishap?'

Well, really! What impudence! Edith stamped her foot, causing it to sink nearly an inch into the mire. 'This is one accident I defy you to blame on me, my lord! The axle broke on *your* carriage, not mine!'

'And I would have been snug in my home if it had not been for you, insisting on this visit to my parents!'

'Insist? *I* insisted on this visit? You must be mad! I had no wish to spend an instant in your company! It was *you* who insisted on the visit!'

'Oh, be quiet!' Lord Whitley hauled Edith into his arms. 'Let me get you out of this. I can't stand here arguing all night. I'm freezing.'

She gasped. It felt so right to be held in his arms. Despite her temper and his oafish behaviour, it felt right. Astonishment robbed her of breath for a moment, but only a moment. Sanity made a hurried return. What did he think he was doing?

'Put me down! Put me down at once!' Being held so close to him made her feel strange. She wasn't sure if she liked the feeling or not. It was impossible to decide how she felt, clasped to his chest like this. It was a mere whimsy, the feeling she'd had that she'd come home. The man despised her, after all.

She needed some distance between them, and quickly. Edith flailed her arms and legs. How dare he manhandle her like a sack of wheat? Anxiety rushed in when she remembered his injury. What of his leg? He would damage himself if he attempted to carry her. Worry added a sharp edge to her tone. 'I demand that you put me down!'

Lord Whitley stopped suddenly and stared at her. 'My absolute pleasure, my lady,' he snapped, releasing his hold with a suddenness that left her gasping.

Edith guessed his intention too late to do anything about it. She tumbled into the stinking, icy ditch, her scream cut off by the sudden flow of water that left her choking. Rough hands hauled her out as the post-boys came to her aid, but not before she had seen the gleam of triumph in Lord Whitley's eye.

'Why, you . . . you . . . ' She could think of nothing bad enough to call him! Filthy, freezing water ran down the back of her neck. Her bonnet had wilted round her face to form a soggy frill. She was weighed down by her sodden clothing and covered in mud from head to foot.

'Charles Ashington, you are going to regret this until the day you die!'

A grin of triumph split his face from ear to ear. 'Never! Anything you might do to me could not possibly give you half the satisfaction I am feeling at this moment!'

Like lightning she stooped down and collected a double handful of mud. Hurling it with a force she would never have believed she possessed, she struck the laughing viscount full in the face.

'I don't see you laughing now!'

Lord Whitley came flying up out of the ditch, ready to do battle. Edith shrieked, but held her ground. She wanted to run and hide behind the post-boys, but that would be cowardly.

The post-boys! Edith sucked in a swift breath. What must they be thinking? Suddenly, it was brought home to her how shockingly improper her behaviour had been from start to finish! Holding out her arms to ward off the advancing viscount, she backed away.

'My lord! You cannot! Not in front of the servants.'

Recalled somewhat to his senses, Lord Whitley stopped and glowered at her. Slimy mud dripped off the end of his nose as he fumbled for a handkerchief. Edith tried to stifle a giggle, then gave up and broke into a gale of laughter. Bending almost double, she clutched at her side. Lord Whitley fumed a while longer, until a wail from Edith proved to be too contagious. He succumbed to laughter himself, trying to wipe the filth from his eyes with a trembling hand.

The post-boys gave up attempting to understand what was going on. Shrugging their shoulders, they turned back to the horses.

Tom looked at his companion. ''Isterical, that's what she be. Although I don't know what maggot's got into 'is lordship's head. I'd best ride to the house for aid. It's not far.'

Tom vaulted on to the back of one of the bays and called over his shoulder. 'Don't ye fret, my lord. I'll be back with another carriage in the shake of a lamb's tail.'

Lord Whitley stopped laughing long enough to gaze after the departing Tom. 'Come back, you fool! Don't alarm my mother!'

It was too late. Tom and his horse disappeared into the gloom. He had only just caught up to them as they prepared to leave The Green Man and had time for nothing more than a quick drink. Nothing was going to keep him from a warm bed now.

Lord Whitley swore in exasperation. 'What's Sam here supposed to do with three horses?'

Edith gasped weakly. She felt sick with laughing so much. This was all too ludicrous for words. Not even a farce at Drury Lane could be so absurd.

'Oh, no! Look at us! What are *we* to do? We can't arrive at Bedebury looking like this! There will be an uproar.'

Lord Whitley shrugged his shoulders. 'We'll have to use the servant's entrance, I suppose. What am I to do with you, Lady Edith? You will freeze in this weather, but I can't leave Sam to lead all of these horses.'

Edith sniffed. *What sort of a weakling did he think she was?*

'Honestly, have you no common sense?

There are three of us, and three beasts, in case you haven't noticed. What could be simpler?'

'You, lead a horse?' Lord Whitley sounded amazed.

Edith had to force herself not to start laughing again. The humour of the situation struck her with renewed force. 'What's the matter? Are you afraid I'll s-soil my dress?'

He simply stared at her. Edith gave up and crossed over to Sam, who had the remaining horses disentangled by this time. Seizing the nearest one by the bridle she started off down the road.

'Come on, or we shall be here all night!'

Ten minutes later, Captain Giles Ashington reined in his pair and stared in astonishment at the procession approaching him along the road. His head filled with lurid accounts of wreckage and injury, he had fully expected to come across a scene of devastation. Was that his cousin, more nearly resembling a scarecrow than a gentleman of noble birth? And surely that bedraggled, filthy creature could never be the enchanting Lady Edith!

Recovering his wits, he leapt from his phaeton and executed an exquisite bow. 'Welcome to Bedebury, my lady!'

7

Edith drifted back to consciousness, becoming aware of the comfort of a feather pillow and the gentle sound of a fire crackling in the hearth. A silent chambermaid had laid a branch of apple-wood on top of the coals and the room was filled with the pleasant scent. Still only half awake, she opened her eyes and contemplated her surroundings. What she had seen last night of Bedebury exuded taste and elegance. Her bedchamber was no exception. The furniture consisted of the finest mahogany, inlaid with a flowered pattern of different coloured woods. Bed hangings of pale blue shot-silk, now partly drawn back, had protected her from draughts overnight, whilst a handsome Chinese carpet in blues and greens covered the floor.

She threw her arms back and stretched.

'Ouch!' Pain shot through her aching muscles. Memory flooded in at the reminder of the dramatic events of the previous evening. Rescued at last by Captain Ashington, she had been rushed off to a warm bath, after which Lady Corbridge herself had tended to her various bumps and bruises. She had hardly been able to eat the delicious supper served to her in this very bed before drifting off to a deep, dreamless sleep.

'Oh, my goodness! Where's the glass?' She slid out of the bed, wincing, then rang for hot water, anxiously examining her reflection for marks or scratches on her face as she waited. Although there was a tender spot high on her forehead where she had struck against the window frame in the chaise, the bruise could not be seen. Satisfied, Edith pondered what to wear. It was difficult to tell the time of day but weak winter light filled the room.

It couldn't be too early. Father and Augusta would arrive at the first possible moment, if they hadn't done so already. She should at least be dressed to greet them. No doubt the gentlemen would be stirring soon. Captain Ashington must not be allowed to see her looking any less than her best.

Just a minute! Edith sat down and regarded her reflection once again. What was she thinking? The gallant captain had seen her looking her absolute worst only a few hours ago. Perhaps it was Lord Whitley she wanted to impress? He seemed to have such a poor opinion of her.

But did his opinion of her matter, anyway? She didn't like him, after all. His temper was foul, his manners atrocious and his attitudes foreign to the way she had been taught to think by her father. They had nothing in common. He'd tipped her into the ditch without a second thought.

Then why did she remember so vividly the feel of his arms around her last night? Or on that night he was so ill, the soft warmth of his lips against hers? Looking at herself in the glass, Edith ran the tips of her fingers over her mouth as she recalled the sensation. A little shudder rippled down her spine.

What made her long to defend him against Lady Louisa's vicious attack on his character? Last night, when he had stood in front of her so furiously angry, with mud dripping off his face and water pooling in his boots, what reason did she have for wishing to pull him into her arms?

'Perhaps I have not been acquainted with many young men,' she mused out loud. 'Perhaps I will feel the same way with Captain Ashington and his friends.'

She grinned mischievously as her maid entered the room. 'Perhaps I shall enjoy finding out!'

The hall appeared deserted as she descended the stairs thirty minutes later, but as if by magic a footman appeared from nowhere and showed her into the breakfast-room. Lord Whitley and Captain Ashington both leapt to their feet as she entered. Lord Corbridge smiled delightedly at her as he, too, rose to greet her. The captain thrust the footman out of the way as he rushed to pull out a chair for her.

'My lady! We had no thought of seeing you before noon at least. Should you be out of your bed?'

She smiled. 'It takes more than a ducking in a muddy ditch to better me, my dear sir. I am made of sterner stuff than that!'

To her delight, she watched as Lord Whitley's ears turned red. So he was embarrassed by his outrageous behaviour, was he? Good! It remained to be seen what gossip about the incident spread from the two post-boys. No one would find out from her, but she wasn't going to tell his lordship that. Let him stew!

Captain Ashington failed to notice the strained atmosphere as he hurried to serve her from the chafing dishes lined up on the sideboard. Lord Whitley took advantage of the distraction and ventured a tentative smile as he poured her some coffee.

'I wish to have a private word with you after breakfast, my lady. If you would be so good as to grant me a few moments of your time?'

She looked him straight in the eye, hugely

enjoying his discomfiture. 'Why, my lord, what could you possibly have to say to me in private?' She batted her eyelids, trying her best to look coy. If only ladies carried fans to breakfast, she could have rapped his knuckles!

Giles intervened as he placed a plate of breakfast on the table in front of her. 'Charles, you dog! Stop trying to steal a march with the ladies. *I* insist on a private word with her ladyship.'

The captain gave her a winning smile. 'We have been invited to a ball on New Year's Eve at the home of Lord and Lady Aston. Will you stand up with me for the first waltz?'

It was a heady feeling, having two such men vying for her attention. Edith's waltzing lessons had come along very well, but she had never imagined dancing with the captain. No, it was his cousin who had filled her thoughts. Would *he* ask her to waltz? By the looks of him, it was doubtful, even if his leg was healed enough to permit dancing. Perhaps just a little goading might produce a reaction.

'*If* my father allows me to attend a ball when I am not yet out, and if he permits me to waltz, I will naturally be guided by my new mama in choice of suitable partners. There is, however, one request I feel I should make.'

Captain Ashington looked hopeful. 'If it is

something within my power, my lady, all you need do is ask.'

As hard as she tried, she could not suppress just a little smile. 'I would wish *not* to go to the ball in Lord Whitley's chaise!'

Lord Corbridge roared with laughter, then hurriedly pretended to choke into his napkin.

Lord Whitley sprang to his feet, almost upsetting his plate in his haste. His hands clenched and opened several times as he glared at her. Edith felt a prickling along her spine at the look on his face. It was exciting, courting danger like this. Her stomach contracted with a mixture of fear and anticipation. Before she could press any further he spat out his reply.

'I think, my lady, that the private word I wished to have with you is somewhat urgent.' He strode over to the door and held it open. 'If you would be so kind?'

Had she gone too far? The fear she felt threatened to overwhelm the anticipation. All she could do now was try and bluff it out. 'Good heavens, my lord, I have not yet had my breakfast! Even a condemned man is allowed a last meal. Am I worse than a felon?'

It was hard work keeping up the innocent expression. Edith stared at the look on Lord Whitley's face. He really would like to kill her!

Lord Corbridge frowned at his son. 'Really, Charles, Lady Edith will think you found your manners in the rag bag! Take yourself off to the book-room and await her convenience!'

There was enough of the autocrat in his manner to give his son pause. He managed a stiff bow. 'I beg your pardon, Lady Edith. If you will excuse me, I will hope to meet with you shortly.'

He stalked off, his limp still present but thankfully not any worse. By the rigid set of the shoulders under his jacket he was obviously still more than a trifle annoyed.

Lord Corbridge chuckled as he spoke to Edith. 'Not *too* shortly, my dear. That hothead of mine needs to cool his heels. Wouldn't you say so, Giles?'

The captain nodded his agreement, although he regarded Edith with a strangely intent expression. 'Charles is not himself. Perhaps that tumble into the ditch addled his brains more than we realized. I have never known him to be rude to a lady. What do you make of it, sir?'

'I think we are keeping Lady Edith from her breakfast! Come, let us talk of more pleasant subjects.' He smoothly started a conversation about the treats in store for the house party. Edith could not fail to notice, however, that he too looked thoughtfully at the door through which his son had made his hasty exit.

She lingered over her breakfast as long as she dared, but at last she found herself outside the book-room. The footman opened the door for her and she saw Lord Whitley standing by the fire, his hands clasped tightly behind him. There was no evidence of a newspaper or any other device to pass the time. Instinctively she knew that he had been standing there like that, waiting for her, ever since he had left the breakfast-room. He forced a ghost of a smile as he strode towards her.

'Lady Edith. Will you not take a seat?'

She ventured a small, tight smile. 'Not until I have apologized, sir. It was very wrong of me to goad you in that manner. I beg your pardon.'

He looked wary, as if he didn't believe her. She tried again, extending her hand towards him. 'Truly, I am sorry.'

He smiled then, a genuine smile filled with warmth. 'No, indeed, I am the one who should apologize. For my attitude, my manner and my actions. I cannot fathom what came over me to drop you in that ditch. It was not the act of a gentleman.'

Sincerity shone from his eyes. Edith could do nothing but respond in kind. Her voice sounded slightly breathless when she spoke, as if she had been hurrying. 'No, it wasn't, was it? I think, however, that it is best forgotten.'

Finally, he took her hand and held it lightly. The desire to suck in a calming breath became an urgent need. His almost casual contact started a warmth spreading along her arm as he spoke. 'You are very generous. I can think of others who would be less forgiving.'

Edith shook her head. Lord Whitley trying to be conciliating was a far more worrying prospect than him in his usual mood. She had no idea how to react to this.

'And no doubt you can think of others who would never have provoked you in the first place.'

A shadow crossed his features. 'That, too, of course. We must make a fresh beginning. I have no wish to be at war with you, my lady. It is entirely too uncomfortable.'

She shook his hand as briskly as she could manage. 'Friends, then. As long as you do not expect me to ride in your chaise!'

'I doubt the need will arise.' He crooked his elbow and tucked her hand into it. 'Come, let me show you round Bedebury. It has some impressive features. The long gallery, for example. Some of the finest artists in the land are exhibited there.'

For the next hour Edith and Lord Whitley wandered from room to room. His knowledge very soon made itself evident as he explained the architecture and the history of many of the finer pieces of furniture. Far from being bored, Edith found herself fascinated by his enthusiasm. He looked so different with his eyes filled with affection as he ran his hand along the rich patina of a Queen Anne chiffonier. Finally, they reached the long gallery.

Sunlight streamed through a row of tall windows on Edith's left, illuminating the colours and gleaming off the gilt frames of a magnificent collection of paintings. Portraits mingled with landscapes and more personal, intimate pictures of favourite horses and dogs. Here a bowl of roses flowed over on to the canvas, so vivid that Edith wanted to reach out and pick one. Further along a cluster of children gathered round their mother, obviously a beauty from the court of King Charles II. In many of the portraits, a definite likeness could be seen to the man strolling beside her.

Edith stopped before a powdered lady in the stiff brocades and panniers of the previous century. Warm eyes smiled down at her, so like Lord Whitley's that she could only stare. 'Your mother, I presume?'

'Yes, indeed. She was a beauty, was she not?'

'And still is, for her beauty comes from within. I have never met a kinder, sweeter lady. You must love her dearly.'

Lord Whitley smiled and laid his free hand over hers for a few seconds. Edith felt a sudden spurt of emotion as he looked down at her. 'Oh, yes, I do love her. At the moment, she is the most important person in my life. I would do anything for her.'

He looked past, and Edith saw his expression change. The warmth faded away, to be replaced by a bleak sorrow. He pulled back and walked to a small sofa, set near the foot of another portrait, this time one of a young couple. The artist had caught Lord Whitley to perfection. He wore his uniform with pride; a pelisse slung over one shoulder to reveal a jacket frogged with gold braid. It was the woman by his side who drew Edith's attention, however. Ethereal beauty clung to her frail form as she gazed up at the man beside her. Edith had seen the face before. There was a miniature on her father's desk, and another, larger portrait in the book-room at home.

'Oh, Charles! My cousin Chloe.'

Lord Whitley sighed. He gestured to the

sofa, waiting for Edith to sit before he did so himself. 'Yes, Chloe. The likeness was taken to mark our betrothal. I left for Spain shortly afterwards. I never saw her again.'

He sat there, lost in thought, until Edith laid her hand on his sleeve. 'She was very beautiful, Charles. It must have been a bitter loss for you.'

If he noticed her use of his first name he gave no sign of it. His mind was obviously far away. 'She died of fever. Louisa told me that she called for me, but I could not come. I knew nothing about it, of course, only that the letters stopped.' He paused, remembering. 'She came to me, when I was ill. I think it was she who saved me. I would rather have gone to be with her, but that would have grieved my mama. I shall never forget her scent, or those eyes, looking down at me, filled with so much compassion.'

Dismay flooded through her. How could she tell him that it wasn't Chloe, but herself whom he remembered? The lump in her throat threatened to choke her as she struggled for breath. Disappointment warred with sadness. The intensity of the feeling surprised her. What right did she have to feel disappointed? Had she hoped all this time that he had indeed known it was she?

Charles looked again at the portrait, then

frowned. 'It's strange. Those eyes are different somehow. I can't quite — '

'You were so very ill,' Edith interrupted hurriedly. The last thing she wanted was for him to recall the events of the night in her father's house. 'And, of course, the light here is not as good as it might be. You remember her as she was, not some artist's impression, no matter how fine the hand.'

He forced a smile. 'You are right, of course. My memories are my own. Even after all this time, I love her so very dearly. I cannot imagine ever feeling that way again.'

It was all so sad. Looking back at his lost ideals and the youthful hopes he had left behind him, Edith sighed. He was still young, not more than thirty, according to Augusta. He could have years of happiness ahead of him. He deserved to be happy. He had given so much for his country. 'Surely you will marry, and learn to love again?'

There was an almost imperceptible shake of his head. 'My mother shares your opinion, but I disappoint her. No doubt I must marry, and soon. I owe it to my family line to provide an heir, but love is something I cannot offer. I will find a girl of birth and breeding, with no romantical notions. I can offer her a great place in the land, but that is all. My heart is in a grave.'

'I cannot comprehend a marriage such as that. I could never be so cold-blooded.'

A spark of genuine amusement lit his features for an instant. 'Oh, I can believe that! You are far too passionate in your opinions. Fortunately, you are in the position where you do not have to compromise those ideals and opinions of yours. Your father would never force you into a marriage that was distasteful to you, and you have the luxury of your private fortune. You do not need to depend on a man. Nor do you have to worry about the succession.'

'Now there you are wrong!' Edith managed a laugh, although she felt closer to tears. 'The thought of the next Lord Cramlington fills me with nothing but worry and repugnance, as I'm sure you must agree.'

'Well, it is not settled, is it? Who knows now what the future may hold?'

'You think Papa and Augusta . . . ' The thought hadn't seriously crossed her mind, but Lord Whitley was obviously in earnest. 'No! You must be wrong. Augusta is surely — ' She broke off, feeling her cheeks go warm. This was no kind of conversation to be having with a gentleman. Lord Whitley misunderstood her confusion.

'What, did you think Augusta too old? You are very much out, I assure you. It is true that she had no children from her first marriage, which was a great sadness to her, but she is just four and thirty, after all.'

She swallowed hard. Of course Augusta wasn't too old. How could she tell him what she'd been thinking? She'd just assumed that her companion was barren. Why didn't he think so, too?

'You are quiet, Lady Edith. Does the thought of a baby brother disturb you?'

Disturb her? No, she wasn't disturbed by the thought. Intrigued and concerned perhaps, but she would love to see her father and Augusta blessed with a child. It was just . . . 'I told Bertram that I wished to hold my brother in my arms before the year was out, but that was simply to enrage him. I had never seriously considered the possibility. You really think they could . . . ?'

It was Lord Whitley's turn to look uncomfortable, as if he had just remembered to whom he was talking. To do him justice, he didn't back away. 'I'm sure they could, but it may turn out to be another daughter, after all.'

Childhood memories caught her with unexpected force. The bewilderment, the desolation, the terror and confusion of a little girl deprived of her mother. Her voice held a lingering echo of her pain.

161

'Mama died in childbed; my brother with her. She was ten years or more younger than Augusta is now. It would be too dangerous.'

'As to that, it is in God's hands. His ways are not for us to see.'

She stared down at her toes, poking out from under her morning gown. The workings of the Almighty had certainly been a mystery to her, no more so than in the past few months.

He rose to his feet and held out his arm. 'Come! We are descending into the dismals! Perhaps you may wish to change your footwear and we can go out to the stables. I wish to reassure myself that Satan travelled down safely, and you, no doubt, must be eager to see your mare.'

More than happy to accept the turn in the conversation she allowed her morbid thoughts to be forgotten on the instant.

'Is it true we are to hunt on Boxing Day?'

'Most certainly! It is a very old tradition hereabouts. The day would not be the same without the Bedebury Hunt.'

'How wonderful! I shall look to your greater experience of the country to give me a lead.'

His laughter sounded full of amusement. 'That is one thing you shall not do! It is expected of me, of course, as my father's son, to be well to the fore, but you must allow that groom of yours to accompany you. The ditches around here were never meant to be tackled by young ladies.'

'As to that, my lord,' Edith replied, stung by the unconsciously patronizing note in his voice, 'I am already intimately acquainted with the ditches around here, or had you forgotten? They hold no fears for me now! Shall we join the others?'

She swept away, torn between annoyance and amusement at the look of chagrin on his face. Rounding a corner in front of him she gave way to a broad grin, but by the time he caught up with her she had her features under control once again.

'I beg your pardon, Lady Edith.' He bowed stiffly. 'My remark concerning the ditches was thoughtless.'

'Not at all, my dear sir! Your remark about the ditches did not concern me nearly as much as the slur you cast upon my ability to ride to hounds. I fear you have underestimated me.'

He sighed. 'Not for the first time, but, Edith, I implore you not to allow my provocation to lead you into anything rash. You will be the death of me yet!'

She laughed. She had driven away the cloud of melancholy that had settled over

163

him. If she could do nothing more, that at least was an achievement.

'Well, my lord, you shall have to wait and see, shall you not? If you will excuse me, I shall change my footwear and meet you in the hall in fifteen minutes, if that is convenient?'

Halfway to her room she stopped abruptly. Her hands felt cheeks suddenly warm.

'He called me Edith.'

Why did his casual use of her name fill her with such delight? She should have been affronted at his temerity, his lack of respect. But no, he hadn't lacked respect. It was more as if he'd been addressing a friend, as if she was more than a formal acquaintance.

Oh, yes! She did want to be more than that, much more!

Absurdly happy, but suddenly more nervous and unsure than she could have believed possible, she raced off to ring for her maid.

8

Glory stamped restlessly on the gravel. She snorted her impatience, warm breath casting a halo of vapour round her head. Riders and horses milled in excited confusion, all awaiting the call to draw off the hounds to the first covert. More than one rider imbibed freely of the warming stirrup cup dispensed by Lord Corbridge's servants as they manoeuvred large silver salvers with one eye on the sidling hooves and another on the demands of the riders.

Edith ignored the crowd and the refreshments both, talking in a soft undertone to the mare, who had caught the excitement from the air. She shortened her rein and settled more comfortably into her saddle. Rogers had taken great pains to check the girths. There was nothing to worry about there. Her skirts were arranged as becomingly as possible. The severe cut of her navy habit was stylish but primarily functional. Not the habit she had been wearing that fateful November morning, this one, but another from the hand of the same tailor. She had been aware of many admiring glances, but flirtation was not one of her priorities today. Not unless, of course, a certain gentleman should wish to speak to her, but that was unlikely.

Apart from a few curt exchanges at the breakfast-table Lord Whitley had been distant and preoccupied. The snub, intentional or not, had hurt. She had believed that they were beginning to be friends, at least, but now . . . now everything had changed. Taking his duty seriously, he had managed to welcome each and every one of the riders now assembled. Not including her, of course. Perhaps he didn't wish to encourage mere females like herself, who were only nuisances in the hunting field. Edith sniffed. Just let him wait, that was all. She'd show him a thing or two!

At last the Master arrived with his hounds. After customary greetings from the party gathered on the front steps of Bedebury to see them off, the confusing mêlée sorted itself out. First the master and his whippers-in, their coats bright beacons as they called and controlled the seething mass of tan, black and white hounds. Noses down, sterns high in the air, the pack surged forwards along the drive towards the home wood. The retinue of gentlemen, ladies and sturdy farmers followed at a respectful distance. Despite her bold words to Lord Whitley, Edith knew better than to push to the front. Nothing was worse than a vulgar thruster, unless, of course, one committed the ultimate sin of heading the hounds. Edith kept Glory to a sedate walk, waiting her chance to break into a smooth canter.

★ ★ ★

'I do hope she will be safe,' Augusta remarked to her husband as she waved her lace handkerchief to the departing riders. 'I worry about her so.'

'Rogers will keep his eye on her. I wish you might see her going over one of these walls; it would set your mind at rest. She is a clipping rider.'

Augusta shuddered at the thought. 'You wish to be out there with them, do you not? Why did you not say so? I am sorry to have spoiled your enjoyment.'

Lord Cramlington cast one lingering look after his departing daughter. His sense of good manners would not allow a single regret to appear in his expression. 'I am grown too old for such gallivanting, my dear. After all, I am a sober married man!'

He didn't fool her a bit. A look of pure mischief crossed Augusta's face as she laid her hand on his arm. 'Old, my dear Richard?

Sober? I wonder? I can vouch for the fact that you are married, however, if anyone should care to ask!'

He turned an interesting shade of pink. 'Augusta!'

'They will all be gone for hours. Whatever shall we do to while away the time until they return?'

He tugged ineffectually at his collar, glancing from left to right to see if anyone had overheard. Augusta slipped her hand through his arm, giving it a discreet squeeze. After one more wave to the departing riders she turned to go indoors. 'Come. You can help me decide what to wear for luncheon.'

★   ★   ★

Edith twisted in her saddle for a last look before she rounded the bend in the drive that would take her out of sight of the house. She saw Augusta wave and her father bend his head to his new wife. A smile tugged at her lips. What a change in Papa! The pair had not arrived at Bedebury until the late afternoon of the Saturday, hours after Edith had expected them. Without a blush Augusta had informed them that they had been unavoidably delayed. The look on her father's face had been priceless. They were so happy.

Could she hope to be half so lucky?

Musing in a similar vein, falling prey to an unaccountable wistfulness, Edith's eyes scanned the assembled company. Such a hodgepodge collection prevented her from seeing the man she was looking for. Breakfast had been bad enough. Once the grooms had brought their mounts to the house he had all but disappeared, leaving her in Rogers' care without a second thought.

The sound of the huntsman's horn brought her out of her reverie. Glory skipped sideways as a chorus of excited shouts rose around her. The chase was on!

She felt the wind whip at her face as she soared over a hawthorn hedge and into a field of stubble. Far in the distance she caught sight of a fleeting glimpse of russet as she let her mare have her head. Glory bounded over the uneven terrain, soon overtaking many of the farmers on their cobs and even some of the gentlemen on their expensive hunters. The thrill of excitement filled Edith with such exhilaration that she laughed out loud.

A raw-boned chestnut ranged up alongside. She glanced over to see Captain Ashington. A ferocious grin lit up his features as he whooped at her.

'Take care, m'lady! There's a regular stitcher coming up!'

Not lost to all sense of prudence Edith allowed him to give her a lead over the first of the famous stone-walled ditches. Glory took the leap in fine style, clearing the water with a foot or more to spare. Others were not so lucky and the field had thinned when she risked a look over her shoulder. One or two riderless horses thundered along aimlessly, while another thrashed in the ditch. Most of the others had sensibly detoured to find the gate.

After only a few more jumps she caught sight of a familiar figure, bent low along the neck of his black stallion, shouting encouragement as he urged Satan onwards. Edith's heart gave a little lurch. Without thinking she altered her line and headed towards him. The stallion pecked as he landed over another hedge into a patch of rough ground. She gasped with alarm at the thought he might fall, but Lord Whitley gathered him upward with an easy skill. The pause gave Edith the chance she needed to come up alongside him. The horns ahead sounded the 'gone to earth' and they reined in.

'Good hunting, my lord?'

He whipped around in the saddle, his face registering first shock and then admiration before he collected his wits.

'Lady Edith! So, you have not yet broken your neck?'

'I would not wish to spoil your day, sir, or mine either, if it should come to that. I have not hunted in an age! The ground is most unlike Northumberland, is it not?'

'I rarely hunt in Northumberland. It's humbug country.'

'Well!' Edith was left speechless. Humbug country? *Humbug country?* How dare he!

'And these trifling hawthorn hedges are good sport, are they? There was only one decent fence on this entire point!'

Edith turned her mount away in a huff. Horrible man!

Satan sidled alongside as Lord Whitley gathered in his reins. 'Unless I miss my guess, you're about to see what we call 'sport', my lady. The fox is running again! Go, Satan!'

Momentarily surprised, Edith allowed the black a fair start before urging Glory forward. Ahead of her she could see at least three of the biggest stone walls she had ever encountered.

The fox shot through a narrow stile with the hounds in full cry. The pause had given most of the followers time to catch up and it was a crowd of riders that approached the first wall. Edith saw Lord Whitley clear ahead of her and then she was over, dropping down across a lane with another massively solid barrier on the far side. Satan flew over as if on wings, but Edith reined hard back. Glory was game for anything, but no match for the broad ditch in front of the wall. Rogers appeared out of nowhere and gestured with his whip.

'Over there, m'lady. A gate.'

Edith urged her mare forwards and over at a sharp angle. A stream of riders followed her line and she was soon hot on the heels of Lord Whitley and the pack. Satan struck a patch of boggy ground, almost bringing him to a stop. Far enough away to avoid the worst of the mud, Edith skirted the area and drew slightly ahead of his lordship. Feeling smug, she galloped away with a flourish of her crop.

The third wall loomed up. Everything narrowed as she concentrated. Only the sound of hooves and her own breathing registered in her brain. No ditch. It must be on the far side, then. Quickly she picked a line and prepared herself.

In almost the last stride, a massive bulk loomed up on her right. With no time to stop and nowhere to go, Edith braced herself. Her mare sprang. Simultaneously an enormous grey gelding launched itself at the wall, ears flat to his head and his eyes rolling wildly. His young rider, hat gone and a maniacal gleam in his eye, looked neither right nor left.

There was nothing to be done. Jumping on

an angle the grey ploughed into Glory's off side with stunning force.

Edith heard a scream as she tumbled sideways. Her own or someone else's, she had no idea. Kicking wildly, she freed her boot from the stirrup as the wall slid past underneath her only inches away. Sparks flew as a shod hoof struck the stone. The ground rose up like a giant fist, slamming the breath out of her. Glory hit the earth a second later, bowled over on to her side by the momentum of the gelding. Edith tasted dirt and smelled the fear in the air. The grey crashed down at the same time, adding to the mayhem. In a nightmare of pain, scrabbling, flashing hooves and the certainty that her beloved mare had broken her legs if not her back, she fought to draw breath and save herself.

Instinctively she cringed backwards. She had to get clear. She had to! One blow from those hooves and she would be dead. Shielding her head as best she could with her arms, she rolled sideways.

The ground fell away. There was a slither and a splash, and she was in the ditch.

The cold made her gasp, but her mouth filled with dirty, frigid water. The foul taste made her want to gag. Choking, struggling desperately to get up, she lost all sense of direction. Everything was black and wet, and filthy. A nightmare of screaming filled her ears. A horse. *Her* horse!

There was a shout, and a hand on the neck of her habit. Edith felt herself borne upwards, away from the water. A strong arm reached round to circle her waist. She clung tight, all the while coughing and choking.

'I have you. You're safe now.'

How well she knew that voice! Yes, she was indeed safe.

'I didn't realize the depth of your attraction for our ditches, my lady,' Lord Whitley remarked in a drawling voice, as he hauled her out of the water to the safety of the muddy bank. 'Some time, you must explain it to me.'

She only groaned. Lying back, her hands reached up to cover her face.

At once, his tone of voice changed. 'Edith! Are you hurt?' He was beside her, outlining her limbs, combing back her bedraggled hair with unsteady, gentle fingers. 'Where is it? Your back? Your ribs?'

The urgency in his voice roused her. She opened one eye to see the sky spinning crazily. His dark gaze, full of concern, looked down.

'Only . . . winded,' she managed to croak. 'I hit — ' She broke off as the memory flowed back. She tried to scramble up. 'Glory! Oh, my God!'

'Shush.' His arm wrapped her in a comforting hug, holding her down against his thigh. 'Stay still for the moment. Don't try to look. Rogers has your mare.'

She paid no heed to his advice, fighting to be free. Anger and despair combined to lend her a furious burst of energy. Wildly she looked around.

'Where is he? I'll kill him! That stupid, lunatic madman! Oh, where is my Glory?'

Struggling to her knees, she beheld the scene. The grey, not Glory, lay on his side, struggling to rise with one leg smashed and useless. The screaming she heard issued from his mouth. Rogers had hold of Glory by the bridle, running his free hand expertly over her near fetlock. Most amazing of all, a snarling Captain Ashington held a cowering young man by the front of his jacket, shaking him back and forth like a sack of rags.

Lord Whitley was forced to raise his voice. 'Giles, Giles, my good fellow, enough! I fear our young friend has learned a painful' — his gaze took in the grey, quieted now by another groom sitting on his neck — 'and expensive lesson. Leave him be.'

Captain Ashington thrust the red-faced youth away with an oath. He strode over to Edith and his cousin. 'I could not believe the evidence of my own eyes when I saw that maniac's criminal behaviour! It is a wonder that you are not killed, ma'am! Thank God that you were right behind her, Charles.'

'Quite.' Lord Whitley had not loosed his hold on Edith. Between the two of them they helped her to her feet. Her knees buckled, but she thrust their arms away.

Fear clutched at her once again. 'Rogers! Tell me.'

The groom looked up briefly, a small smile of relief on his face. 'A bad strain, my lady, but nothing broken. There's a nasty graze on her hind quarter from the wall, but we'll have that right in two shakes of a lamb's tail.'

A huge sob exploded from her throat. 'Oh . . . ' The relief affected her so badly she thought she would fall. The fields and the sky lurched drunkenly around her. She could do nothing but hide her face in her hands and shudder, completely out of control.

For the second time in as many minutes she felt an arm encircle her shoulder. Whisked off her feet, she had no energy left to resist. Weakly, her head found a broad and comforting resting-place.

'Come out of this. Rogers can take charge. We need to get you home.'

Lord Whitley strode over to a grassy bank, somewhat drier than the surroundings. Instead of lowering her to the ground he sat down himself, holding her tightly. His hand came up to clasp her head to his chest, obscuring her view of the scene. Bewildered, Edith tried to protest his treatment of her.

Before she could make herself heard a loud retort rang out. The agonized squeals from the grey cut off as the groom ended his suffering. A deathly silence ensued.

Fresh tears poured from Edith's eyes. Try as she might, there was nothing she could do to quell them. Vaguely she heard Captain Ashington's voice, talking to Lord Whitley.

'We can get the mare to Farmer Tyler's barn. It's only a few furlongs away yonder. What we're to do with her ladyship is a different matter. Should we try her saddle on my horse? If he was to walk we could manage. Or shall I ride to Bedebury for the carriage?'

'No need for either. The carriage would take too long and she's in no fit state to sit a horse right now. I'll take Edith home. Can you bring Satan over for me?'

Feeling like a parcel at the receiving office, Edith was handed to Captain Ashington and then upward on to Satan's withers. Lord Whitley eased her back until she was as comfortable as possible, hard up against the solid wall of his chest.

'Be a good fellow and take my place with

the hunt, Giles. Try what you can to quell the gossip, also.'

'I don't think we'll have to worry about that. Plenty of people saw what happened. They're only thankful that her ladyship isn't badly hurt. It'll be a cold day in hell before the Master allows that cub of Aston's to ride to hounds again, once he hears the story, which won't be long. You were too far ahead to see what happened at the first wall, but he caused mayhem there, too. The boy's a menace!'

'That 'boy' is only three years younger than yourself, my dear Giles. But yes, I agree with you. He has to be taught a lesson. My father informs me that he's ruined two horses already this season, before the cubbing was even over. I think we can rely on Lord Aston to do the necessary.'

'Perhaps you're right.' The captain glowered after the departing miscreant, who could be seen trudging along a muddy farm track. 'I wish I had him in my Company for a month, that's all I can say!' He shook his head. 'Enough of this. You must get Lady Edith home. Take care.'

She attempted to raise her head to tell the captain that she was perfectly capable of looking after herself, but her body refused to obey her commands. Did they think she was deaf, these men? A shiver ran through her, not entirely from the numbing cold that was creeping up her arms and legs. No, not deaf, merely not worth their consideration. A nuisance of a female, to be tolerated and nothing more. The black depression which had been clawing at her threatened to overwhelm her completely. She was only to be tolerated because of her eighty thousand pounds, of course. Otherwise she'd still be floundering in the ditch!

Some more talking went on over her head, but Edith neither knew nor cared what was said. All she wanted was to be home, curled up in the study at the vicarage, watching her father write his sermon. They could have her eighty thousand pounds and be done, if only she could know those carefree days once more.

'Edith, you are not attending. I asked if you were comfortable.' Lord Whitley's voice broke into her thoughts and she shook her head to clear it.

She summoned up her manners. 'I am perfectly well, thank you. I am sorry to have caused you so much inconvenience.'

'Don't be missish, Edith. It doesn't become you. Hold tight.'

Stung by the reprimand, she did as she was bid. They progressed in silence for some time.

Still only mid morning, they were alone in the world as Satan walked home along a muddy farm track. The sun had finally warmed the air, but there was little power in it to dry the ground. Here and there they disturbed a blackbird or a thrush in the leafless hawthorn hedges, but the fields were bare of cattle or sheep or any trace of humanity. Those with no pressing obligations had followed the hunt, leaving none to watch their passing.

She might even have drowsed off, if she had not been so cold and so uncomfortable. His lordship's hunting saddle had little in the way of a pommel, but it was most definitely not designed to carry two persons. There was little she could do about it however, but walk, and she had not felt her feet for some time, so cold were they. She doubted she could manage a single step.

'Cold?' His voice broke the silence, echoing her thoughts. 'Here, see if this will help.'

He somehow managed to unbutton his coat as he spoke, drawing her closer to the heat of his body as he tucked her hand inside the coat and under his arm. She felt the smooth texture of his waistcoat against her cheek and smelled the scent of the starch his valet had used on his neckcloth. It was a curiously intimate thing to do and for a few moments Edith felt confused by his gesture.

Embarrassment warred with gratitude.

As he made no further movement she managed to relax. Gradually she became aware of a faint heartbeat and the rise and fall of his breathing. It was a soothing rhythm and she felt herself sinking towards him. His arm around her tightened.

'Don't go to sleep.'

By twisting her neck she could look up at his face, scant inches away. He glanced down and smiled, whimsically. 'I know what you are thinking. It is the height of impropriety for us to be riding along like this.'

Edith had been about to slide her hand along his jaw, oblivious to anything but the feel of him so close to her. She wanted to kiss him, to hold him closer still and never let him go.

I love him.

She had never known anything with such a certainty. She loved everything about him. The line of his jaw, so strong and uncompromising. His generous nature, so carefully guarded by the veneer of coldness that had fooled her for so long. Yes, even his bad temper, for she had provoked him severely. His unswerving loyalty to his friends. Warmth rose into her cheeks and ignited low in her loins as she considered his magnificent physique. Oh, yes, it was indeed the height of impropriety to be thinking such thoughts.

'I've embarrassed you. I beg your pardon. You are perfectly safe with me, Lady Edith. My friendship with your new mama must be your reassurance.'

He paused, but when she could think of nothing to reply he tried again.

'I assure you, you can with confidence regard me as nothing more than an older brother.'

She wanted to scream, or kick him, or both. The idiot! Couldn't he see that that was the last thing she wanted to do? But there was a shadow between them, an enemy she couldn't fight. Charles Ashington would never regard her as anything other than a younger sister when the ghost of Chloe lay between them.

9

Her first ball! Edith looked down at her elbow-length kidskin gloves and the rich ivory satin of her gown. Embroidered with gold *fleurs-de-lis* around the hem, the under-dress was covered by a three-quarter robe of lace, open down the front and fastened with pearl clasps. Short, puffed sleeves complemented the pin-tucked bodice. The low neckline was modest by some standards, but still felt alarmingly revealing to the demure daughter of a clergyman. Augusta had approved it however, and her taste was impeccable.

A row of pearls around her neck with matching drops in her ears was the only jewellery she wore. The most elaborate feature of the whole toilette was her hair, cunningly wrought by Lady Corbridge's dresser into a waterfall of curls descending from a wreath of silk lilies-of-the valley. Edith had never believed she could look so elegant.

Just then a knock sounded at the door and the dresser returned holding a bouquet in a gold filigree holder. Edith breathed in the scent of carnations, rosebuds and snowdrops. Who had managed to find flowers for her in

December? Her breath caught as she examined the handwriting. Could it be him?

She had seen very little of Charles since her return in ignominious fashion from the hunt. After a warm bath she had retired for the day, feeling as though someone had beaten her with a stick. Twice since then the gentlemen had ridden to hounds, including her father, but she had been too stiff and sore to want to make the effort. With her mare out of action, there really wasn't a suitable mount for her anyway.

Lord Whitley had taken her out in a phaeton on the second day to let her see for herself that Glory was progressing well, but it was impossible to have any sort of a conversation with a groom perched up behind. Edith felt very unsure of what to say, anyway. These feelings she had started to experience were too new, too overpowering for her to rush in as was her usual manner. She felt a reserve, a shyness, which was most unlike her normal self. For the first time, Edith didn't know what to do. Charles, after all, remained as stubbornly blind as he had ever been. Or was she mistaken? Had he, like herself, not known how to handle the situation? Her pulse beat faster at the thought.

There was a tremble in the fingers that

opened the card, as she hoped against hope that he had thought of her. 'Flowers for the rose within our midst', read the note. The signature was that of Giles Ashington.

'Oh.' How absurd to feel so let down! Of course, it was so much more in the dashing captain's style to have ransacked his aunt's hothouses. After all, one didn't send one's almost-sister flowers, did one? And when had Charles not been in charge of a situation? Fool even to think it! She had never seen him at a loss. He had probably dismissed her as a tongue-tied bore, and nothing more.

With a sigh of disappointment, she tucked the note away in her glove drawer and slipped the ribbon of a fine ivory fan over her wrist. The posy was, after all, the first she had ever received from an admirer! It wasn't Giles's fault that he wasn't the admirer she desired.

Pondering on her situation, she made her way down the sweeping staircase to join the others in the drawing-room. She felt vulnerable, almost as unsure of herself as she had been that first day in the inn-yard. There would be so many strangers at the ball tonight, so many young women who would know exactly how to act in genteel company. What if she embarrassed her father? Worse still, what if she gave Charles a disgust of her? He held a low enough opinion of her behaviour as it was.

Edith shook her head as the footman opened the door for her. She was being stupid. She'd had dancing lessons from the finest masters, a gown that would be the envy of all and the benefits of her father's title. She was equal to the best in the land, as Lord Whitley was very soon to find out, if he didn't realize the fact already. Just let him dare look down that aristocratic nose of his!

Ready for battle, a bright smile pinned to her features, Edith had the wind knocked out of her sails by the reaction of the gentlemen. Lord Whitley and Captain Ashington sprang to their feet as she entered, followed more slowly by the two earls, who nonetheless looked openly admiring. Her father turned away for a second or two, apparently to cough, but his eyes looked over-bright as he came forward to greet her.

'Edith, my dear! How wonderful you look! For a moment you reminded me . . . Your dear mama was just such a beauty. She would have been very proud of you tonight, as am I.'

She felt her own throat close over at the obvious emotion in her father's voice. She blinked rapidly, but was saved from having to make an immediate reply as Captain Ashington offered her his arm to escort her to a chair. His admiration was of a very different kind. There was a warmth in his expression that could not be disguised. She felt her cheeks grow hot under his intent scrutiny.

'You will be the belle of the ball, my lady,' he told her. 'I have no doubt about that whatsoever.'

She looked away in confusion, only to find Charles's gaze fixed upon her. To her surprise, he smiled. 'Giles is right, for once. May I compliment you, ma'am? You have turned out in very fine style indeed!'

★ ★ ★

There was a slight awkwardness about the travel arrangements, as seven was too many for one coach unless one of the gentlemen sat on the box and even then they would be crowded. With two, courtesy and precedence demanded that Augusta and Lord Cramlington travelled with their hosts, but unfortunately that left Edith on her own with the gentlemen.

In Edith's opinion, Augusta once again allowed her partiality to overcome her scruples.

'You will be more than safe with both Charles and Giles to accompany you, my dear, and it is not as if the two coaches will not be in close company all the way. I am sure the gentlemen will keep you well entertained.'

As they were to dine with Lord and Lady Aston before the ball began, the party set out early for the journey, which would take them the best part of an hour. Edith donned a dress mantle of heavy velvet edged with swansdown. The generous hood covered her coiffure without damage, as long as she refrained from twisting her head this way and that. With hot bricks under her feet and a carriage closed up against the chill she felt snug and warm, warmer still each time she thought about Charles beside her, devastatingly handsome in his immaculate evening dress. His stark black swallowtail coat contrasted vividly with the pristine white of his shirt and neckcloth. A tasteful waistcoat, satin knee-breeches and silk stockings completed the outfit, covered now as she was herself in a travelling cloak. Captain Ashington in his dazzling regimentals looked as showy as a peacock in her estimation, although he, too, must be admitted to be a strikingly handsome man.

The captain had lost no time in handing Edith up into the second carriage. He had clambered up to sit beside her, only to be ousted to the forward seat seconds later when Charles made shameless use of his rank.

'The son of an earl to sit in the maidservant's place, my dear Giles? I think not!'

The captain grumbled good-naturedly as the horses pulled away.

'May I remind you, my lord, that I am myself the grandson of an earl? And, what's more, only one life away from being in direct line?'

'I'm sorry that I am not prepared to die to further your ambitions, my dear cousin. Perhaps I should be employing a food taster from now on?'

'Oh, I think a simple duel would suffice, Charles, if I had any such ideas.'

'Ha ha! And what did you have in mind? Swords? The thought of you with a pistol in your hand fills me with abject terror!'

There was just enough light for Edith to make out Giles's rueful grin. 'And why do you suppose I have not attempted this stratagem earlier? Swords or pistols, it makes no difference, does it?'

He shifted his attention to Edith. 'You must forgive us, my lady. Perhaps you are not aware that my cousin is one of the finest shots in the whole of England. If that was not enough, his skill with a blade is, much as I am loath to admit it, so far above mine as to render any such engagement highly imprudent. I shall have to make do with my lowly station in life.'

Another rude sound from Charles forced Edith to hide a smile behind her fan as the banter went on.

'Lowly station? With a fortune greater than many a duke to come to you from your mama? My heart bleeds for you, Giles. It truly does.'

With conversation in a similar vein the journey passed in a flash. Before she knew it she was entering the drawing-room at Aston Hall to be greeted by her hosts for the evening. Just beyond them, a shock awaited her. Looking for all the world like a sullen schoolboy, she beheld the man who had so recklessly endangered her safety on the hunting field. Lady Aston made her intentions plain immediately.

'May I present my son Wilfred, my dearest Lady Edith? Naturally you will open the ball with him, as our guest of honour. I have placed you beside him at dinner, so that the two of you will become friends in no time!'

The party made its way into the dining-room, strictly according to rank, but once there the machinations of the hostess became obvious. Dinner became a purgatory to be endured, with Lord Whitley and Captain Ashington banished to the far end of the vast table, Augusta and Papa almost as distant and only Wilfred or a very deaf chaplain to talk to.

An enormous silver epergne, laden with fruit, successfully hid her view from anyone opposite, even if she had been tempted to talk across the table.

Liveried footmen served the meal in austere silence, zealously surveyed by the formidable butler. The room was lit by so many candles that the glassware and cutlery gleamed with a thousand reflections. So oppressed by the splendour that her appetite deserted her, Edith nibbled at a sliver of chicken.

The Honourable Wilfred looked about as pleased with the arrangements as she herself felt. When he had finally assuaged the worst of his hunger, he at last deigned to talk to her, instead of grunting at the two remarks she made before lapsing into despairing silence.

The incident between them in the field he dismissed with a casual, 'Demmed waste of a day, the brute breaking his leg like that. By the time that fool of a groom brought up a remount the hunt was miles away!'

No idea of a word of apology or enquiry as to her health or the welfare of her mount entered his mind for a single instant. Wilfred, it appeared, had no opinion of anyone other than himself. She listened to a monologue of his exploits on the hunting field, his prowess with a gun and the superior slashing ability of his best fighting cock without managing more than a 'yes' or a 'really?' in reply. His lack of sensitivity was so astounding she could not believe her ears.

She watched in amazed horror as he consumed a vast quantity of wine with his meal, which by itself would have sustained her for a week. By the time the ladies came to leave the table, his legs weren't quite steady under him as he rose. She had to open the ball with this lout? What an evening lay in store for her!

By the time those guests not privileged enough to be invited to dine arrived, Edith had recovered some of her equanimity. Giles Ashington rescued her from the worst of the Honourable Wilfred's excesses, turning a deaf ear to any attempts by Wilfred or his mother to get rid of him. As the ballroom filled and the musicians took their places there was little even he could do, however. Resigned to her fate, Edith accepted the proffered arm and allowed herself to be led on to the floor. Wilfred looked her over as he might have done one of his horses.

'Demmed flat, these country dances. Far too tame for my taste. Still, duty is duty. I'll show you a good time when the waltz comes round, though. I've given orders for lots of them tonight. You'll like that, eh?'

The leer he gave her, combined with the suggestive squeeze of her hand, sickened Edith. Saved from replying immediately by the movement of the dance she tried to collect her wits. At hands across she managed a response.

'I regret, sir, that I have promised several of the waltzes already. And also, as you have said, you have your duty. There are many ladies here tonight.'

'I don't give a fig for any of them. You're the sort of filly to suit my taste!'

She held her tongue, vowing not to let the creature near her for the rest of the evening. Luckily, Wilfred was not the only young man to admire her, or her fortune as the case may be, and she was soon besieged at every turn.

Not until the third pair of dances did she have the opportunity to look about her. There were about thirty couples presently on the floor, with as many more sitting round the room or lounging against the pillars which held the lofty roof. Captain Ashington had been correct. Although there were several pretty girls in the ballroom, none of them had as fine a gown as she wore. Like a flock of pastel butterflies they fluttered round in more or less graceful style, set off by the sombre coats of the gentlemen with here and there the scarlet of regimentals or the equally smart blue and white of the three naval officers present.

True to his word, Giles Ashington claimed her for the first waltz, frustrating the Honourable Wilfred once again. Edith let out an audible gasp of relief as he led her on to the floor.

Giles smiled down at her as he slid an experienced arm around her waist.

'Enjoying yourself?'

Too confused for the moment to answer, she tried to absorb the sensations of a man holding her so intimately. Nerves fluttered in her stomach as her mouth went suddenly dry. Dancing masters were one thing, Captain Ashington entirely something else! Truly, after Wilfred and the pimply youths she had endured, the captain appeared in an entirely different light. How handsome and strong he was, how broad in the shoulder and long in the leg. With his looks, his fortune and his magnificent record at Waterloo and in the Peninsula he was the epitome of her childhood dream.

Suddenly she smiled. 'I am now. You cannot believe the toadies and flatterers it has been my ill-luck to dance with! You are much more comfortable to be with, Captain.'

The amusement vanished from his eyes, to be replaced by the same intensity of regard that had caused her to blush earlier in the evening. The hand at her waist tightened for a few seconds before he recovered himself.

'Thank you, my lady. I regard that as a compliment of the highest order!' The sincerity in his voice quickened her heartbeat.

'Oh, now you are funning! I simply meant that I do not regard you in the light of the likes of the Honourable Wilfred, for instance.'

'If you mean that I am not a fortune hunter, you are quite right. I will say no more, but you must be aware that my feelings are anything but shallow, Edith.'

How could she not be aware of it? She trembled, almost missing a step as she struggled to find a reply.

'Oh, please, do not — '

'Hush. I apologize. Of course it is too soon. You regard me as a friend, and for that I am grateful. Much can be built on friendships, after all. What is your opinion of the purple volcano yonder?'

Edith glanced over to see a dowager in an astonishing turban of purple silk trimmed with yards of gold lace. The captain's apt description brought a smile to her face as she allowed the conversation to be steered on to much safer ground. His sentiments however remained very much on her mind. With only a few words of encouragement their friendship could well indeed develop into much more. Is that what she wanted?

Her eyes sought out Charles, lounging against a pillar in conversation with a stout gentleman a few years older than he. No! It was impossible. She had no finer feelings for Giles. Friendship was all she could offer. He was everything that was good, and gentlemanly, but he was not Lord Whitley.

Edith felt a little awkward and strove for another topic of coversation. The least she could do was match Giles's good manners. 'Did you meet often with Lord Wellington in Belgium? I think he must be such a wonderful man. I admire him tremendously.'

Captain Ashington smiled. 'Perhaps that is because you have never been on the wrong end of one of his *looks*. It is not pleasant, I assure you, but I do acknowledge him to be a very fine general.'

'Perhaps it is best not to meet one's heroes. That way there can be no disappointment.'

'Indeed. Perhaps you are right.'

She smiled up at him. 'And I am *convinced* it is best not to meet people like Wilfred.'

His eyes lit up with merriment. 'You'll get no argument from me on that score, Lady Edith.'

She managed to avoid Wilfred right up to

the supper dance, but by the look on his face when he claimed her arm almost roughly he would not be fobbed off this time. Rudely turning his back on her other suitors he pulled her on to the floor without as much as a by-your-leave. As his arm closed around her, she could see the dangerous glitter in his eyes. There was a pervading odour of sweat about his body vying with the taint of alcohol on his breath.

'I have you now, my pretty. Playing hard to get, eh? You must know my love of the chase.'

She attempted to ease herself away from him. 'I have no idea of your meaning, sir! Pray, do not hold me so close.'

'You women are all the same, leading a man on all night, then showing him a cold shoulder. Well, not with me.'

His breath seared her ear as he grew closer yet. The heat from his sweaty palm where it lay low on her back burned through his glove and the fabric of her gown. He pressed against her breasts, almost slavering as lust overcame him. He was going to kiss her, here, in public, on the dance floor. She felt a surge of revulsion and mortification. Wildly she looked around. The people nearby were all strangers. What could she do? Cause a scene? Faint? Allow him to kiss her and pretend nothing had happened?

One look at his face sent the disgust surging through her again. No! She would not!

Deliberately she missed her step, at the same time deftly grasping the fan hanging from her wrist. She trod as heavily as she could on his foot, swiftly bringing the fan round to dig into his stomach as he faltered. They cannoned into another couple, causing a flurry of confusion.

Offering profuse apologies to the other lady, Edith pulled away. Wilfred swore under his breath as the choler in his face mounted alarmingly.

'Bitch! You did that on purpose.'

Those within earshot froze, stunned expressions on their faces, both at the language and the unmistakable venom in his voice.

'You have said quite enough.'

Edith whipped around to see the imposing figure of Lord Whitley looming over her. Instinctively she reached out for his aid.

'I have been sent to find you by your mama, my lady.' His voice sounded quite matter of fact, but the tone hardened immediately as Wilfred moved to intervene. 'Take yourself off at once, sir! If this was not your own roof I would meet you for the insult I just heard you utter to the lady. Do try not to make a further exhibition of yourself!'

Wilfred spluttered with rage. Edith shrank back before the display of wrath, only to feel a calming hand slide over hers where it rested on his lordship's arm.

'No doubt you will accept the apology this cub is about to utter, Edith. *You* are not lacking in civility or good conduct. We are waiting, sir.'

'I'll be damned if I will!'

'You will most certainly be damned if you do not.' Lord Whitley's voice positively dripped menace. 'I will see to it personally. Unless I am much mistaken, I do believe there are several others of the same opinion, also.'

Wilfred glanced round, uncertain. The shocked faces of the ladies within earshot, and the grim, stony looks of the men convinced him. He muttered unwillingly, 'I beg your pardon, ma'am. I forgot myself for the moment.'

'As we shall forget you, on the instant.' Deliberately Lord Whitley turned his back and led Edith from the floor. With a smile here and a word there he guided her back to Augusta, smoothing out the awkwardness with practised charm.

A shudder ran along Edith's spine at the thought of the scene Wilfred had created. If it had not been for Lord Whitley . . .

'I thank you, sir, for your assistance.' Edith cringed as soon as the words left her mouth. The wooden tone in her voice sounded so ungrateful.

'Think nothing of it. You appeared to be managing fairly well on your own, but young Wilfred Aston is an ugly customer. I thought he would have had more respect for his father than to behave like that here, though.'

Lord Whitley's tones were stiff and clipped, but there had been genuine concern in his actions. Edith shook off the effects of the incident and smiled at him more sincerely.

'No, indeed, that sounded as if I did not care what you did, but I was so frightened. I am truly grateful.'

'In that case, we shall have to see to it that he does not disturb you any further. Giles has already danced with you more than he ought, so will you permit me the next two after supper?'

Waltz with Charles? Edith felt her heart pound. Captain Ashington had sent her pulses into a whirl, and she felt only friendship for him. Could she stand in Lord Whitley's embrace and not give her feelings away?

She had to breathe deeply before she could

find a reply. 'Is that wise, sir? Surely your wound . . . ?'

He shrugged off her concern. 'I've taken greater risks in my time, my lady. It is you who will be the one in danger.'

Quite out of character in his dealings with her, his gaze twinkled down, filled with amusement. 'I have not waltzed in some time. Your toes may be in mortal peril.'

She made a quick recovery. 'Never. I have nothing to fear at your hands, sir, or even your feet. You forget, there are no ditches here!' Although her words were funning, meant to provoke a reaction, she knew them for truth. She could trust Lord Whitley with her life.

The shaved ham and champagne at supper could have been bread and water. She tasted nothing. Midnight came and went. The old year ended and the new one started as she sat there and sipped her wine. So he went by a grand title and in the fullness of time would become an earl. What did that matter? It was not the trappings of wealth and privilege that attracted her. Indeed, had he but a few hundred a year she could have been happy with him. The question was, could he ever be happy with her?

Locked in a battle with her sensibilities, excitement warred with nerves, whilst common sense cautioned her all the time. It was only to be a dance, for heaven's sake! He was merely keeping an eye on her, out of a sense of duty.

All the same, she could hardly wait for the moment when he would take her into his arms.

As they made their way back out to the ballroom she could see her fingers tremble where they rested lightly on his arm. Her legs felt as if they would give way at any second and anticipation caused her breath to come in short, uneven gasps which almost robbed her of the power of speech. She'd read of romantical swooning females, but never had she thought that she might be one of them!

Good gracious, this would never do! She wasn't some bashful miss out of the schoolroom. Taking a deep, calming breath she looked around her, eagerly seeking a harmless topic of conversation. There, in front of her, a gentleman led a lady on to the dance floor. She stopped abruptly, clutching at Lord Whitley's sleeve in a manner which would have caused his tailor to wince. Only her rigorous training stopped her from pointing.

'Charles,' she hissed, 'Look! Over there. Can you believe what we are seeing?'

Startled by her actions he looked up. He

caught sight of the objects of Edith's attention but instead of sharing in her shock he smiled. A look of satisfaction crossed his features.

'I thought for a minute the Honourable Wilfred was bearing down on us with a horsewhip! What could be more normal than for a newly married couple to take to the floor? I'm surprised only that they waited until after supper.'

She shook her head, bemused. 'But . . . but you don't understand. That's my *papa*, and . . . and he's going to *waltz* with Augusta. He never dances. He doesn't know how!'

Charles laughed outright. 'If you could see your face, my lady! I'm sure Augusta will take care of him. I enjoyed many a dance with her in winter quarters in Spain. The waltz was still very much frowned upon then, but it didn't deter her. With so few ladies available she always made time for her husband's junior officers. Many's the occasion she never sat down all night. If anyone knows how to waltz, she does.'

By this time they too had moved on to the floor. Edith slipped into his arms, intent on her parent. Before she knew what was happening they had almost completed a full circuit as she stared and marvelled. Truly, Papa *could* waltz, and quite well, too!

'Ahem.'

Recalled to her partner, Edith felt a sudden bloom of heat in her cheeks.

'Oh, my goodness! I beg your pardon, my lord! You must think me abominably rude.'

Humour lurked in his expression as he gazed down at her. 'No, merely amusing. You truly never have seen your father as a person, have you? He finds himself very happily married to someone who can share all his deepest concerns. As a result, tonight he does not have a care in the world. I doubt that he remembers that you or I exist.'

Edith looked again, with new eyes. 'Augusta appears happy too, do you not think, Charles?'

'Oh, yes. She has told me as much. Her feelings for her first husband ran deep and she was with him for more than ten years, but I do believe that in a very short time she will love your father just as much.'

A small sigh escaped her. 'He is such a fine man. It would be hard to do anything else but love him, but then I have a marked partiality, myself.'

'Which is very natural in your position, but yes, I share your opinion. I see much to admire in Lord Cramlington. His is a difficult position but he has behaved admirably.'

She felt a glow of satisfaction at his praise

of her father. Indeed, she felt so favourably inclined towards his lordship that all of her previous awkwardness disappeared. She, too, no longer had a care in the world. Dancing in the arms of the man she loved, with a fine orchestra playing and a thousand candles glittering and gleaming all around her, what else could she ask for? Except . . . had she really called him Charles? It was the way she thought of him now, but only his mama or dearest friends had the right to address him as such. How forward of her! Had he noticed? Of course he would have noticed! Did he think her a bold piece, wanting in manners and decorum? Best not to let him dwell on it.

'You have deceived me, my lord.'

Those eyes twinkled again. 'Oh, and in what way is that, Edith?'

So he *had* noticed. She shuddered inwardly, wishing herself a thousand miles away. There was nothing to do but make the best of it.

'You led me to believe that you were not skilled in the waltz, yet here we are, perfectly in tune and not a bruised toe between us. You have just admitted to dancing with Augusta in Spain, also. You are a man of many talents, are you not?'

'I confess I surprise myself, but with such a fine partner what else could I do but excel?'

'Now you are teasing. I will change the subject. Do you plan to go to town soon?'

'Not for some time. I have affairs to see to in the country. No doubt you will be preparing for the Season, however.'

She nodded. 'Can you imagine it? Both Augusta and I will be presented at the first drawing-room. If the rumours are true, Princess Charlotte is to be married soon. It will all be very interesting.'

He gave her a cynical look. 'I'll believe the marriage when I see it. The last time it was tried nothing much came of it.'

'Prince Leopold is said to be enamoured of her.'

'Or her position.'

'You are too hard, but at least I shall be able to see them. Papa has already met the Regent. He says he is grossly fat.'

The hand round her waist tightened fractionally. 'I am sure he said nothing of the sort! Such an opinion must not be bandied about in public, Edith. Kindly restrain yourself.'

Aware of uttering an indiscretion Edith looked up at him, just as the music ended. Relief washed over her as she curtsied. He was smiling. He had been teasing her, again!

* * *

The velvet cushions in the carriage felt wonderfully soft as Edith sank down for the journey home. She'd experienced such varied emotions tonight that exhaustion claimed her almost immediately. It would be hard to keep her eyes open.

'Lie back. If you would care to rest your head against my shoulder you may be able to sleep.'

Any thought of rest fled immediately at Lord Whitley's suggestion. But he sounded so matter-of-fact, as if young ladies draped themselves over him every day of the week. If he saw nothing improper, why should she? Greatly daring she allowed her body to relax. The velvet of her mantle cushioned her cheek against his shoulder as she gave herself up to the wildest of imaginings. Nothing that had gone before could compare to this! How wonderful to have the right to do it every day. She felt rather than saw him adjust the folds of her cloak where it had fallen away from her lap. With a murmur of content she drifted off to sleep.

★ ★ ★

Silence pervaded the carriage for some time, until a tiny sound, almost a snore, penetrated the air.

'You're a lucky dog, Charles.' Captain Ashington spoke softly so as not to awaken the fair slumberer. Lord Whitley inclined his head.

'You have nothing to fret about with me, my dear cousin! I leave the field entirely open to you. Although I must think of marriage soon it will not be to one such as Edith. She deserves far more than I can offer her.'

The captain made an impatient noise. 'Don't sell yourself short, man. I have the distinct and unwelcome suspicion that she's taken a decided partiality to you. You're not exactly the worst catch on the market, are you?'

'Edith deserves someone who can love her, and beat the devil out of her when necessary. I believe you capable of both, Giles.'

'As to the love, yes, I am capable of that. It was not me her gaze followed round the room, though.'

'I must go away, then, and soon. Lady Edith should be happy in her marriage, and I would make her miserable.'

'So, I have your permission to seek the lady's good opinion?'

Lord Whitley laughed. 'Since when have you ever required my permission, Giles? I wish you luck in the chase. And if you catch her, you're going to need every bit of it!'

10

Agnes Fenwick, housekeeper's keys ajangle, bustled in to the breakfast-room with her face flushed and her lips compressed. Two weeks after their return from Bedebury, Augusta and Edith were lingering over their meal, perusing some of the correspondence newly arrived that morning. Agnes was not happy.

'I have had to send off the second housemaid, my lady,' she told Augusta. 'Wicked gossip she is spreading, and poking her nose where it don't belong. Spying, that's what she's been doing, and passing on secrets. She's been having dealings with that Mrs Anstey.'

Edith didn't need to be told what it was about. Just that very morning her maid had told her about the rumour currently spreading. There was betting in the clubs as to when Augusta would bear a child. Plenty of money had been laid on her producing a 'seven months' baby. That a baby existed was, apparently, not in doubt. What did these horrible people with nothing better to do believe? That her stepmama had had an improper relationship with her father? Or

209

even worse, that she was palming off some other man's by-blow on the unsuspecting earl? As the lady in question had not even so much as dropped a hint of being in an interesting condition, Edith could only swallow her wrath and turn her mind to other pursuits more fitting than common gossip.

Augusta looked troubled. 'I had thought our servants realized where their loyalty lies. I will not have Lord Cramlington disturbed by petty bickering or gossip, Mrs Fenwick. You did the right thing. Do you wish me to come down to the servants' hall?'

'No need for that, ma'am. I think they all know where they stand, now. Between Hartley and myself we've managed to convince them.'

'Good. I have every confidence in your management. Hopefully everything will be peaceful from now on. Lord Cramlington goes to Northumberland soon and I do not want him worrying about us in his absence.'

Edith waited until the housekeeper had left. 'I did not realize that Papa was planning a trip home. Is that wise, at this time of the year?'

She took a quick glance out of the window. Even at ten o'clock the sun was still struggling to make an impression on the chilly morning. Grey clouds threatened rain at the very least, if not stinging sleet or snow.

'Not wise, no, but I thought it best not to dissuade him. He wishes to visit your mother's grave.'

Edith felt a pang of sorrow. 'It is her birthday soon, in February.' Memory raced back over the years as she recalled other times. 'We . . . we used to put snowdrops on her grave. In the apple orchard there were always a few early blooms. I didn't know what would happen this year.'

'It will take him at least a week to travel, so now is the best time to set out. We shall miss him, shall we not?'

She gave a watery smile. 'You are very good, Augusta. Others would not be so understanding.'

'Others are not married to your father. He is the best of men. And now, before we fall quite into the dismals, shall we go to Hookham's?'

★　★　★

They were subjected once again to stares and conjecture as they entered the library. Lady Louisa had done her work well. Select little titbits, dropped by her loyal confidantes Miss Berwick and Mrs Anstey into the ears of companions, ladies' maids and valets alike, gave all the more credence to snippets passed on by the second housemaid. Only Lord Castlereagh's correspondence with the Prince of Coburg and the definite date for a royal marriage caused more comment in the drawing-rooms of the *ton*.

Even at this early date, before the start of the season, Edith's circle of acquaintance widened every day. She began to appreciate the true worth of Lord Whitley and his cousin Captain Ashington. Many of those she met made it their first business to ascertain her prospects to the last farthing. Penniless young men were thrust upon her by ruthless mamas at every opportunity, much as Lady Aston had done. Others were bolder, relying on their own resources to further their causes with her. When she received an offer of marriage from a gentleman she had not seen above three times in her life her sense of humour was the only thing that saved him from a box on the ear. As it was her laughter proved to be a much more stinging refusal.

Captain Ashington did not look on her suitors with favour. The captain, Edith realized to her dismay, had taken a proprietary attitude towards her. True, she had begun to rely on his company at social gatherings, but Edith knew in her heart that he could never be more than second best. If

Charles had been present, she would not have been so keen to talk to Giles. Indeed, if she were to be honest, she often sought him out in the hopes that he would have news of his cousin. It was not fair or honourable to build up his hopes of a more intimate relationship. Somehow, she would have to speak to him. How could she do such a thing, though? There was nothing in his speech, or his actions, that she could point to as being out of line. How could she accuse him of having nothing more than a certain look in his eye, and a way of — crowding — other gentlemen who wished to address her?

Augusta only smiled when asked for her advice. 'Until he declares himself, Edith, there is nothing you can do.'

She heaved a despairing sigh. 'Cannot you hint him away? I do not wish to lose his friendship, but friendship is all I feel for him.'

It was Augusta's turn to look troubled. 'Then I am sorry for him, my dear, because his feelings for you are writ large on his face whenever he catches sight of you.'

'I do not wish to give him pain, Augusta. I *must* speak to him.'

'No. I think, perhaps, it will be best coming from me. I shall endeavour to speak to him alone when next he calls.' She paused, considering. 'I doubt we will have long to wait.'

Whether Augusta managed to talk to the captain, Edith did not discover, as his regiment was posted to Norwich with what seemed to be indecent haste. When he came to make his farewell he appeared almost despondent.

'I have become too used to fighting the French. The idea of turning on my own countrymen fills me with repugnance, but I have my orders. Does not our Parliament realize the level of discontent at the Corn Laws? This civil unrest could well lead to revolution.'

Edith shared his concern. 'One reads of so much distress and suffering, but what can be done?'

'Nothing but our duty, ma'am. And pray that heads wiser than ours can find a solution.' He smiled, took her hand and kissed it. 'Think of me when I'm gone, Edith, as I shall be thinking of you.'

Shocked, she stared up at him. There could be no mistaking the note in his voice, or the unspoken sentiment so clearly displayed. There was silence in the room as she struggled to find the right words to say. The glow in his eyes faded as he observed her reaction.

'Do you send me away with no hope, then?'

Unhappiness replaced the shock. She would have to hurt him. There was no other way. 'I cannot return your regard, Giles. Believe me, I am honoured, for you are a very fine man. In other circumstances . . .'

He continued to gaze into her eyes for what seemed like an age.

'It is my cousin, is it not?'

She felt a flush creep into her face. 'Please, do not press me.'

He shook his head, as if trying to come to terms with her refusal. 'No, of course not. Forgive me.' He sighed. 'It is not my place to do so, is it? Believe me, ma'am, that you will always rank high in my affections and if there is ever a time that you need my services I beg you to call on me.'

Edith had to turn away. She crossed to stand in front of the fire. Plucking up her courage after a few moments to compose herself, she looked at him steadily. 'You are too kind, sir. I regret very much being the cause of your pain. I know . . . I know you will not thank me when I tell you that I very much regard you in the light of the brother I never had.' She paused to swallow hard. 'Thank you for not making this difficult.'

Giles tried to laugh, but there was little mirth in the sound. 'You didn't expect me to make an ass of myself, did you? No doubt I shall recover, in time.' His eyes looked bleak. 'I shall have plenty of that in Norwich.'

She tried to ease the tension, somehow, anyhow. 'You will be flirting at the assemblies within the month, I am sure.'

'Flirting is an entirely different matter, ma'am. It is an officer's duty to flirt, but my heart will not be in it. My heart will be here, in town.' He stared at her as if he was trying to memorize every detail. His hand reached out, and then dropped to his side in an attitude of defeat as he shook his head. 'Goodbye, I'll take myself off.'

He left abruptly before she could reply.

There was nothing to be done. She paced around, wondering what she could have said, how she could have acted, to have kept that look off his face. She honoured him for his courage. He had been deeply wounded, but he had not ranted or raved, or beseeched her in any way. Truly, he was a man worthy of her love.

By this time she had wandered into her father's study. The picture of Chloe caught her eye, bringing a renewed spurt of longing and frustration. Why did she have to love Charles Ashington? Life would be so much simpler if she did not. Why did Chloe have to die? The two of them would have been happily married, and she would never have formed this deep attachment for the sound of his voice, or be wrestling with the feeling of loss and incompleteness she felt whenever he was not near her. The liking she felt for Giles would have had a chance to blossom into something stronger.

She clenched her fists. 'I want to go home! I want to climb in the apple tree and take flowers to my mother's grave and worry only about finding a plump chicken for Papa's dinner!'

★ ★ ★

Augusta frowned over the note that had been delivered before breakfast. Edith waited as she read it twice, but it was set aside without comment. Her manner seemed strange, as if there was something to conceal.

'You look, concerned, ma'am. What's amiss?'

Augusta managed a weak smile. 'Oh, nothing, my dear. It is merely an old acquaintance from the Peninsula. She has fallen on hard times and seeks my help. I really should go and see her at once, so I fear we must put off our outing.'

'Oh, very well. I'll take Glory out instead. Now that she's back, I long for a ride in the park. I doubt if the fine weather will hold until tomorrow. The rain is enough to give one the dismals, is it not? If you will excuse me, I'll send a message to the stables and change into my habit.'

Edith left the room, mystified, her brain working fiercely. There had been a seal on that expensive, hot-pressed notepaper, not merely a common wafer. No lady in financial distress had written that missive! And, as sweet as she was, Augusta could not lie to save herself! Something was amiss. Edith tapped her fingers against her lips.

'I am determined to find out what it is.'

Rogers accompanied Augusta's barouche from the stables, leading the now-recovered mare. Edith made her farewells and waited until the carriage disappeared round the corner before hurrying to mount. Feeling like a spy and acutely conscious of the puzzled looks being cast her way by her groom, she set off in furtive pursuit. They had not travelled very far, only a few streets, when the barouche drew up outside an imposing house. Looking neither right nor left, Augusta alighted and hurried up the front steps to be admitted immediately. No penniless lady lived in that prosperous mansion!

'Rogers, do you know that house?'

The groom shook his head. 'No, my lady. It

won't take me long to find out, though.'

In a few moments he returned. 'The housemaid yonder says Lord and Lady Seaton live there.'

Lord and Lady Seaton! But that meant . . . Edith tried to hide her surprise and failed. 'Rogers, why in the world would the countess want to visit Lady Louisa?'

He forgot himself. 'To give her a piece of her mind, my lady! As I would like to do, an' that's no error!'

Edith gazed at him in astonishment. 'And why, pray tell, would you want to do such a thing?' The groom coloured to the roots of his hair. 'I . . . I beg pardon, my lady.'

He wasn't very forthcoming. Intrigued, Edith pressed further. 'Come, Rogers, you are not in any trouble. What is it that you know?'

He sighed. 'I got talking to Lord Whitley's groom in the 'Royal Oak' last night. There are things being said as shouldn't be said. If they should happen to be repeated in my hearing I shall know what to do! There's not a finer lady alive than her ladyship, and let anyone dare call me a liar, that's all I say!'

Edith sucked in a sharp breath. She'd known about the gossip concerning the baby of course, but this had to be worse for her groom to take offence. His anger indicated tongue-wagging of a scandalous sort. There had been gossip about Lord Whitley and Augusta before. Her mind raced through several lurid possibilities. Could it be that Lady Louisa was going to spread a worse lie? Perhaps she had made a threat? Or even, could it be she had stooped to blackmail and that was why Augusta had come here? She had to find out more.

'Rogers, you must tell me the rumours. Indeed, they must have been bad for you to be so fierce. What could — ' She broke off suddenly as the full import of his words registered. A flood of sensation in her stomach left her short of breath. 'Did you say you spoke to *Lord Whitley's* groom? Is his lordship back in town, then?'

'Yes, my lady, just arrived yesterday, at dusk, it was. Jack, the groom, was given the evening off as they'd come all the way from Peterborough that day.'

The excitement she felt drove worries about Augusta out of her head for a brief moment. Charles was back. Surely he would call on them soon? Perhaps that very day! She should hurry home to change. What about the blue merino gown? No, that had been spoilt when he dropped her in the ditch. Perhaps her red twilled silk, with the Prussian spencer, just delivered?

'Beg pardon, my lady.'

'What? Oh, Rogers, I am sorry.' Edith came back to reality. She flushed as she saw the amusement on her groom's face. Indeed, she had been wool-gathering, dreaming of meeting Charles again.

'I only wondered, ma'am, about that gentleman yonder. Do you know him?'

Luckily for Edith the hat she had chosen was equipped with a fairly heavy veil. She turned away just in time as her cousin Bertram paused at the top of the entrance stairs of Lord Seaton's town house. He looked carefully in all directions before pulling the bell. Something in his manner struck her as so secretive that she felt danger prickle at the base of her spine. What was Bertram doing here? Could it be a coincidence, or was something more sinister afoot?

Abruptly she made up her mind. There was nothing she could do here, but Augusta must be made to take her into her confidence as soon as she returned. Perhaps Lord Whitley would call. She could ask him for his advice. Anything that concerned Augusta's wellbeing would surely be a primary concern to him, too.

'Rogers, I am returning home. I want you to stay here and wait for the countess. Make sure she is safely upon her way home, then ride ahead and give the message to Hartley. I

221

can manage Glory well enough by myself. It's not far.'

He reached over to hold Glory's bridle as Edith made to turn away. He looked torn between his desire to help the countess and his duty to his mistress.

'My lady, wait! What is it you fear? If you think the countess is in danger I'll go in there right now and fetch her out. You know you can rely on me.'

She tried to smile. 'I don't know what I fear, Rogers. I just know that something is amiss. Cousin Bertram's intentions are not honourable, of that I am sure. There can be no danger to my stepmother in broad daylight and in the middle of London, but I still feel concerned. If you can but wait for her, that will be enough.' She paused to look at him. 'Thank you for your loyalty. I shall not forget it.'

His gaze lingered for a moment or two longer as he assessed her words, and then he released the bridle. 'Very well, my lady. Don't you ride round to the stables, though. Have one of those good-for-nothing footmen lead the mare.'

He sounded like Agnes! He couldn't have been more than five-and-twenty at the most, but his responsibilities obviously weighed heavily on his shoulders. Edith felt humble as she urged her horse away. Such loyalty and concern were heart-warming.

There were no notes or messages waiting for her on her return, and Hartley could not give her any reports of callers. Disappointment bit sharply as she realized she had been hoping for something more. Obviously Charles did not long for her company as much as she did for his, then. He had probably dismissed her from his mind.

Nearly an hour later Augusta still had not returned. Edith's concerns grew stronger by the moment. Her stomach churned with nervous apprehension as she watched the clock. She had just made up her mind to enter Augusta's room and search for the letter when there was a commotion in the hall. Hartley's voice rose in protest, but the voice that shouted a reply was familiar. An awful premonition of danger made her bolt out to the upstairs hall to find Rogers halfway up the first flight of stairs in search of her.

'Trouble, my lady!' he burst out. 'Lady Cramlington has been carried off by that villain! I saw her bundled into a postchaise, looking like she was nearly senseless. Drugged or something, I think. There were two men inside, and two post-boys, so I couldn't do anything to get her away from them. I followed the carriage to the Great

North Road then rode back to tell you as quick as I could.'

'Augusta!' Dread clutched at Edith like a living beast. Was Bertram so desperate for the succession that he would risk an abduction?

She pressed the heel of her hand to her forehead as she tried to think. She had to go after them. Augusta's life might depend upon it.

'There's not a moment to be lost! Rogers, Glory will not do for this. Fetch our two fastest hunters from the stables. Be quick! Hartley, I shall want someone ready to take a message to Lord Whitley, but we cannot wait for him. He may be away from home.'

Dashing into the book-room she scribbled an urgent note, calling for her travel cloak, gloves and crop at the same time. She tried to think, to plan. Money! She needed money. Who knew how far they might have to ride on their search? Papa's strongbox! It was locked, but she seized a poker from the fireplace and hammered at a paperknife until it broke the hasp. Panting a little from her exertions, she looked around the room. There! In the corner stood a glass-fronted cabinet containing some of her late cousin's personal possessions, including his sword. She dismissed that immediately as impractical, but on the shelf below lay a case containing a fine pair of duelling pistols. Seconds later they were safely in her possession. Very carefully and deliberately, only ever having seen it done before and never having attempted it herself, she loaded them. One fitted snugly in the inside pocket of her cloak, and the other she kept to give to Rogers.

Scarcely fifteen minutes had passed before the groom returned to the door leading a fresh horse. With a roll of banknotes in one pocket and the pistol in the other, Edith scrambled into the saddle, not waiting for help. She stared down at the perturbed Hartley.

'Tell Lord Whitley . . . ' She stumbled to a halt, not knowing what message to send. 'Tell him I depend on his aid. We will leave word as often as possible, but I have no notion where Lady Cramlington has been taken. A team of bay horses and a chaise with a tan body and wheels picked out in green is all the description we have. Beg him to hurry, Hartley.'

Hartley slipped a package into a saddle-bag. 'There's some food and drink. My lady, take care, I beg you. I will go myself to Lord Whitley. I wish I was young enough to come with you now.'

'I'll take care of Lady Edith,' Rogers interjected, as he checked the pistol she had given him. 'I'll take care of that villain, too, when I catch him!' He nodded to Edith, then urged his mount forward.

Speed was impossible in the crowded streets. The gelding Edith rode was quite unused to a female rider. His paces were definitely more suited to a male. She had to battle for control until the houses began to thin and they could ease from a most uncomfortable trot to a canter.

No word was forthcoming until they reached the first of the posting houses on the Great North Road. Bertram had not stopped, but the ostler remembered the carriage for that very reason. Rogers reported back to Edith, shouting the news as they cantered along.

'The offside leader was sweating up badly and looked blown, he reckons. Should have been changed, but they were in too much of a hurry, he told me. That were an hour or two back, so no doubt they've a fresh team by now. Have you any idea where they might be going?'

She shook her head, near to despair. 'None at all. We must press on. We have to find them, Rogers. We just have to!'

'Oh, we'll find them, my lady! Don't you fret about that, or my name ain't Jimmy Rogers. It's just *when* we'll find them that I'm worried about.'

She urged her mount forward once more. Poor Augusta. What had that maniac done to her?

Nearly three hours later, utterly weary and completely disheartened, Edith staggered as she climbed down to change her mount once again. They had ridden almost sixty miles in their search and had gained considerably on the carriage, always presuming they were following the right one. Feeling weak at the knees she collapsed on a bench in the inn yard as she waited for Rogers to deal with the ostler. The cold chill of the afternoon seeped into her weary bones as she sat there. It would soon be dark, the brief winter day drawing to a close, and she was far from home.

It took all her resolution to climb up into the saddle one more time. Rogers, too, looked weary; but no less determined.

'Since they're not here they must have pressed on to Baldock, or to Hitchin. We'll run them to earth yet.'

She dragged up a smile from somewhere. 'We must, Rogers, but if they're not at Hitchin or very close by I can go no further. We shall have to put up there for the night.'

Darkness had fallen by the time they reached the outskirts of Baldock. With the sky obscured by cloud and a light, freezing rain falling, it was impossible to go further. All Edith wanted was a hot drink and a bed. She had long since lost any feeling in her fingers and toes. She felt cold, and wet, and dirty.

There, in the yard of the White Horse Inn, they saw a post chaise, heavily stained with mud and dirt, drawn up in a corner. The light was uncertain, but it was definitely midbrown in colour. Rogers rubbed at one of the filthy wheels with his coat sleeve.

'Green, my lady! This has to be it.'

Strength arrived from somewhere as Edith slid to the ground. Ignoring the curious stares of the boys and the pain of returning circulation she straightened her clothing and her hair as best she could. Taking a firm grip on her crop, she marched up to the door and entered the inn with Rogers only a step behind her.

11

Assaulted by a hundred smells, Edith paused on the threshold. Stale beer, horse, smoke, wet clothing, wet feet and who knew what else, combined to render the warm air thick and redolent. She passed a weary hand across her eyes in an effort to accustom herself to the light of the oil lamps that burned here and there, doing little to brighten the sombre effect of the dark oak panelling, bare floorboards and smoke-stained ceiling.

Loud talk and a burst of laughter sounded from the taproom to her left as Rogers shouted for the landlord. A door opened and closed, wafting in the aroma of mutton being roasted. Edith's stomach growled in protest. They had not stopped for the food so carefully provided by Hartley and she had had nothing to eat since breakfast.

A balding man bustled up to them, halting in astonishment as he took in his new customer. His expression changed from jovial welcome to one of shock. He opened his mouth, but Edith forestalled him.

'I am Lady Edith Backworth, and I

demand to be taken to Lady Cramlington at once!'

Something in her manner, or perhaps it was the grim look on the face of her groom, made the landlord blink and hastily alter his opinion about the kind of female now confronting him. He made an attempt at a smile as he bowed. She might look like a wanton, but she was equally obviously a lady of quality.

'Indeed, your ladyship, we have no one here at the moment apart from a gentleman and his wife. Taken ill she is, and lying down in my best bedchamber.'

'Ill she may be, but his wife she is not! Fetch the magistrate at once. That lady is the Countess Cramlington and she has fallen into the clutches of a black-hearted villain.'

She pushed past him towards the stairs. 'Don't just stand there, man! Fetch help at once. Come, Rogers, we must find her.'

Just for a second as she pounded up the stairs Edith wondered what she could possibly say or do if the travellers did indeed turn out to be an innocent married couple. The embarrassment and scandal would be like nothing she had ever faced before. No, it could not be! Augusta had to be here. She had to be safe.

Thrusting open the first door she came to

she found nothing but a private parlour, shrouded and dark. The next was the same. As she slammed the door the landlord finally caught up with her.

'I tell you, my lady, we only have Mr Earsdon with us, in the best bedchamber. He didn't take a private parlour.'

Edith stamped her foot. 'Take me to him at once! Instantly, do you understand?'

The landlord must have thought she had run mad. He threw up his hands and led the way up another flight of stairs. When he stopped and made to knock it was Rogers who shoved him out of the way and burst through the door.

A meagre fire burned in the grate whilst a solitary candle cast a faint glow over the figure slumped in the chair drawn up to the heat. A bottle of brandy stood open and half-consumed on the small side table at his elbow. On the bed, face down and with one arm limply dangling over the side, lay Augusta.

'You monster! You scoundrel! You wicked, evil villain! She lashed out with her crop, taking the startled Bertram by surprise as he tried to struggle up out of his chair. His expression of dismay turned to one of blazing anger as the crop caught him full across the face. He leapt up, overturning the chair and

231

table both. The bottle and the candle crashed to the floor. Like magic a double-barrelled pistol appeared in his hand. Edith saw her death in his mad eyes and knew a moment of paralysing fear.

Before she could move, Bertram was sent sprawling sideways as Rogers launched himself forwards, grappling for the weapon.

Chaos reigned in the room. Broken furniture slammed about as the two bodies heaved and rolled amidst shattered glass. With the candle out, only the flickering flames of the fire lit the chamber. Fumes from the spilled brandy filled the air as Edith desperately tried to distinguish between Rogers and Bertram. How could she help if she could not identify which was her groom and which her villainous cousin?

Another man entered, pushing the hapless landlord aside just as a deafening retort rent the air. One of the combatants sprang to his feet whilst the other remained ominously motionless. Smoking pistol still in his hand, his finger on the other trigger, Bertram kicked at the inert body of Rogers. His breath heaved in and out of his chest.

'Don't just stand there, Moyle. My cousin and I are leaving.'

Too horrified to even think, Edith found herself seized by a pair of strong arms.

Bertram pointed the menacing pistol at the landlord.

'Have a fresh team of horses put to the carriage. Now!'

When the landlord failed to move, he deliberately pulled the hammer on the pistol back to full-cock. 'If you value your miserable, snivelling life, you'll do as I say! Call for the ostler.'

'Rogers! Oh, God! Let me go! I must help him, I must!'

Edith strained towards the inert figure. A dark stain began to spread on the floor as she tried to reach him, only to be dragged away by Bertram's accomplice.

'He doesn't need any help.' Bertram seized her straggling hair and pulled her cruelly towards him. Her hat tumbled to the ground to be kicked to one side. 'You've interfered once too often, my lady. And now you're going to be my safeguard out of this little imbroglio.'

'What about the countess?' Moyle interrupted, jerking his head towards Augusta, still lying motionless and uncaring.

'Leave her! She'll sleep for hours, yet. Or can you think of a way to carry her down the stairs and still keep a hold on this one?'

Helpless, Moyle still holding her arms and Bertram with a pistol to her head, Edith was

233

forced down the stairs and out into the yard. Two of the stable-lads rushed up at the commotion but stopped in a hurry at the sight of the weapon.

Bertram snarled at them, 'A team, if you don't want to end up like the one upstairs.'

His chest heaved in and out from his exertions, but the sound now in his voice was one of elation and excitement. He truly was mad. Edith felt bile rise in her throat. He'd enjoyed shooting Rogers. He would shoot either of these two, or herself, and never turn a hair. In fact, he would gain tremendous satisfaction from it. The lust for blood-letting held him tightly in its grasp.

He handed his pistol to Moyle. From out of his coat pocket he produced a second weapon and waved it under Edith's nose. His grasp on her hair tightened as he motioned the valet away.

'I'll take care of this one. You go to the stables and make sure the team is all we require.'

In quite a conversational tone he addressed Edith as he jammed the new pistol against her temple. 'We don't want tired horses, do we, my dear?'

Watching the three of them head off to the stables, he called out after them. 'Have them fit reins, Moyle. You'll have to drive, and don't tell me you can't do it. We shall not require any witnesses where we're going.'

He wrenched Edith's hair back further towards him as he spoke. She could smell foul brandy on his breath as his lips moved close to her ear. Sickened, she summoned up her fortitude to withstand the pain. She'd never cry out in front of this monster, never!

The landlord stood at the top of the front steps, wringing his hands, obviously half-paralysed with shock.

She called out to him, desperate for assistance. 'Help my groom! He may not be dead! Go to his aid, man. There is nothing you can do here.'

More than willing to distance himself from the pistol the landlord disappeared, to find refuge or to aid Rogers she had no idea. In the suddenly silent yard she waited, trembling with fear, helpless in Bertram's hands, eyes filled with tears at the pain in her scalp.

She felt cold, colder than the dank weather warranted, as she fought for control. She had to think. What could she do to prevent herself being dragged into that carriage? If Bertram succeeded in making off with her, all would be lost. Edith harboured no illusions that he would let her go.

As the team was brought out and manoeuvred into the shafts, a little whimper escaped her throat.

'Charles, where are you?'

Bertram thrust her up the step and in to the musty vehicle. Thrown roughly to the floor, a sharp pain in her hip screamed a message to her brain. Of course! The pistol! What a flea-brain not to have thought of it before.

Edith scrambled into the corner, making herself as small as possible. Hopefully Bertram would be too preoccupied with his escape to worry about her for the time being.

The chaise lurched and swayed out of the inn-yard. Bertram let down the window and leaned out. His pistol cracked in the night air, dissuading any would-be pursuit and at the same time startling the team into an uncontrolled gallop down the High Street.

St Mary's church flashed past, a dim, looming shadow as the chaise thundered along. The violent swaying and jolting soon had her clinging on for dear life. Bertram laughed aloud in triumph.

She stared at him. Hatred welled up. 'Yes, laugh, Bertram,' she muttered. 'We shall see who laughs the last!'

The tears came unbidden. Poor Rogers, lying on that chamber floor with none save ignorant fools to aid him. Please God, let him not be dead. Please God, let her avenge his fate!

Under the cover of the darkness her hand found and caressed the butt of the pistol in her pocket. Even a faint chance of escape sent her spirits soaring. If she could not outwit this lunatic then she deserved the doom he had planned for her. She smiled, just a little. Bertram had failed. Whatever happened now, Augusta was saved.

Moyle finally managed to bring the team under control, but not until they were blown and content to trot. In a very short while they would be too tired to do even that. How they had managed to escape an accident Edith had no idea. What with the moonless night and only a feeble glow from the carriage lamps they must have been plunging headlong to disaster. Perhaps the leaders knew the road well. It certainly hadn't been Moyle's skill that had saved them.

Where were they going? Hitchin? Surely not. Even Bertram must realize that he would be pursued. A side road, then. Some village with an inn, but not a posting house. Perhaps he was foolish enough to think he could return to his own home in Norfolk. No! Not even Bertram could be that stupid. Somewhere quiet, that was it. Her thoughts raced.

He wouldn't be able to obtain a fresh team

if he left the Great North Road, but they could transfer to a smaller vehicle such as a gig and slip quietly along the back roads to King's Lynn. Ships left from there bound for the colonies. Bertram could evade capture in Canada, or even slip over the border and reach America. He would never be brought to book there.

Her resolve hardened. Her cousin would not escape if she could help it! Quite calmly Edith extracted the pistol from her pocket, pulled back the hammer and squeezed the trigger.

Nothing happened.

Shocked, she tried once more as Bertram threw himself towards her. Again, only a loud click sounded inside the chaise. What had she done wrong?

He wrenched the pistol from her grasp and threw it from the window.

'Bitch! You'll pay for that!'

With as much force as he could muster, he drew back his arm and slapped her hard across the mouth. Pain exploded like fire. Edith felt the taste of blood as she was knocked to the floor. Dismay and shock left her witless as the torment overwhelmed her. She had failed! The thought screamed loud inside her head. Failed, and now she would die. She would never see Charles again. She would never talk to her father, or lay those snowdrops on her mother's grave. All was lost.

Despair blotted out any other feeling. Bertram's mood changed once more as apparently the clouds of madness slowly retreated from his mind. His hand stroked over her hair as he addressed her.

'There now, my dear, I'm certain you would never have meant to hurt me. We are cousins after all, are we not?'

She gritted her teeth as her flesh recoiled from his touch. 'Give me your pistol, then, and we shall soon see whether I would hurt you or not!'

He laughed again. 'The she-cat has claws! Never fear, I shall tame you. It is late, and we must find lodging for the night. Moyle will guide us to an inn, although I fear it may not meet her ladyship's exacting standards. What a pity if you should take a chill from damp sheets.'

Was that not the least of her worries? Edith thrust the self-pity aside as she cast around for a plan of action. She'd made a pretty botch of the job up to now. Her hero, the Iron Duke, had had his reverses, but triumphed in the end. She could do no less than emulate him. What would Wellington do in such a situation? Her strategy had to be faultless this time. She recalled reading his dispatch to Lord Bathurst from the field at Waterloo. Indeed, like his troops after the battle, she was overcome with exhaustion. It became harder and harder to think as her brain filled with cotton and her headache threatened to overcome her entirely. Under her breath, she whispered to herself.

'Yes, that is it. I shall rely on reinforcements to press the action. I am sure they will come. I must . . . I must delay until then.'

The cracked leather of the seat was under her cheek somehow. There was nothing to be done. Sleep. That was it. Sleep.

★   ★   ★

Lord Whitley could not remember ever being in so foul a temper. His wrath was boundless, fuelled every passing mile by the rash imprudence of the chit who had been sent to plague his every waking hour. To think that he had actually contemplated their next meeting with anticipation. Indeed, the visit he had made to his estates had been damnably flat. He muttered an oath under his breath. Look at how he had pressed his horses so hard from Peterborough. Fool!

Instead of sitting quietly in her mama's drawing-room to receive morning callers she was dashing all over the countryside with nothing but a groom to lend her any consequence. And who would have to sort out the repercussions? He would, of course. How many times had he come to her aid already? Would she never learn?

As the day drew to a close and a light rain began to fall his anger was further compounded with anxiety. What if he did not come up to them before nightfall? No doubt Augusta was by now safe at home and worrying herself sick over Edith's safety. What a wild goose chase! That fool of a butler with his ludicrous tales of kidnapping. If he was not dicked in the nob he was undoubtedly senile and should be put out to pasture. Did no one possess any common sense at all?

An extra-sharp twinge from his maltreated leg sealed his ire. If he did not find them before Baldock he would dine there and be damned. She didn't deserve his concern!

The scene at the White Horse on his arrival soon changed his mind.

Lit by a dozen torches, there was hustle and bustle as a burly man, obviously some official, stood shouting orders as a carriage was prepared for him. Half-a-dozen militiamen milled about in aimless fashion, succeeding only in adding to the confusion, whilst a soberly dressed individual carrying an apothecary's case was on the point of descending from his own smart little gig.

Lord Whitley found himself ignored until he summoned up his parade voice.

'Landlord! Landlord! Is Lady Edith here?'

His demand had every eye turned towards him. There was silence for a few seconds, then a veritable torrent of explanations and excited exclamations. He could make nothing of it, until a sentence reached his ears.

'Shot? Shot did you say? Who?' He roared for silence, and then addressed the man who had caught his attention.

'Is Lady Edith hurt?'

The landlord, for it was he, almost sobbed at the thought of the ruin to his reputation. 'Not her, sir, but the groom. She has been carried off by Mr Earsdon. And the other lady, the one she called the countess, is still insensible from the laudanum.'

God, it was all true! His world lurched about him as he digested the information. These gapeseeds were standing about here, whilst Edith was in danger.

'Get me a horse, and someone who knows which direction they took. There's no time to be lost!'

Never a quick-witted man, the landlord's reactions were too slow. Charles slid down from his mount and stared coldly at the hapless man. 'I am Viscount Whitley. If any harm comes to her ladyship I shall hold you directly responsible! I said, get me a horse, or are you deaf as well as an addle-pated blubberhead?'

The landlord gaped. 'At once, your lordship. The magistrate will accompany you.'

Lord Whitley spied the mount belonging to the officer of the militia.

'Only if he can catch me,' he threw back over his shoulder, as he vaulted into the saddle, deaf to protests. 'Where away?'

The ostler shouted out directions as the horse danced around for a few seconds until he brought it under control. A savage jab with his heels shot the animal forward into the night.

12

Pain. Edith became aware of pain. Her head ached, her lips felt swollen and bruised and her muscles cried out in torment. Dragging her unwilling eyes open had never been such a task and she had to try more than once before she at last discerned her surroundings. A chaise! She was in a chaise. But what was she doing here?

Memory returned with a rush. She jerked upright on the seat, only to almost sink again as the pain blossomed into an agony that flooded through her. She fought to overcome her confusion. Memory returned at last. What was the excitement now?

Bertram had thrust his upper body through the window to yell fiendishly at Moyle. Something was happening, but what?

He pulled himself into the chaise again as it picked up speed, but only to extricate his pistol. Was someone in pursuit? She felt a surge of excitement. Surely that was a horse galloping along the road behind them? The creaking of the coach made it hard to be certain.

Her cousin knew someone was chasing

them. He took careful aim out of the window. Was he to kill another man? Not if she could help it! Edith lunged forwards just as he pulled the trigger, sending the shot harmlessly into the night.

With a snarl of fury he turned on her, his hands encircling her throat to shake her like a terrier with a rat. Through a haze of red, Edith heard vague sounds, horses protesting and loud voices, as the chaise was forced to a stop. Bertram flung her to the floor once more as he leapt from the vehicle. Gasping and choking, Edith could only lie there, desperate to draw air into her burning lungs.

Even that respite was not granted to her as she was suddenly seized and hauled out into the night air. Bertram held her before him like a shield, the pistol once more to her head. Locked in combat, Moyle and another figure grappled in the roadway, rolling over and over amidst the trampling feet of the sweating team.

Edith stared. Hope sprang to life once more as she watched the fight. Surely . . . oh, yes, it was him!

'Charles! Oh, Charles, please help me!'

Her voice issued forth as little more than a croak. He could not possibly have heard. She could only watch, and pray.

The valet was no match for Lord Whitley. A

mighty blow to the jaw rendered him senseless, then his lordship scrambled to his feet and stood over him, panting, fists clenched and an expression of utter fury on his face. Edith opened her mouth to call again, but her throat was so dry and bruised that she could make no sound.

'A veritable Corinthian!' Bertram sneered.

Lord Whitley whirled around. He froze at the sight that met his gaze. He examined Edith in detail, his mouth grim and his fists clenching and unclenching as testament to his impotent fury.

'Considering your options, my lord?' Bertram tugged on Edith's hair. 'I fear you have very few. *I* hold all the aces in this round, I do believe. Unless you are desirous of seeing my cousin's brains splattered in a most unbecoming manner.'

'Let her go!'

The command issued forth as a low-pitched growl that would have had any sane man quivering in his boots. Bertram only snickered.

'I think not, and it ill behoves you to be making demands of me in this predicament.'

A groan sounded from the huddled form on the ground as Moyle began to stir. Bertram immediately switched his attention.

'Moyle! Moyle, get up, you useless cretin!

Get up this instant!' He sighed. 'It is near impossible to find reliable servants, is it not?'

Moyle scrambled to his feet, feeling his jaw and weaving unsteadily around, still not in full possession of his wits. Bertram stamped his foot.

'Where is your pistol, idiot?'

Moyle fumbled in his pocket and produced the weapon, although its muzzle wavered around in a most distressing manner.

Only then did Bertram relax.

Edith gasped. At last her voice returned. 'His pistol! He has already fired two shots! Oh, Charles, it was not loaded!'

Lord Whitley ground his teeth in despair. 'God, woman, could you not have told me that before now?'

Bertram threw down the useless weapon, laughing wildly. 'Fools, the pair of you! Shoot him, Moyle, and we shall be on our way.'

'Shoot his lordship?' The order sobered Moyle on the instant. 'Sir, I could not possibly.' He gulped. 'Not in cold blood. In the inn, that was an accident, but this . . . this would be murder!'

'Since when does that make a difference? Stop dithering, you oaf! I want him out of the way, and I want it done now!'

Edith intervened, desperate to give Charles a chance.

'Like you wanted your father out of the way, Bertram? Like Catherine?' It was a wild guess, as she had no real knowledge of the circumstances surrounding either his father's or his wife's death. It struck the mark, however. Bertram made an exclamation of contempt.

'What use was Catherine to me, when I was to inherit the earldom? Of course she had to be put out of the way. A pretty countess she would have made. An ironmaster's daughter, indeed! I would have been a laughing stock.'

Edith noticed the effect on Moyle, who looked blank with shock. She pressed on.

'And so you killed her. Tell me, did you break her neck before or after you pushed her down the stairs?'

'Before, of course. The noise might have brought the servants running before I could finish it. It certainly brought Moyle running, didn't it, man? Very touching, I thought it, the way you gathered her up into your arms.'

Moyle gulped in a mouthful of air, and then another. His face looked ghastly in the dim light.

'You killed her? You *killed* her? No!' He let forth an agonized cry. 'No more! I will not permit you to mock her memory.'

'You will not permit? How dare you! Do as

you are told at once, or it will be the worse for you.'

All the while, Lord Whitley had been sidling closer and closer to Edith. Seizing his chance, he leapt forward and pulled her from Bertram's slackened grasp.

'Shoot! Shoot, you fool!'

Bertram backed up hurriedly as his command was ignored and Charles thrust Edith away. Like two wild animals the men stared at each other, assessing, calculating. Moyle watched from the sidelines, saying nothing, as Charles advanced on Bertram. Evading a blow, Edith's cousin made a dash for the riding horse, which was contentedly cropping the turf a few yards away. Just as his hand reached out to seize the dangling rein, the quiet of the night was shattered by Moyle's pistol. A flock of birds erupted from a nearby elm, screeching into the night in panicked confusion, whilst the horse let out a neigh of terror and bolted. The carriage team, close to exhaustion, tossed their heads and stamped wildly, but stood their ground.

Bertram pulled up short, a look of pure astonishment on his face as a stain blossomed across his ribs. Slowly, slowly he crumpled to the earth.

Moyle dropped the pistol. Trembling violently, he sank to his knees. Quietly, he spoke to his master.

'Too long have you lived on this earth, Mr Backworth.'

Charles hauled Edith into his arms to hide the sight from her eyes. Fervently, she clutched at him, glad to be alive, brimming with joy that he too was safe. The feelings of relief and content that swept over her were short-lived as he proceeded to hustle her into the chaise and drag down the window shade to hide the view.

'Stay here, and for once do what you are bid!' he snapped in his most ferocious voice, slamming the door with almost enough violence to wrench it from its hinges.

Shuddering, gasping with shock, Edith huddled into a corner. She had no desire to approach her cousin! Oh God, how awful! Let him be dead! Let the monster rot in hell!

The realization of just how close her own death had been seized her with powerful force. She closed her eyes and gave way to a flood of scalding tears.

Charles appeared at the door again a short time later. His manner was brisk to the point of rudeness.

'What money do you have?'

Edith tried to gather her composure. She sniffed once or twice and swallowed the lump that had lodged in her mangled throat.

'Money? Why, I don't know — '

'For goodness sake, woman, we must get this valet away before the pursuit catches up with us, and unless I very much mistake I can hear them even now. Or do you want him to stand trial? What a fine time you would have in the witness box, not to mention Augusta! Who do you think will suffer most when your dirty linen is hung out for all the world to see?'

Oh, goodness! Moyle! Of course he must be got away, and at once. He deserved no punishment for his actions. He had done them all a favour. Edith fumbled in her pocket and found the remains of the roll of bills she had stolen from her father's strongbox. Blindly, she thrust them at Lord Whitley.

'Here, send him away, and quickly. He saved our lives.'

'Mine, perhaps. Yours only until I wring your neck. Wait here!' He stamped off.

Edith gazed after him in utter astonishment.

Soon all was confusion. The magistrate arrived, together with the militiamen and two of the stable boys from the White Horse. She vaguely remembered assuring people that she was unharmed, and more clearly registered the disbelief that showed in their faces. There was noise, and shouted instructions, then the sound of horses riding away. The chaise swayed as someone mounted to the box, then swayed again as Lord Whitley took his place beside her.

Scarcely managing a trot, the team made its way home. In ominous silence, Charles stared out of the window. There was no discerning his expression in the dimness, but his body was straight and stiff in the seat, his fists clenched tightly where they rested on his knees. Just as they turned into the yard she plucked up her courage.

'Do you think they will catch him, my lord?'

He almost spat out his reply in a terse voice that boded ill for the future.

'As I sent them in completely the wrong direction I very much doubt it. I hope, for my sake, that they do not apprehend him before he takes ship for Canada. I have now compounded my sins of omission by lying to the authorities. Fortunately the magistrate is an acquaintance of my father and is much shocked by this business. He will do everything he can to hush it up. Now that you are back safely perhaps nothing will come of it all.'

There was little conviction in his voice, but Edith scarcely noticed. What about Augusta?

And Rogers, too! Oh, God! Poor Rogers! Edith leapt from the chaise before it came to a halt, frantic to discover his fate. She pushed her way through a gaggle of gaping bystanders and ran up the stairs to the scene of the confrontation.

Augusta lay quiet. Tucked under the sheets, dressed in a nightgown and with her hair brushed down and fashioned into a long plait, she looked liked a young girl. A redoubtable female sat by the head of the bed. Edith was subjected to an intense scrutiny before the woman nodded. She rose to her feet and sketched a curtsy.

'Lady Edith? My name is Mrs Barnstaple. I am the landlady here. Such goings on I would never believe. We are respectable folks here, and none may stay under my roof who cannot say the same.'

'And you have my gratitude, indeed, my undying thanks! You shall be well rewarded for your care of Lady Cramlington. Tell me about my groom. Is he . . . ?' Her anxiety was so great she could not voice the words.

'In the next bedchamber, and the surgeon with him. They have hopes that he will live.'

For some strange reason, Edith found herself on the floor. She blinked, trying to make sense of it, but it was so much easier not to think at all.

A voice sounded far off. 'For goodness sake, the poor lamb!'

Someone plucked her from the floor. There was the enfolding luxury of a feather bed, and then she knew no more.

The shrill protest of a recalcitrant horse awoke Edith the next day. Immediately she regretted her first instinct to sit up and open her eyes, as it caused a devil to commence work with pincers and a hammer in her head. She lay back in the bed and pressed her hands to her aching forehead. A second, more cautious attempt allowed her to take in her surroundings.

Solid, country-made oak furniture met her gaze, while a small fire burned in the open grate. Her habit, sponged and pressed, hung to one side of the bed.

How . . . ?

Edith gasped, thrusting back the covers to discover what she wore. Someone had undressed her and she was now covered from head to foot in a respectable flannel nightdress made for a much larger person. Thank goodness! It must have been the woman she vaguely remembered from the night before. The landlady, wasn't it?

Thoughts of the landlady brought other memories to mind. 'Oh, Augusta! Rogers! How could I have forgotten?'

Scrambling out of bed, determinedly ignoring her throbbing head, Edith searched for something to wear. Her mouth hurt where Bertram had struck her and her neck hurt too from lying crammed up in the chaise. She could still feel his hands about her throat. There must be bruises. But what were these trifling complaints compared to Augusta's ordeal? What about Rogers, lying somewhere with a bullet in his body? That bullet had been meant for her. Where was a wrap? Her underclothes? Her shoes? Nothing could be found!

She could wait no longer. Edith poked her head out of the bedchamber door, trying to remember the room where Augusta lay. The upper floor of the inn was quiet, the only sounds issuing from an arrival in the yard and what must be the kitchens below, judging from the smell of baking bread, which filled the air. Edith sniffed appreciatively before daring to venture forth.

The gown threatened to trip her, being several inches too long. Holding it clear of the floor with one hand she tiptoed to the chamber near the head of the stairs. Cold from the boards struck into her bare feet as she shivered in the chilly air. What if Augusta was still sleeping?

Without bothering to tap she slipped

quietly inside the door. Augusta sat to one side of the fire, pale but composed. On the other side of the fire she beheld a gentleman she knew well. Deep in earnest conversation, it was a moment or two before he looked up to see who had disturbed him. He did not succeed in hiding his shock. Lord Whitley regarded her appearance with utter disapprobation, if not abject horror. His gaze shifted from her face to her feet and then back again.

'Oh, my lord! I did not know . . . didn't realize . . . ' Edith's voice positively squeaked. Embarrassment deluged through her as she tried to stammer an apology. Augusta leapt from her chair to enfold her in a warm embrace, and lead her to the fire, completely thwarting her intentions of either sinking through the floor or turning tail to flee.

'My dear! My poor, poor Edith! Look what that monster has done to your face! You should not be out of your bed! We did not expect to see you so soon. Indeed, I have not long since breakfasted myself, and Charles has been so kind as to keep me company and inform me of last night's events. I am so greatly in his debt, and in yours, my dear, for I know now that it was you who saved me.'

'Permit me,' his lordship interrupted. 'I shall withdraw at once and inform the landlady that you are awake.' He almost scrambled for the door in his haste to depart, stumbling slightly on his poor, maltreated leg. 'I will see you in the private parlour I have engaged for your use on the floor below.'

Without once meeting Edith's gaze, he bolted from the room.

Edith hid her face. 'I shall die, I know I shall. What must he think of me?'

Augusta laughed. 'Why, nothing, of course. This situation is so bizarre why should you not appear looking like a . . . well, like a — '

'Positive fright! I must get dressed, at once.'

'Are you sure you do not wish to return to bed? You have been through a terrifying ordeal.'

'No more than you, and I must see for myself how Rogers does.' Her voice cracked and she determinedly fought back sudden tears. 'Look at me! I am a watering pot, am I not? I am so anxious for his safety.'

Augusta laid a comforting hand on her arm. 'All is well! The surgeon has seen him this morning and is pleased with his condition. Of course he is very ill indeed, but he is a strong man and we have every hope that he will recover.'

Edith sighed. Some of the tension left her. 'Thank God! Still, I must see for myself. Will you wait for me in the private parlour, ma'am?'

'Of course, and I will send the chamber-maid with your clothing and some hot water, if it is not already in your room. The landlady has been most obliging.'

Some half-hour later, Edith descended to the private parlour. Rogers had not managed to speak in his laudanum-induced state, but she had seen recognition in his eyes as he squeezed her hand. The ball had passed completely through his arm, causing a great deal of bleeding and shock. The bone was broken but not badly shattered, and should mend provided infection did not set in. She had been pleasantly surprised at the surgeon, a quiet, competent man whom she trusted almost immediately. In his spotless bed, with a chambermaid provided for his sole use, Rogers stood the best of chances. Let him only live and she would reward him handsomely. His own farm, perhaps, or a livery stable. Papa would know what was best.

Rogers was safe, but what of her own situation? With her hand upon the doorknob she paused. Every instinct bade her turn tail and flee, but it was no good. She would have to face his lordship some time, although she would by far prefer to have a tooth drawn. Better get it over with.

All unprepared, she came upon a scene that quite astonished her. Marching up and down, waving her hands around and declaiming loudly, Lady Louisa held the floor. Lord Whitley stood to one side of the fire, a look of utter fury on his features. Augusta appeared completely shattered, whilst a lady Edith had never seen in her life shook her head and tut-tutted every other second.

'You will never succeed in convincing me of your innocence! I have long suspected this, my lord! You waited only until my uncle, Lord Cramlington, left for the North and then you planned this assignation! I was never so deeply shocked in my life.'

The scales fell from Edith's eyes as she stood there, taking in Louisa's display. This had been arranged! Of course Bertram had not thought that he could get away with abduction and murder. He and Louisa had hatched a plot between them to destroy Augusta's character utterly. Who would ever believe Augusta's tale? She could hardly credit it herself, and she had lived through the worst of it. No doubt it should have been Bertram who was 'discovered' at the inn, but Lord Whitley's presence suited Louisa's purpose even better! And, of course, this unsuspecting woman had been brought along as a witness. She was probably a patroness of

259

Almack's; by the look of her attire, she obviously held a very high position amongst the *ton*. Well, Louisa the harpy had backed the wrong horse this time!

'Good Heavens, you have a very bad habit of making yourself odious, Louisa! What person in her right mind would bring her family along on an assignation?'

Louisa whirled around, her face an absolute picture. The look of utter chagrin convinced Edith, as nothing else would have done that she had been correct in her suppositions.

Lord Whitley took his lead from her appearance and pressed home his attack with withering scorn. 'As I told you, Louisa, before you so very kindly honoured me with your opinion of my honesty, I am escorting these ladies on a private visit. We are only in this place because Lady Edith has had the misfortune to have a slight accident.'

He paused to come forward and draw Edith into the room. His hand squeezed her arm with an urgency that gave her an inkling of the seriousness of the scandal they were all facing. 'My lady Edith, I do not believe that you have been introduced to Mrs Drummond Burrell. Mrs Drummond Burrell, may I present Lady Edith Backworth? I could only wish that this meeting had been under somewhat more auspicious circumstances.'

Mrs Drummond Burrell! Right again! Edith nearly laughed aloud. How had Louisa ever persuaded this high-in-the-instep lady to undertake such a journey?

She favoured Edith with two fingers and a very cold look. 'I am most extremely thankful to discover that my worst fears have not been realized. When my dear Louisa desired us to stop here, and then swore that she had seen Augusta's face at the window, I did not know what to think!'

'I am sure Louisa is as much relieved as you, ma'am.'

Louisa completely lost her head. 'All I am sure of is that you would stoop as low as aiding and abetting this pair! What else can we expect from you, you vulgar creature! Parson's daughter, indeed. You are no better than you ought to be!'

'Be silent!' Lord Whitley's command left Louisa open-mouthed with amazement at the anger in his tone. 'You have said quite enough! I have borne with your spite and shrewishness for too long, Louisa. I will not permit you to malign my future wife in such a manner!'

13

A chair. There was a chair by the window. Edith fixed her attention on it. *Best not to think right now. Cross the room carefully. Sit down and smile.* That was it. All the while, her heart cried out with pain. He had sacrificed himself to save Augusta's reputation, noble idiot that he was. He had sacrificed her chance at happiness, too, without a by-your-leave. He would never love her if he were forced into an unwanted marriage.

She tried to keep a quizzical note in her voice. 'My lord, was that wise?'

There was an unfathomable expression on his face as he turned to look at her. 'I am sorry, Edith, to blurt it out in such a manner, but I will not permit Louisa to talk about you in that way. It is completely beyond the line of what is acceptable. She has to be made aware of how things stand between us. I am sure Mrs Drummond Burrell will respect our privacy until the announcement has been made.'

One glance at Mrs Drummond Burrell was enough to disabuse Edith of any hope that the lady would hold her tongue. She was almost quivering with the excitement of having a monstrously interesting *on-dit* to spread amongst her friends. To be the first with the news of Whitley's wedding! If her feet had sprouted wings she still could not have been back in London fast enough.

Louisa looked as if she had swallowed a lemon. Her skin had a greenish cast to it, rather like a gooseberry fool. Her mouth opened and closed; she could think of nothing to say. The knowledge that the harpy had been utterly confounded at last did very little to ameliorate Edith's despair as she stared at Charles.

'Well, and I am sure you are wishing us at Jericho!' Mrs Drummond Burrell began to pull on her kid gloves. She looked around her, searching for the enormous muff she had cast on to the table. 'I rather think that we might return to town, my dear Lady Louisa. This morning's events have quite driven anything else out of my mind. You may rely on me, my lord, to be the soul of discretion. Not a word of Lady Edith's accident shall pass my lips.'

She crossed the room with all the pomp of a queen at her drawing-room and held out her hand to Edith. 'I wish you well, my *dear* Lady Edith! Permit me to send you vouchers for our little assemblies. Such grace and vivacity as yours can only lend consequence to our gatherings. Such a pity about the stairs! How you came to trip I do not know, but it has quite spoilt your beauty for the moment, has it not? Might I recommend arnica? It is most beneficial. I shall call on you in a few days to find out how you go on. I trust the bruising will have faded by then.'

She barely paused to draw breath before continuing in a like fashion. 'How soon will you be returning from the North?'

His lordship intervened, taking her arm and steering her towards the door. 'I regret we will not be continuing our journey at this time. Naturally Edith wished to seek her father's blessing, but her unfortunate accident compels us to return as soon as she is sufficiently rested. I believe she should consult a physician, just to make sure there are no lasting effects. You may look to see us in a very few days, my dearest madam.'

Somehow, Mrs Drummond Burrell found herself escorted out. Lord Whitley conveyed her down the stairs and into the yard. Louisa trailed behind, pausing at the doorway to cast Edith a look of pure venom.

At the sound of the chaise pulling out of the yard, Augusta drew in a sharp breath.

'Well!'

Edith burst into tears and raced from the room. Later, as she lay on the bed, staring with unseeing eyes at a crack in the ceiling, there was a tap at her door. Augusta poked her head into the room, and then slipped in when she saw that Edith was awake. Without speaking, she sat by the bedside and folded her hands in her lap. Edith twisted and tugged at the damp rag in her fingers that had once been her handkerchief.

'Am I so sunk beyond reproach, ma'am,' she choked out. 'Could he think of no other way to rescue my reputation?'

Augusta reached out to still her twining hands. 'Hush, Edith. I thought you had a decided partiality for his lordship. Your father and I have discussed the match, you know.'

'What?' Edith sat bolt upright. She moaned and hid her face in her hands. 'Has it been so obvious? If he had but wished for this I would be the happiest woman in the kingdom, but he has been driven to it by Louisa's meddling. He does not wish to be married to me! I know his opinion too well. Papa, also! What must he think of me now?'

Augusta looked puzzled at this far from coherent speech. 'Who? Your father or Lord Whitley? Your father had no thought in his head of your marriage to anybody. You are still his little girl, I think, but the announcement will not come as a surprise to him. Indeed, he will find it quite convenient to further his acquaintance with Lord and Lady Corbridge.'

Edith dragged air into her strangled lungs. Her throat still felt raw and bruised, and a prolonged fit of tears had not helped. 'Not Papa, Lord Whitley. I must cry off, somehow. I cannot let him make such a sacrifice!'

'Sacrifice? What an absurd ninnyhammer!' Augusta laughed out loud. 'Charles will be very happily married to you, my dear. I know he cherishes some long-lost memories, but you will soon drive that ghost out of his head. Who could live in the past with you around? He will be entranced before the honeymoon is over.' She looked sideways for a moment, a sly smile playing around her lips. 'I have no doubt that the wife of Charles Ashington will think herself a most fortunate woman! His address is all that one could wish for, and when he sets himself to be pleasing, as I well remember he did in Spain, there were so many hearts a flutter you can have no idea!'

Edith closed her eyes in despair. If only! If only once he would look at her with love in his eyes she would die a happy woman.

'You don't understand. He told me himself that he could never love another, but that it is his duty to marry. He is merely being noble.'

'Pah! Not even so complete a gentleman as Charles would be *that* noble if he did not at least hold you in affection. I do not know where all this talk about sacrifice has come from, either. You have done nothing wrong. All blame in this whole case must lie with your cousin, and now that he is dead it must rest with him in his grave. There will be an inquest, of course, but I doubt you will be called. Charles assures me that he will be able to deal with the magistrate.'

'Why should he have to? None of this has been his affair, from start to finish. We have imposed on him so much. I repeat, he does not wish to marry me. I am sure of it.'

Augusta sighed. 'There must be a marriage now, Edith. Think what mischief Louisa will make. Not only my reputation is at stake now. And . . . ' she paused, considering her words, 'now there is your brother or sister to protect, also.' She blushed, casting down her gaze in confusion.

'What? Augusta, is it true?' Edith could not hide her astonishment. All the rumours and the innuendoes! Heavens, there could be no whisper of impropriety permitted now! She flew up off the bed to stand and stare.

Augusta held up her hands in an appealing gesture of confusion. 'Indeed, I think so. Your father does not know, and perhaps . . . perhaps nothing will come of it, after all, but I am almost sure.' She shook her head. 'I am quite bewildered. With my Henry it was our dearest wish for so long, but nothing. I . . . we . . . thought it could not be — '

Her words were smothered as Edith seized her in an embrace and danced her round and round. 'Oh, how wonderful! I am so delighted for you!' Tears came to her eyes again, but tears of joy this time. She drew back suddenly, memories rearing their unwelcome head.

'But you must be careful! We must take you back to London at once, to consult a physician. Papa can afford the very best now. We must take no chances with you or the child. Why did you not say something before? What if Bertram's evil has harmed your baby?'

Augusta smiled. 'What a fuss! I am not an invalid. I am merely tired, as are you! We will spend the rest of today in complete quiet. Charles has left us to rescue his stallion, which is causing him some worry, and he will arrange for a more suitable chaise for us tomorrow. We will be back in London by nightfall.'

Edith sat down again. Her depression, which had lifted momentarily, rushed back more profound than ever. 'Lord Whitley has left? He did not wish to speak to me, even? It is worse than I thought.'

'Now, now. Do not fall into the dismals again! Everything will turn out well. I promise you. Charles will speak to you when you are rested. He told me he thought it better not to discuss matters when you were still overwrought. He was quite correct, in my opinion.'

'He merely wished to be out of my sight. No ostler would dare mistreat a horse of such obvious quality. Satan is only an excuse. Perhaps he will run away and never come back, like Moyle.'

'Now you are being fanciful. Why do you not go and see how that groom of yours goes on? The serving girl told me that he is awake.'

She sprang up once again, in a torment of remorse. 'Oh, Rogers! I had forgotten the poor man! I must go at once. Pray, excuse me, ma'am!' She dashed from the room, her troubles forgotten in her anxiety.

★   ★   ★

His lordship, accompanied by an imposing travelling carriage, complete with post-boys and an armed guard on the box, arrived back at the White Horse at eleven the next day.

269

Edith flushed to the roots of her hair as he entered the room. Overcome by a most uncustomary shyness she could not meet his eyes, but sat staring down into the fire as Augusta greeted him. Vaguely she heard a few words of murmured conversation, and then the closing of a door.

A pair of glossy boots entered her vision. She glanced up, then away again. As always, his dress was immaculate, from the perfectly cut riding breeches and jacket to the snowy neckcloth tucked into his elegant waistcoat. He had stopped to put off his gloves, hat and greatcoat and could have been dressed for any morning-visit. He must be so tired, but he did not have the appearance of it. As she well knew, he had ridden all the way to town and back again in the space of a few hours.

'Edith, look at me, please.' There was no anger in his voice. It was a command, nonetheless. She had to obey. Drawing in a breath, she stood up and faced him. He regarded her for a few moments. Her surroundings faded from her attention as she gazed into his eyes.

'You are not to blame for this. I know you are naturally impulsive. It would have been your first desire to rescue Augusta, as it was mine. Prudence is not to be expected from one as young as you. None of us knew the extent of Bertram's wickedness.'

She regarded him dully. He sounded like a schoolmaster. 'Or of Louisa's wickedness also. Bertram took Augusta from Lord Seaton's house after Louisa lured her there with a letter. That oh-so-unexpected meeting yesterday was designed to ruin her.'

He shook his head. 'Louisa? I cannot believe it of her. She is spiteful and malicious, yes, but that is all.'

There was no point arguing, after all. She sighed. Nothing would change. He was blinded by his memories.

'I cannot marry you.'

He reached out for her hand. 'Would it be so bad? There is no going back now. We have had our differences, I am aware. They are nothing we cannot overcome. Think of the advantages I can offer you. As Lady Whitley you will hold a fine position in the land. My parents admire you. Indeed, my mother will be delighted! I must marry soon, so what objections can there be?'

She shook her head. So cold, so business-like. An arrangement for their mutual benefit. What objections? She could think of several without really trying.

'You do not love me, sir.'

He led her over to the chair by the window, where he could better see her expression.

Going down on one knee he chafed her cold hands between his own warm and powerful ones. His look was direct.

'No, Edith, I do not love you in the way I loved Chloe. Perhaps love will come when we know each other better. I do have a certain affection for you. You have many fine qualities. I admire your loyalty and your bravery. You are not exactly an antidote, either. You are very easy on the eyes, you know. You will grace my home with your beauty. But if it does not work, I will not stand in the way of your happiness, once we have an heir.'

Could he say anything worse? A certain affection for her? Offering her a *carte blanche* to lead the kind of life she so despised in the society around her? Would there be rumours about the fathers of her children, just as there were about so many others? And yet he had just admitted that he admired her loyalty! No, Impossible! There must be someone he had in mind for himself. In giving her permission to look elsewhere, he could do the same himself. They would be trapped in a loveless match for convenience, to save Augusta from disgrace. To save herself and him from scandal. Could she live with him, knowing that he was not faithful? That his heart belonged to Chloe and his affections to some nameless, faceless woman in a little cottage in Chelsea, or Richmond?

She pulled her hands away. She *could* live with him, of course she could. How could she live without him? She loved Charles, utterly and completely. Who could think of his courage and his unswerving devotion to his friends and not love him? He had lost so much. She would make him happy, or die in the attempt. She could, at the very least, give him a well-run home. Oh, yes, she could do that, and give him a family. The thought sent a thrill of heat surging through her.

'Very well, Charles. I will marry you. You have my word.'

He reached out to cup her cheek with his hand. The unexpected tenderness of the gesture nearly undid her as no amount of his anger would.

'Do not look so sad, Edith. We shall rub along comfortably together. You will see. I shall not make any unreasonable demands on you. Do not think I will be pressing my attentions on you on our wedding night, or anything of that nature. It will all take time.'

Stupid man! A spurt of anger flashed round her body. Was she to be a wife and not a wife? If she could not have his love, then she would at least love his child. She poked him in the chest with her forefinger.

'If I am to be your wife, then I must be your wife in every way, Charles. *I* will want a family, and an attentive husband.' Each word was punctuated by another poke. 'I . . . cannot . . . settle . . . for . . . second . . . best!'

He drew away, rising to his feet to look down at her. His expression was impossible to read. 'Very well, Edith, if that is your wish I will do my best to accommodate you. I hope you will not be disappointed.'

He turned on his heel and left the room.

She gazed at the closed door for an age, her thoughts in turmoil. What had she done? Could any good come of such a match? Would he ever love her the way she loved him, to desperation and beyond? Perhaps that would never happen, but it would not be from a want in her if it did not.

★   ★   ★

Lady Edith Backworth took to the floor of Almack's Assembly rooms one Wednesday night at the end of March with her hand on the arm of the man she was to marry. Augusta had presented her at the Queen's drawing-room, where among others she had met the Charlotte, Princess of Wales. And now, with the benevolent eyes of Mrs Drummond Burrell upon her she was to receive the ultimate seal of acceptance. The light strains of a waltz filled the air as Charles slipped his gloved hand round her waist. He smiled a little, softening the austere look that enveloped him so often.

'Waltzing at Almack's, Edith. Every maiden's dream, is it not?'

She could almost feel the warmth of an August day as recollection flooded through her. Without effort she could picture the little motes of dust dancing in the air and that bold songthrush searching for snails as she knelt by her mother's grave and told her of her wish to dance at Almack's with one of Wellington's heroes. But she had imagined a dashing guardsman in a red coat, or a bewhiskered hussar decked out in miles of silver frogging with perhaps a pelisse slung over his shoulder. Lord Whitley, in his sober black coat and satin knee-breeches had no need for arrogant display. He was as great a hero as any in her imagination. She was the object of envy of every single woman in the room. Why then was she not overcome with joy?

Because he did not love her in return.

Since that disastrous episode with Bertram nothing had gone right. The scandal over his sudden death had largely been hushed up, forgotten in the general excitement caused when notice had been published of her betrothal. Rumours of Augusta's condition had firmed into certainty, delighting all but the most spiteful. Charles, however, had changed. He treated her with a formal courtesy as chilling as it was correct. She longed to pick a fight with him, or provoke him into some outburst. But that would be childish, not worthy of her.

'Nothing to say?' His voice brought her out of her reverie.

'Oh, I am sorry. I was wool-gathering, was I not? Indeed, I have imagined this occasion often.'

'And the reality?'

'It is nothing like my imaginings. How could it be? Not even the wildest of imaginations could conjure up the events leading to tonight. It is like something out of a romantical novel.'

He did not look especially pleased. The film of ice descended behind his eyes once again, hiding his thoughts.

'Not to worry, my lady. No doubt our wedding will give your thoughts a new direction. I know it has been on my mind every waking moment.'

She wanted to hit him. 'It is not a death sentence, you know! All you have to do is say the word and I will cry off immediately.'

That startled him. He looked down at her with a rueful expression on his face.

'I beg your pardon. I must have sounded quite insufferable. I didn't mean it like that. There is such a lot to do that I had not thought of. Lawyers to deal with, finding somewhere to live, servants, and a host of other details. I cannot find a pair suitable for the barouche I have in mind for you, and then I thought you might like to learn how to tool a phaeton. Not a high-perch one, of course, but none of my cattle would do for you.'

Her irritation disappeared in a flash. He was trying so hard to do the right thing by her that she felt like crying. She didn't want phaetons, and servants, and settlements. She wanted him.

'Please, Charles, I do not wish you to go to so much trouble. All these matters can be dealt with later, when we can discuss them.'

'Some, perhaps, but not all, and the wedding is only three weeks away, after all. How are your preparations progressing?'

She shuddered eloquently. 'For once, Augusta and I are nearly pulling caps with each other! Her ideas do not match with mine. Four hundred guests! It is a nightmare.'

'But necessary, considering your status, and the status you are about to assume. You will be a countess, one day.'

A countess. When had she ever wanted to be a countess? What did that matter?

'I am well aware of all that, but it is *our* marriage, after all. It is much more important to me to be a good wife to you, than all this fuss.'

The music ended before he could reply, though the thought crossed her mind that he had been about to say something. Bowing formally, he led her back to Augusta and made way for the bevy of well-wishers who pressed around her. Edith watched him as he stopped to talk to an acquaintance. How could she bear to marry a man who did not love her? But could she bear not to marry him when that man was Charles Ashington?

'Oh, my darling,' she murmured under her breath. 'What will become of us?'

14

'I don't know why we have to go to Rundle and Bridge's this morning, Ma'am,' Edith remarked to Augusta, as they awaited the arrival of Lord Whitley in the drawing-room. 'There really is no need to choose a betrothal gift. It is such an unnecessary expense.'

Augusta shook her head and laid down her embroidery. 'Nonsense! It is quite the custom. Apart from which, Charles wishes to do so. And when you look so becoming, my dear, I'm quite sure any man would wish the same.'

The outfit Augusta referred to consisted of a dashing new walking gown of sapphire blue with a matching, chinchilla-trimmed pelisse and enormous chinchilla muff, lined with sapphire silk. Her hat was a fetching, high-crowned creation with no less than seven egret feathers falling from the brim to frame the left side of her face.

Edith regarded herself in the looking-glass over the mantel.

'Well, at least I look like a future countess, even if I do not feel like one! I can see my married life as one long visit to milliners, and tea parties and assemblies. It will be Town in the spring, summer at Bedebury, Northumberland for the shooting and Leicestershire for the hunting! I hope his lordship will approve.'

Her stepmother laughed out loud. 'What purgatory you have in store! My dear, you will have a purposeful and happy life. I am sure of it. If you are only half as happy as I, you will be content.'

She sighed. 'Oh, I know, but I feel so . . . so . . . I do not know how I feel. I cannot explain it.'

Charles arrived at exactly the appointed time. Dressed in a morning coat of navy-blue superfine and pantaloons of a delicate biscuit hue, he looked every inch the gentleman of fashion. He raised an eyebrow as he beheld his betrothed.

'I am astonished. I thought I would be kicking my heels for an hour, but I see that you are quite ready. Your taste is impeccable, Edith. I shall be cast into the shade.'

She glanced at the clock. 'Is not punctuality a virtue to be cultivated, sir? You regard it, should not I?'

'Ah, but I am, or should I say, was, a military man, my dear. The Duke would have flayed any man late on parade. Shall we go?'

Too startled at being addressed as 'my

dear' to think of a suitably crushing reply, Edith meekly submitted to being ushered out of the house and into the waiting carriage. By the time she had recovered her wits the moment had passed. Suddenly she smiled. She liked it! Charles could call her his *dear* any time he wished. And one of these days, he would mean it, too.

★   ★   ★

They left the carriage at a convenient vacant spot not too far away from the jeweller's shop and strolled, arm in arm, along the street, encountering several acquaintances upon the way. Charles stopped to converse with a formidable dowager he introduced as a friend of his mother. Not sure that she liked the level of attention being bestowed on them, Edith dwelled for a moment or two on the memory of her obscurity in Northumberland whilst he talked. Well, that quiet life was gone forever, so no use repining. Recalled to her surroundings by the pressure of Charles's hand on her arm she smiled, nodded, and said all that was proper.

'Cap'n Ashington! Cap'n Ashington, sir!'

They turned as one at the urgent note in the voice that called out. Two men sat huddled in a doorway, one blind and one missing an arm. The blind man held a battered violin, with two of the strings broken and the sound board cracked. Both wore the filthy remains of uniform, and both had the grey look of men worn down by poverty beyond the limits of endurance.

'Good heavens, does that disreputable beggar mean you, Charles?' the dowager exclaimed, staring down her haughty nose. 'How dare he have the temerity to address you? A constable should be found, at once. These wretches should not be permitted to accost people of our stamp. Why do they not frequent the stews where they belong?'

Lord Whitley raised his hat a bare inch to the dowager. His eyes blazed with an anger that made Edith gasp. 'I will make my farewell to you, ma'am. I am acquainted with these men, who have given everything they possess to make this very street safe for you to walk on.'

He promptly turned his back on the woman, a snub that was as unmistakable as it was final. In a somewhat agitated state, he held out his arm and snapped at Edith. 'My lady, may I escort you somewhere while I speak to these men? Foster was my sergeant at Salamanca. I cannot abandon him.'

She ignored the arm, and the tone of voice. 'Of course you cannot abandon him! I should very much like to meet one of the soldiers who served with you, my lord. Who is the other one?'

In a second she had crossed the few paces to the men to hold out her gloved hand to the one with the marks on his empty sleeve where the stripes had been.

'Sergeant Foster? How may we help you?'

She gritted her teeth and tried very hard not to look at the sergeant's companion, whose hideous wound marred not only his eyes but quite half of his face as well. To have given that for his country, and then to be left to beg in the streets! Her temper soared, although she smiled as sweetly as she could manage in the circumstances.

The old soldier glanced rather wildly from the magnificent creature confronting him to Lord Whitley and then back again. He wiped a grimy hand on his equally grimy breeches, then thought better of holding it out. He appeared apprehensive, but at the same time pathetically determined.

'I beg pardon, sir. I didn't never mean — '

'That's perfectly all right, Foster.' Edith had never heard Charles use quite such a tone. She glanced quickly over to him, staggered to see the look on his face. His complexion had paled and he seemed, for once, to be at a complete loss as he regarded

Foster with a mixture of anger and appalled compassion. Perhaps she looked the same way herself. Something had to be done.

'I am Lady Edith Backworth, Foster. You were very right to talk to us. I think you might require some assistance for your friend. Am I right?'

Foster swallowed hard and cast her a grateful glance. He nodded.

'Yes, ma'am, I mean, your ladyship. Tom here ain't able to get no work, and I don't rightly like to leave him. He used ter play, like, on the street corners, but some young ruffians . . . ' Tears came into his eyes, to be roughly brushed away. 'He's hungry, my lady. I'm only fit for holding horses and such like meself, so I can't earn much to help him.'

He added, somewhat bitterly, 'They won't even let me sweep a crossin' now.'

Edith waited for Charles to speak. He remained silent, struggling with his emotion. His hands clenched into fists and then relaxed again as she watched. Suddenly she understood. He could not speak. The shock of seeing this man, and the depths to which he had sunk, had affected him in a way she could not begin to imagine. More than pity held him silent. Obviously, she must be the one to deal with this. She smiled warmly at the sergeant.

'I am sure that we can find some employment for you, and then you may be able to help Tom. Lord Whitley should very much like to lend you some money so that you can buy him a hot meal and perhaps a lodging for the night. You will need a neat, plain jacket for the job I — we have in mind, so he will advance you the cost of that as well. It will come out of your wages, mind you!'

They stood there, the two of them, looking at her, while Tom clasped his violin and listened intently. What was the matter with them? She refused to be embarrassed.

'Come, Charles, give Sergeant Foster your card, so that he will know where to call in the morning. Not too early, now. Shall we say at twelve o'clock? He will need a guinea or two for his expenses, also.'

Lord Whitley pulled himself together. Coins changed hands, a dull gleam of gold with some silver as well to pay for an immediate meal, and then Sergeant Foster accepted a visiting card, squinting to make out the address. He held it very carefully by the edges so as not to mark it. His breathing was not quite steady when he looked up again.

'All I need is a job, Cap'n. Tom and me, we're very grateful.'

Lord Whitley found his voice at last. He

gripped Foster by the shoulder and held his hand firmly. 'No. Thank *you*, Foster.' He shuddered slightly as he was gripped by emotion. 'Forgive me, Matthew. You must think me entirely stupid. To see you like this . . . you have put me in mind of my obligations. I must take Lady Edith out of this wind now, but I shall expect you tomorrow. Do not fail me, for if I have to search the streets of London, I warn you now I shall not be best pleased. Shall I summon a hack for you?'

Foster let out a cackle of laughter. 'A hack? I'd like to see the jarvey that would take us anywhere! No, sir, we'll manage, now. God bless you. And God bless yer ladyship.'

Edith slipped her hand round Lord Whitley's elbow and gently urged him away. The two of them remained silent until they reached the jeweller's shop. His lordship managed a normal tone as he conducted his business with the proprietor, but he appeared much preoccupied. Edith kept her attention strictly on the array of rings set before her, although she longed to take Charles in her arms and hug away the hurt that lingered in his eyes. Now was not the time.

At last she selected a band of three diamonds and two sapphires, all very fine stones, most elegantly mounted on figured gold. Charles tested the fit himself, waiting patiently as she stripped off her glove, then sliding the ring into place on her third finger. A thrill shot through Edith as his fingers touched her skin, magnified a thousand fold as he raised her hand and kissed it.

'I have found a treasure. I do not think I quite realized it until now.'

In front of the sentimental gaze of the proprietor and several awe-struck assistants, he then proceeded to take Edith into his arms and lower his lips to hers. The hands around her shoulders tightened briefly.

'Thank you so much for what you did.'

She felt heat boiling into her face. Swamped with embarrassed delight, for a moment she could only blink and stammer. She raised trembling fingers to her still-pulsating lips, blinking back scalding tears, which threatened to overflow.

'Oh, Charles! What a thing to do!'

He gazed down into her eyes, on the point of saying something more, when the shop door opened and a pair of gentlemen swept in, bringing a blast of the March gale with them. The moment was broken. Edith turned hastily aside, disconcerted by the realization that she was about to blurt out her feelings in a jeweller's showroom. She must not confuse his gratitude with love. His emotions were not the same as hers, after all. But, oh, if only there could be love between them!

She summoned up a smile. 'Shall we return home? We need to talk.'

Leaving the ring upon her finger, she pulled on her grey kid glove.

'Allow me, ma'am.' Taking possession of her hand, he deftly fastened the buttons at her wrist. Reluctant to let her go, his fingers slid down to grasp hers as he stood there, ignoring the curious stares of the newcomers. Edith was obliged to nudge him into action once again.

There was no sign of Foster when they reached the street. Notwithstanding their need to discuss the sergeant, Edith was too full of half-formed schemes and plans to make conversation. Memories of the kiss refused to go away, either, leaving her in a complete turmoil. Charles appeared to be struggling with demons of his own and was perfectly prepared to sit quietly in the carriage. She gazed out of the window, filled with a strange sort of elation. Inside her muff, her fingers played with the hard outline of the ring inside her glove. A purpose! She could see before her now a purpose to her life, one that she could never have achieved as plain Miss Backworth. Indeed, it was one that she could fulfil better than even Charles himself.

But she had to make plans. There were people to see, and things to do.

Just before the carriage arrived she turned to Lord Whitley. 'Charles, when your cousin Giles was posted to Norfolk, did the whole regiment go?'

Recalled to his surroundings, Lord Whitley blinked a time or two. 'I beg your pardon! I have not been attending. You must think me sadly ill-mannered. Giles, did you say? Only a company was required, or so I believe.'

Excellent! Edith thoughts raced ahead once again. So, the colonel would still be at the Horseguards. All she needed was his permission, and if she could not bring a mere colonel around her thumb then she was not her father's daughter! She would visit him this very day, and take Augusta with her. No colonel would refuse to see a countess! Especially not when the countess was a very old friend indeed.

Not until they were back in the drawing-room did Charles refer to the incident with Foster. Augusta had left to make calls, and they were quite alone, a circumstance Edith found most delightful. Being betrothed had its advantages.

'I really must thank you once again for the way you handled Matthew Foster,' he said, as he handed her a glass of ratafia. 'I was so nearly overcome by my emotions that I did not know what to say. That man saved my life on more than one occasion. Indeed, we were friends, as much as I could be friends with a man who was a subordinate. He taught me much of what I knew about soldiering. When we were both wounded at Salamanca I lost track of what became of him. I never thought . . . Edith, his wound was not nearly as bad as mine. I received the best of care, but look what happened to him. I am so ashamed.'

She felt a pang of compassion at his distress. 'Do not be! You had your wound, and your terrible loss at home. There was much to occupy your mind. Indeed, if you were in any way like me, you would have thought that a grateful country would take care of a man like Sergeant Foster.'

He strode over to the fireplace and stared down into the flames. The light flickered across his features, highlighting the deep creases between his eyes. 'Alas, I know better. They are cast upon the streets, far from their loved ones, with no hope of making their way home, and I have permitted this to happen to men once under my command. I was quite at a loss how to deal with him. You managed so beautifully not to injure what pathetic pride he has remaining.'

She could sense the depth of his

bewilderment. It would seem that Charles Ashington was not used to feeling inadequate. No doubt, in time, it would do him good. But he could not be allowed to fall into the dismals over this affair. It would not do to dwell on the past as it would recall Chloe too painfully, just when she had hopes of driving her from his mind.

'You forget I am a parson's daughter! I am very well used to dealing with such people. When they have fallen so low, through no fault of their own, all that they have left to them is their pride. It would not do, for instance, to have him believe he was in any way dependent on *me* for his relief. *You* he can accept, as the welfare of your men is your duty.'

Charles ran his fingers through his hair. 'Yes, but what am I to do with him? He is bound to regard as charity any scheme to send him to one of the family estates. And what about Tom? I cannot even remember the man.'

'I have a different scheme in mind. No, I will not say more about it now. I must consult with Papa. Please bring Foster to see me tomorrow, when everything should be settled.'

He sought her hand once again to kiss it warmly. 'You are most generous. I should not be leaving this affair to you, when you have the wedding preparations to make, but I do think that you will manage better than I. You may call on me for any assistance you may require.'

She couldn't help it. A giggle escaped before she could stifle it. 'Ah, thank you, sir! You call me generous, but I am not nearly as generous as you are going to be!'

By the time Lord Whitley arrived the next day with a much-improved Foster in tow, everything was ready. Edith had flown around the town in a whirlwind of activity, from Horseguards, to the City to see Sharples, then to Chelsea to meet with the superintendent of the hospital there. Augusta had followed in her wake, more than a little bemused at the outpouring of energy.

'But don't you see,' Edith had tried to explain, 'the thought of living a life of languid ease was just too much to bear! One must have a purpose. My charity will be that purpose. Charles will never object to my furthering such a worthy cause!'

Augusta, once she had grasped the outlines of the plan, thought she began to see very clearly indeed. Edith would no doubt have drifted into some sort of philanthropic activity once she was married, as it was her very nature to do so, but to find a cause that would bring her the interest and the deep gratitude of her husband was of no mean consideration. There would always be something to discuss, his escort to beg on visits, or his opinion sought on a multitude of topics. Oh, yes, Augusta was quite as aware of the future possibilities as was Edith!

★ ★ ★

'A regimental hospital!' Lord Whitley exclaimed. 'Are you serious?'

'Very much so! I warned you that you were going to be generous. Your colonel has given his approval. My father will help, and I plan to approach all of the better families with ties to the regiment. Sergeant Foster here is the perfect person to employ as your agent. He obviously cares deeply about the plight of his comrades, and is a resourceful and competent man, or he would never have risen to the rank he obtained. But it will not be just a hospital. Some will remain there, perhaps forever, to be cared for. Some will merely pass through the gates on their way to other opportunities, once they have been given training to suit them to life away from the army. Then, they will make contributions, too, to help others.'

His lordship looked stunned. 'You have seen the colonel?'

'Yes, indeed! He thinks it an excellent scheme. We must find a suitable building as soon as possible. I had thought of commissioning an architect, but the need is immediate. Perhaps in the future the board of governors, with you as the chairman, my dear sir, will consider such a proposal, but not until the legalities have been finalized. Sharples will see to all that is necessary.'

'I cannot take it in. You have planned all this since yesterday?'

'Indeed I have. The person to talk to is Sharples, who will explain to Sergeant Foster the terms of his employment, and who will consult with you as to finances. He has agreed to act in a voluntary capacity. Was that not good of him? You had best go now, as I have a million things to do!'

Sergeant Foster burst out laughing at the look on Lord Whitley's face. He tried his best to turn it to a cough and to avoid his lordship's gaze. A meal, a hot bath and a suit of clothes had almost overnight restored him to his normal, good-humoured self, although his health would take much longer to right itself. It was the prospect of work, and meaningful, honest work that had him looking forward to the rest of his life. It was to Lady Edith that he owed his good fortune, and well he knew it.

'Come on, sir. We've had our marching orders. We could have done with her ladyship in the Peninsula, and that's no error!'

'Wait, just one moment!' Edith crossed to a side table and picked up a long case. 'Sergeant, would you please give this to Tom with my compliments? I came by it quite by chance. He will need it when we employ him at the hospital.'

'Employment, miss, for Tom?' He sounded incredulous.

'Why, yes. I will need him to entertain those too sick to leave their beds.'

Foster accepted the violin, his subjugation complete. 'My lady, you might be young enough to be my daughter, but I've never met anyone like you. There'd better not be a man alive that would wish harm on you, that's all I can say. Not as long as I'm around to hear of it. You've got enough compassion, aye, and the courage too, to take on the whole regiment and care for them. You ever need me, all you have to do is ask.'

His throat worked for a moment until he could find his voice. 'I'll wait for you downstairs, my lord.' He departed quickly, before his emotions became too obvious.

She watched him go, then turned her attention to Lord Whitley. The expression on his face made her want to smile. He looked utterly stunned.

'You have not said much on the subject, sir. I thought you would be pleased.'

He shook his head. 'I do not know what to think. I am quite bewildered. I had thought to settle down to a quiet married life. I think now that I shall have to revise that opinion.'

She laughed. Greatly daring, she closed the space between them and kissed him on the lips. 'Go find Foster, Charles. Your married life is not going to be quite so settled as you supposed!'

15

The day of the wedding dawned a perfect, early-spring morning. Edith awoke at first light, surprised that she had managed to sleep at all. She had tossed around in her bed for hours, so excited by ideas, fears and suppositions that there had been no bearing it. At two o'clock she had crept down the stairs, candle in hand, only to see a ribbon of light under the door to the book-room. Her papa sat there, gazing into the past, a familiar, framed miniature in his hand. In the quiet of the sleeping house he had told her of his own wedding day, more than twenty-one years before. Not until nearly four o'clock had she climbed back to bed, leaving her father with his memories.

There was already a bustle in the house, a hushed, stifled excitement that threatened to burst out at any moment. She forced herself to lie abed until the maid stole in to make up the fire, but once the door closed as silently as it had opened she thrust back the covers and leapt up. Over by the window she drew the curtains and gazed out into the square. What was Charles doing at this moment?

Since the meeting with Sergeant Foster, he had had to deal with the inquest at Baldock. He had arrived back from there with that set look about his jaw and the distance in his eyes. She knew him better, now. That habitual, almost impersonal stand-offishness he assumed was his way of dealing with people or situations he would rather avoid. It was as if his actions were governed by duty alone. This time was different, though. She could cope with his withdrawal and help him to overcome it. Only a few days before she had seen more in his eyes. Of course she had!

By some miracle he had managed to keep both Augusta and herself out of the scandal, but the strain must have been great. Just the thought of Bertram made Edith feel sick. It must have been so much worse for Charles, forced to relive the events of that day before the coroner. Well, she wasn't going to think of Bertram ever again. She would *not* allow him to ruin her day!

She yanked the bell-wire to summon her hot water. It was time to dress. She prowled around as she waited for a response, filled with a vast nervous energy that threatened to burn her with an inward fire. Soon, soon she would be married! She would never return to this bedchamber, or indeed, to this house, except as a visitor. It would be her home no

298

more, just as the parsonage was no longer her home.

The door opened.

'Agnes!' What was she doing, answering the bell? But of course Agnes would come. She had dressed her for all of the occasions in her life so far. Her birthdays, her confirmation in the cathedral at Newcastle. Agnes had taken her to say goodbye to her mother, all those years ago. Of course Agnes would come today.

'Well, my dear, and here we are.'

Edith smiled. The satisfaction in Agnes's voice spoke much more loudly than her words. 'Yes. Here we are. *At last.*'

The twinkle in the housekeeper's eye deepened in response. 'Now, Miss Edith, you know I've only ever wanted the best for you.'

'And now I have it, Agnes. I shall be very happy.'

'I hope so, my dear. I so truly hope so.'

Undemonstrative Agnes startled Edith by folding her in a huge embrace, brief but full of meaning. They broke apart as a procession of servants followed the housekeeper with the bath and can after can of hot water. Someone had been up betimes to bank the fires. Perhaps no one in the house had slept last night!

When Edith's hair was washed and combed

out and her beautifully embroidered under-clothes in place, Agnes summoned Augusta to the dressing-room to supervise the arrangement of her hair. In this, as in the choice of dress, Edith had been allowed to have her way. Drawn back into a simple knot on the top of her head, only a few ringlets curled down to soften the stark simplicity of her coiffure. Nothing should detract from the ceremony and the sacrament she was about to receive. She smiled at Augusta's quizzical look.

'I have the rest of my life to be fashionable, ma'am. Today I am making a promise before God.'

Her dress might be simple, but it was a stunning creation of finest white satin with an overlay of Honiton lace opened down the front. The neckline was only moderately low, whilst the long sleeves were caught together with rosettes along their length. She wore pearls in her ears and round her neck, and in her hand she carried a posy of white rosebuds, violets and lilies of the valley. Similar flowers in silk circled the crown of her bonnet, which was tied under her left ear in a fetching bow of matching satin. A fine lace veil attached to the crown covered her face.

Before Edith quite knew what was happening the carriage had drawn up at the steps to the church.

Her knees trembled as her father helped her down from the coach. These were the last moments of her life as a carefree girl. A sudden thumping in her chest caused her to draw a deep breath. Her father's smile looked strained, but she took courage from the reassuring warmth of his hand over hers.

The interior of the church was dim after the bright spring sunlight outside. Shafts of coloured light speared down from the stained-glass windows, illuminating here and there the crowded congregation.

Edith blinked. So many people! Surely the half of them had not been invited. But then, she was marrying a man of consequence. Sometimes, it was hard to remember. All she wanted to do was marry the man. The only person she recognized with any certainty was Sergeant Foster, resplendent in a new dress uniform. Charles must have provided it for him. Her heart swelled a little more as she returned her gaze to the front of the church.

She caught sight of him at last, waiting for her by the altar, and all other considerations flew out of her head. He looked so handsome, yet so remote. Dressed in a dark blue morning coat and dove-coloured pantaloons, the stark contrast of his starched neck cloth highlighted his features. As she drew closer the expression on his face softened. Looking directly into her eyes, he smiled.

Nothing more mattered to Edith. She heard the measured tones of the priest, then Charles, clear and concise as he made his responses. Her own vows echoed through the ancient building.

They were married.

The rest of the day fled in a blur only half-remembered. There was the wedding breakfast, the farewells, and then the ride in the chaise. Not the one that had ended up in the ditch half a lifetime ago, or so it seemed, but another, brand new and upholstered in the softest leather with a pillow for her head and a hot brick for her feet. The team was changed twice upon the journey to Bedebury and nothing delayed them for a moment. They were whisked along the roads and through the tollbooths as if on wings. Before she ever believed it possible the chaise bowled through the lodge gates and up to the house, lent to them for the occasion.

Charles handed her down. 'Welcome back to Bedebury, my lady. You must consider it as much your home as I do.'

They endured the congratulations and welcomes from the butler and housekeeper with a good grace, before Edith was taken away to her new chamber, a much more spacious apartment than the room allotted to her on her last visit. A door led from one dressing-room to another. The housekeeper tilted her head. 'Lord Whitley's dressing-room. There's none as shall disturb you this evening, my lady, unless you ring. Dinner will be served in an hour, and after that you may be quite private.'

Edith considered dispensing with the formality of dining in state, but then decided against the notion. Charles might be hungry after the journey, after all. There was much still to be learned of his habits. She smiled into the mirror. 'And all the time in the world to do it.'

She thought she looked her best some forty minutes later, attired in a silken gown of a deep rose pink hue, most becoming to her newly acquired status. Indeed, a flush of anticipation had added a bloom to her complexion, a fact not lost on her maid. She giggled as she handed Edith a fan.

'His lordship has already gone down to dinner, my lady. I passed him in the hall just now.'

'Then I must not keep him waiting, must I?'

A shawl of Norwich silk and a simple turban of pink velvet completed her toilette. She waited for the footman to open the door into the salon, conscious of a delicious flutter of anticipation below her breast bone.

Such a disappointment then, when the room proved empty. Where was Charles? Edith waited a few moments, then set off in search. Not in the book-room, or the estate office, nor in the billiards room. Surely he would not have gone into any of the morning-rooms, so where was he?

She had just decided that the maid must have been mistaken about his coming downstairs when at last she caught sight of him, leaving the gallery.

'There you are, Charles! I thought I had lost you.'

He started at the sound of her voice, whirling around to face her. There was a mingled expression of surprise and dismay on his countenance, almost instantly wiped away as he schooled his features to a welcoming smile.

She frowned. Why had he looked so guilty?

He bowed. 'I beg your pardon, Edith. I had thought to be in the salon before you. I am so sorry to have kept you waiting.'

Why the formal manners? He was obviously uncomfortable about something. Edith slid her hand into his proffered arm, puzzled by his attitude. He laid his free hand over hers for a moment. The warmth of his touch sent all other thoughts out of her head. Today was her wedding day, and soon, soon it would be her wedding night. She smiled.

'Shall we go to dinner?'

★ ★ ★

Later, in her chamber, Edith's fingers trembled as she removed her jewellery. The flutter in her chest had increased, so much so that she could almost hear her own heart beating. She remembered nothing of the meal she had eaten, nor of the conversation they had held in the drawing-room before the tea tray was brought in. Her breath came in hurried little gasps as she fought for calm. Excitement mixed with apprehension as all of Augusta's advice whirled through her head. How she managed to speak normally to the maid she had no idea. At last she could stand it no longer and sent the girl away, deaf to her protests.

'Thank you, Mills, but that will do. I am perfectly capable of brushing my own hair.'

Clad in a silken nightdress and dressing gown cut low in the front and sheer enough so that her form could be distinguished through the delicate folds, Edith fiddled about with the items on the dressing-table in front of her. She brushed her locks until they shone, dabbed some of her favourite violet perfume behind her ears and along the line of her throat, then added a few more drops to her wrists. With nothing to do she brushed her hair again. The array of bottles in front of her was still not to her liking, so she changed them about, then promptly changed them back again.

'Oh, for goodness sake!' Exasperated, she sat down and folded her hands in her lap. Seconds later, she jumped up again to look at the clock on the mantel. Where was he?

An eternity later there was a discreet knock on the dressing-room door, even though she had left it invitingly ajar. Her heart beat wildly as she felt the blood rush to her face. She pressed her hands to her cheeks in a vain attempt to cool them before she turned in her seat to welcome her husband into the room.

Charles wore a long brocade dressing-gown over his nightshirt, tied at the waist with a sash of crimson satin. In his hand he carried a tray bearing two glasses and a misted green bottle. He hadn't bothered with a cap for his hair, which gleamed like polished ebony in the firelight. The fire reflected in his eyes also, preventing her from reading his expression.

She swallowed, twice, forcing away the lump in her throat that threatened to choke her. 'Champagne? I am being spoilt.'

He found a vacant corner on a side table and proceeded to pour the effervescent wine. Their fingers touched briefly as he handed her the glass. He felt warm against her nervous chill.

Charles raised his glass in a toast. 'To us, my lady.'

'To us.' The bubbles bit at the back of her throat. The wine was dry, but not overly so. 'We managed quite well, I thought. Nothing went wrong today that I noticed.'

He nodded. 'As you say, except that I wished Giles might have been with us. It is a pity that his duties kept him in Norfolk.'

Of course, Charles knew nothing about his cousin's proposal. He couldn't be allowed to think Giles would so easily abandon him.

'I don't think that Giles wanted to come to the wedding.'

He frowned. 'Not wish to come? Why ever do you think that?'

Edith felt the colour mount to her cheeks again. This was awkward. 'I think it might have been too painful for him. I did not speak of it before, my lord, but Giles made me an offer.'

The disclosure had a startling effect on Lord Whitley. He set down his wineglass with a snap. 'Giles asked you to marry him? And you refused his offer? When was this?'

He sounded almost incredulous.

'Shortly before he was posted to Norwich.' Edith watched her husband pace up and down the room. What was the matter?

Suddenly he turned to face her. 'Why didn't you tell me of this before now? This could have changed everything! If I had known that *Giles* had made you an offer . . . '

A coldness stole into her chest. If he had known, he would never have felt obligated to offer for her himself. Perhaps he believed she had trapped him into this marriage. Well, that could not be changed now.

'You are forgetting something, Charles. I refused Giles. I had no wish to marry him. He accepted that. So must you.'

Charles spun round away from her. He marched over to the fireplace and leaned on the mantel, staring down into the flames. His expression was hidden by the flickering shadows, but it was obvious that a battle was going on inside him. At last he turned. Edith waited. Every second sent her disappointment and dismay spiralling deeper and deeper. Finally he spoke.

'You are right. My reaction was hardly flattering to you, was it? You must think me an ill-mannered oaf. I beg your pardon. I quite see why Giles felt unable to come to our wedding, but I am glad that it was your sentiments which came between him and his dream and not me.'

He walked towards her once again, a curiously fixed look about his face, as if he had come to a resolution. 'Shall we go to bed?'

Reaching out, he took hold of her hand and helped her to her feet. By the side of the bed he turned back the sheets before untying the sash of her dressing gown and slipping the silky folds from her shoulders.

Feeling incredibly awkward, nervous and yet excited Edith sat down and hurried to slide her feet under the covers. Her tongue began to move almost of its own accord.

'Your mother's servants are so thoughtful. See, they have scented the sheets with lavender.' She watched with some apprehension as Lord Whitley removed his own dressing-gown and sat on the side of the bed beside her.

When he made no reply she continued. 'Don't you think the smell of lavender reminds you of a summer's day and the sun striking warmth and freshness into everything it touches?'

He smiled a little. Perhaps he recognized her nervousness and was willing to go along with it.

'I'm afraid the smell of lavender reminds

me of more unpleasant times. Whenever I am ill I have lavender-water compresses on my brow. But the odour is very faint here. I shall not mind it.' He reached out once more for her hand and brought it to his lips. Edith's breath disappeared in an instant, leaving her shaken and gasping as he kissed her fingers and then pressed her palm to his lips.

'I prefer your scent. Violets. Sweet violets.'

Edith hurriedly moved over in the great bed as he climbed in beside her. Her breath returned with a tremulous gasp as he eased himself down before reaching over to take her in his arms.

'Don't look so scared. I'm not going to bite.'

She felt better now. The nerves fled as her love for him welled up once more. Greatly daring, she raised herself up on one elbow to look down at him. 'And what if I were to bite you?'

A crack of surprised laughter escaped him. His reaction was swift as he pulled her down to lie across his chest. He reached up to comb her hair back from her cheek as he looked into her eyes. He opened his mouth to say something, but then a look of shock sprang into his face.

'Those eyes!' He closed his own, breathing in deeply to absorb the scent surrounding him. He looked at her again, appalled.

'My God! It was you. All those dreams of an angel bending over me. Those beautiful eyes, and the scent of lavender and violets. I thought it was Chloe, but the eyes were always somehow wrong. How can this be?'

She didn't like the way he was looking at her, but this was a time for honesty.

'In November, when you were injured, you suffered a terrible fever. You called out to Chloe. I could see how much you loved her, but I could not bring her to you. There was nothing else I could do, Charles. I pretended to be her. It gave you some ease, but when your fever abated I knew you would not like me to mention it. You obviously had no recollection of what had happened.'

He looked grimmer than ever. 'What exactly did happen?'

She swallowed. 'You held me in your arms. Before I could free myself, you kissed me. I feared for your life, Charles. We all did.'

'Who else knows about this?'

Hurriedly, she shook her head. 'No one. I promise you, I told no one.'

There was silence for a few moments. Edith's heart raced madly in her chest as she waited for a reaction. When it came it surprised her. Charles rolled on to his side and out of the bed.

'I must think. I cannot believe this. What have I done?'

He snatched up his robe and strode out of the room, without so much as taking a candle with him.

16

Somewhere in the distance a clock struck four. Edith lay rigid in her huge bed, the faint scent of lavender that surrounded her only adding to her pain. The tears had long since dried on her cheeks, but sleep refused to release her from her misery. She had heard no sound but the clock for hours now. The room lay in total darkness, only a faint glimmer from the stars creeping through a chink in the curtains.

She laid a hand on the pillow where his head had rested so briefly, speaking her thoughts aloud.

'Where are you Charles? Why didn't you come back to me?' Did he hate her so much?

Finally she could bear her fears and doubts no longer. She had to find him, to talk. Greatly daring, she fumbled for the tinder box and struck a spark. At last her candle was alight and she could see to find her gown. Not waiting to find her slippers lest her courage deserted her she crept through her dressing-room and tapped softly at the door to Charles's rooms.

There was no answer. She tiptoed through

his dressing-room, all the while aware of the pounding of her pulse. The door to his chamber was closed. Once again she knocked, then reached out a trembling hand to turn the knob.

The bedchamber was deserted. There was no sign that he had ever been in the room at all, apart from a few remaining embers in the fireplace. Edith did not have to search for her husband. She knew where he would be, although the knowledge filled her with an aching sadness. Holding her candle high to illuminate the way, she left the room.

Her bare feet made no noise as she crept along, the only sign of her passing the flickering candlelight as it cast distorted shadows ahead of her. It was cold in the pre-dawn hours and the ghosts of a hundred ancestors pressed around her as she walked the corridors. At last the dim glow ahead of her confirmed her suspicions. There was someone in the gallery.

Two stands of candles, now guttering towards the end of their usefulness, still provided enough light to illuminate the portrait. The emotion in Edith's breast threatened to choke her as she looked at him. She felt sad, yes, but to her surprise she also felt a mounting anger. How dare he treat her this way?

Some noise alerted Lord Whitley. He turned, jumping up from the sofa when he saw Edith standing there. He advanced towards her with his hands held out, but she backed away.

'Do not touch me!'

He stopped, a stricken look on his face at the angry command in her voice. Standing a few feet away, his eyes pleaded with her.

'Edith, please. Let me explain. This is not — '

'I do not wish to hear,' she broke in. 'How can you have an explanation for this insult? This is where you went before dinner, too, isn't it? On our wedding night, to be mourning the only woman who meant anything to you. The woman who will continue to mean more to you than your wife.'

He started forward again but she backed away. If he touched her she would scream! She felt defiled, unclean even, that her love had been rejected in such a manner.

'I should have married Giles Ashington when I had the chance. He would never have treated me in this way. You are despicable; do you hear me? Despicable!'

She whirled around, desperate to escape before she broke into tears. She fled back to her chamber, conscious of the heavy footsteps pursuing her. The candle blew out, plunging her into a darkness at once absolute. She blundered along for a few steps before crashing into a piece of furniture unseen in the inky blackness. She cried out in pain, then cried out again as she felt his hands close around her arms. She tried to pull away, sobbing and crying, as he helped her to her feet.

'Edith, please. You don't know what you are doing. You will hurt yourself if you continue like this.'

'More than you have hurt me, do you mean?' She could hear the bitterness in her own voice, the sure knowledge that all her dreams had turned to dust. 'Such injuries as these will heal, given time.'

The anger left her as suddenly as it had come. She slumped, exhausted, and would have fallen save for the strength of his arms around her.

'Let me go.'

Far from complying, his hands tightened their grip. His voice sounded urgent, yet somehow distant in the darkness, as if he was calling to her from the end of a long, dark tunnel. 'You must listen to me. You must.'

She opened her mouth to speak, but no sound came. Tiny red sparks danced before her eyes and she heard a roaring in her ears.

Edith fainted.

★ ★ ★

There was silence when her eyes flickered
open. She knew with a certainty that she was
alone. Disoriented at first, Edith sat up and
stared around at the unfamiliar room, until
suddenly the events of last night crashed back
into her mind. She was in her bed. The nearly
full bottle of champagne stood on the table
where Charles had left it, but the fire glowed
with a cheerful blaze that did nothing to lift
her spirits. He didn't want to be married to
her. He would never allow his dead fiancée to
be forgotten. He . . . she swallowed hard. He
wished that she had married his cousin.

She pulled the bell cord by the bed. As she
waited for the maid her thoughts whirled. She
would not stay in a house where she was not
wanted. She had no intention of speaking to
him ever again, no matter what it was he had
wished to say to her last night. The last thing
she needed to hear was his apology. How
could he ever apologize for preferring a dead
woman to her?

Too full of nervous energy to lie still, she
could wait no longer and jumped from the
bed. Feverishly she searched for her riding
habit. She needed to be alone, to think. To
have the fresh air blowing in her face and no
unfriendly walls crowding in on her. When at

317

last the maid arrived with a can of hot water Edith nearly snapped her head off.

'Quickly. Help me to dress. No, wait. Have a message sent down to the stable. I want a horse saddled and waiting for me in fifteen minutes. In the stable yard, not at the house. What are you standing there for? Hurry up and do as you are bid. I shall expect you back here in five minutes, sooner if you can make it.'

Edith was driven by the fear that Charles would interrupt her before she could make her escape, but fortune was with her that morning. Thanks to her prior knowledge of the house she slipped out by a side door without anyone attempting to stop her. Clutching her crop in nervous fingers, with her hair bundled up almost any old how under her hat and a thick veil to hide her features she arrived at the stable yard breathless but unnoticed.

Her luck did not hold. Pacing slowly up and down, leading a good-looking hack with his one sound arm, was Jim Rogers.

'Rogers! What are you doing here? You should not be out of your bed!' Edith felt the tears well up afresh at the sight of her groom. 'Oh, Jimmy, it is so good to see you.'

'Now, now, my lady, none of that. It isn't fitting. You call me Rogers, same as always.'

He cast a furtive look round the yard before flashing a beaming grin. 'But it do feel good to see you again, all the same. His lordship sent me down here from Baldock, once the inquest was finished with. Do you remember Jack Baker, his groom? Escorted me down here like I was a lord meself. To have a holiday, he said. Keep me out of the way until the fuss died down, more'n likely, but they treated me right, and that's God's own truth.'

Oh, he was so good to her, and so loyal. Not a word of blame for having been the cause of him being hurt by her maniac of a cousin. Edith knew without a doubt that this homely young man had been prepared to die for her. She tried to choke out some sort of response, but all she could manage was a watery smile and a ragged, 'I must thank my husband.'

Her groom coloured. 'I forgot to wish you well on your marriage, my lady.' He gazed over her shoulder as if expecting to see someone else behind her. 'Is Jack bringing out another mount for his lordship, or will I get one of the lads to go with you?' He paused a moment. 'I'm not up to riding myself, like.'

Edith placed a hand on his forearm. 'Oh, Rogers, of course you're not ready to ride. I don't need anyone to go with me. I won't be leaving the estate.'

A stubborn look came into his eyes. 'Oh no you don't, my lady. Your father, I mean Lord Cramlington, would have my hide for letting you out alone, not to mention Lord Whitley. Ain't he comin' with you?'

'I just need to get some fresh air, Rogers. I won't be long.'

His only response was to tie the gelding to a ring set in the wall. 'I'll get one of the lads to saddle up. You're not goin' on your own, and that's final.'

She stamped her foot and clenched her hands into fists in frustration. How to get away?

Nothing if not resourceful she spotted a wheelbarrow, not yet put away after the stalls had been cleaned. Within seconds she had it upended next to the horse and was climbing rather precariously up into the saddle. The stirrup iron wasn't quite right, but it would have to do.

The noise of the shod feet on the cobbles brought Rogers hurrying to the stable door, but he was too late. Edith heard a loud shout carry through the still morning air, but she was away. Putting the hack to a brisk canter she set off for a copse she could see in the distance.

320

Her elation at having escaped her groom was short-lived. The evils of her situation pressed down on her once again as soon as she pulled her horse to a walk through the trees. There was nowhere to go, and no one to confide in. Angrily she brushed moisture away from her eyes. She would not cry. She would not!

Breaking through the trees she found a farm lane and turned to follow it, not caring where she went. Rapidly she sifted through her mind for someone who could help her. Giles? No. She dismissed him at once. She could not drag Giles into this imbroglio. It would be utterly unfair. Sergeant Foster? Of course not. His first loyalty would always be to Charles, which was only fitting. No, she had to face it. There was no one.

'Well, well! What have we here?'

Startled, Edith twisted in her saddle at the sound of the unfamiliar voice. She had been so lost in her thoughts that she had not heard another horse's approach.

Her heart plummeted. Surely the last person on this earth that she wished to have dealings with right now was the Honourable Wilfred. She tried to ignore him and urge her mount on but he wheeled his own horse across the narrow lane, blocking her progress.

'Not so fast, my pretty! We have unfinished

business to discuss.'

Edith eyed him coldly. He looked dishevelled. His nose was red and swollen and even at this early time of the morning she could smell spirits. Most likely he'd been out all night, carousing, and was only now making his way home.

She drew herself straighter in the saddle. 'There is nothing I wish to discuss with you, sir. I reserve my conversation for gentlemen. Kindly allow me to proceed on my way.'

By now, Wilfred had summed up the situation and realized that she was on her own. His hand reached across to grasp her mount's bridle.

'You'll regret that remark before I've finished with you. Run away already, have you? Shocked by the demands of a husband, perhaps? Married life not what you imagined, I'll have no doubt. Or was it his limping lordship? Wasn't he the buck you expected? Perhaps you need a real man to show you a good time.'

Thoroughly frightened by now, more at the look on his face than the crudeness of his speech, Edith attempted to break free. Reining her gelding back suddenly, she threw both horses into agitation. They milled around in the deserted lane until Wilfred's bay reared on his hind legs. Forced to loosen his hold to control the animal, he swore loudly. Edith seized her chance. With a spur from her heels and a slash from her whip at Wilfred in passing, she darted off down the lane. Perhaps she could make the farmhouse. Urging her mount to a gallop she sped away, only to discover that she had been headed away from the farm and not toward it. She came across a much broader roadway, lined on both sides by ditches and the famous walls. Not sure of her direction she hesitated before turning left. Surely she could not be far from Bedebury?

The sound of hooves loomed loudly behind her. Edith's unfamiliar mount and less than perfect seat on the horse had her at a disadvantage, but he would have to catch her first. She had her whip, and her two hatpins. She would claw his eyes out before she let him touch her!

Almost neck and neck they thundered down the lane. What she could see of the fields on either side were deserted. Not even a plume of smoke from a kitchen fire rose in the air to indicate habitation. As a hand reached for her bridle she screamed.

'Charles! Charles, help me. I need you.'

Wilfred hauled both mounts to a halt, but Edith was out of the saddle in a flash, running for all she was worth down the road.

He couldn't control a horse and catch her at the same time and once he was on the ground she had a chance, of sorts. The sound of hooves came closer, closer still, and the morning air was rent with another shout. But oh, surely, surely she knew that voice?

Lungs bursting, a red haze clouding her vision, Edith screamed once more for help. She tripped, sprawling in the road as a hand reached out to seize her. Her hat was wrenched away, allowing her hair to spill down her back. Wilfred cursed his luck and threw the battered hat down as savagely he wheeled his horse to ride her down.

An avenging fury rounded a curve in the road, tearing along in a reckless gallop that sent dirt flying in his wake. Lord Whitley bore down on Wilfred, a look of ferocity in his face that sent Edith scrambling for the safety of the ditch as soon as she caught sight of his expression.

He hurled himself from the saddle, bringing Wilfred off his horse in a crashing heap. First to recover, he hauled the shocked Wilfred to his feet then delivered a stunning blow with his fist that sent him staggering backwards, blood streaming from his nose. A second blow followed, then a third, until at last her would-be attacker lay in a snivelling heap, begging for mercy. Lord Whitley seized him by the collar once more, throwing him in the direction of his maltreated horse as he aided him on his way with a well aimed kick to his breeches. Wilfred scrambled after the beast, gasping for breath as he groped for the reins. Thoroughly panicked, the horse bolted for home, ignoring Wilfred's curses as he stumbled along behind. Lord Whitley watched him go, his fists clenching and unclenching in a fury.

'Edith! Oh, my God! Edith.' He whirled around, scanning the roadway. 'Where are you. What — ?'

He strode forward to gaze down at her, his face unreadable. His chest rose and fell rapidly, proof of his exertion, or perhaps of some strong emotion. His eyes blazed as he fought for control. Was there another emotion there that had aroused his fury in some way? Before Edith could say a word, or even pull herself to her feet he had jumped down the bank and hauled her into his arms.

Crushed to his body, she moaned as his lips descended on hers. No kiss she had ever imagined came anywhere close to this one. His hot breath seared down to her soul as his mouth sought hers in a passionate outpouring of feeling. Hands roamed over her body, pulling her ever closer, moulding her bones into a pliable form that fused them together in an unshakeable embrace.

When at last he let her go, she clung to him, gasping and panting. Her knees felt like India rubber as she fought for breath and a semblance of composure. His arms closed round her again, not frantic this time, but nonetheless with a proprietary embrace that left her with no choice but to stay precisely where she was. She buried her head in his shoulder, aware of his scent, his solid comfort and of the pain that tore at her heart.

His voice sounded resigned. 'I might have known that I would find you in the ditch. Thank God there is no water in it this time. I shall have to give orders that one is constructed solely for your own use much closer to the house. This is by far too fatiguing before breakfast.'

She smiled a faint, sad smile at the absurdity of the situation.

'What are we going to do about Wilfred? It is his fault I am here, after all.'

'Wilfred can go to hell, which he most assuredly *will* do if he crosses my path again. But on second thoughts, perhaps we should marry him off to Louisa. They deserve each other.'

He slid a hand under her chin, tipping her head up so that she was obliged to look into his eyes. What she saw there made her gasp.

There was no anger. There was sadness, mixed with something else. Something she hardly dared give a name.

'Edith, when your groom came to tell me that you had fled the house, a knife turned inside me. I can never let you go, my darling. I love you. I love you more than life itself. Promise me you will never, never, you hear me, do such a foolish thing again. Wilfred could have killed you.'

Edith gazed up in utter astonishment. A tiny bud of hope started to unfurl in her heart. Her brain refused to accept the message given to her by his eyes and his words.

'You . . . what?'

'I love you, my darling. Last night you found me saying goodbye to a dream, a foolish, youthful fantasy that had nothing to do with the creature who so fills my heart. You infuriate me, insult me, drive me almost to violence or insanity, but I find I cannot live without you. Giles cannot have you. I will not permit it. Say that you can forgive me. Nothing else matters. You are my wife, till death do us part.'

He fell silent suddenly as a rueful grin spread across his lips, although his eyes still held the glow that kept her transfixed, staring up at him in growing delight.

'Your penchant for ditches may well hasten that event.'

At last she found her voice. 'I love you too, my darling. I have loved you for so long. Since first you held me in your arms.'

He swept her off her feet and clambered out of the ditch. 'But you wished to rend me limb from limb, and do not attempt to deny it.'

She allowed her lips to quirk as she held on more tightly round his neck. 'Not as often as you had to force yourself to remember *your* upbringing! Admit it.'

'I admit nothing. I have absolutely no doubt that mere weeks from now when you are shamelessly manipulating me to grease the wheels of your hospital project you will use such disclosures against me.'

Edith laughed. She turned her face into his chest as he hailed a passing farm cart. Embarrassment threatened to overcome her desire to hold on to him forever and never let go.

'Charles, you cannot! You must find the horses. Don't call him over, please. Look at me. I resemble some wanton more than I do a parson's daughter. I will never be able to hold up my head again.'

Lord Whitley set his bride on her feet as the farm boy, full of concern, hurried over to them.

'My beautiful Edith. The horses will no doubt be back at their stable by now. You have changed my life forever, and if this lad or the London Mail itself should take us home I shall be forever proud to stand by your side.'

Just as her eyes filled with tears at his wonderful, heart-filled words he bent over to whisper in her ear. The sensation of his hot breath against her skin sent a shock of longing through her entire body.

'And don't try to faint on me this time. When we reach Bedebury we have some unfinished business to settle, madam wife.'

Edith smiled. 'Not yet your wife. But soon, Charles, soon. I promise, my love.'

We do hope that you have enjoyed reading this large print book.

Did you know that all of our titles are available for purchase?

We publish a wide range of high quality large print books including:
Romances, Mysteries, Classics
General Fiction
Non Fiction and Westerns

Special interest titles available in large print are:
The Little Oxford Dictionary
Music Book
Song Book
Hymn Book
Service Book

Also available from us courtesy of Oxford University Press:
Young Readers' Dictionary
(large print edition)
Young Readers' Thesaurus
(large print edition)

For further information or a free brochure, please contact us at:
Ulverscroft Large Print Books Ltd.,
The Green, Bradgate Road, Anstey,
Leicester, LE7 7FU, England.
Tel: (00 44) **0116 236 4325**
Fax: (00 44) **0116 234 0205**